Averted

Lena Knight

A note from the Author

Please note that this is a work of fiction, created by my imagination. Naturally, some scenes were inspired by personal events. The story may also entail some triggering subjects, such as emotional abuse and mention of death, so be advised.

Thank you in advance for giving my story a chance. Hope you like it... Happy reading.

Lena

For those who don't want to sit still and look pretty…
Instead, want to get their hands dirty, in more ways than one…
This one's for you.

Playlist

Available on Spotify

1,2,3 - Oliver Cronin, Topic
Ride the biker - Ruby Darkrose
Tik Tok - Kesha
Run for the HIlls - Tate McRae
Miss Independent - Ne-Yo
Ruin My Life - Zara Larsson
Dirty - Christina Aguilera
Just a Lil Bit - 50 Cent
Get the Party Started - Pink
Rumors - Lindsay Lohan
Crazy - Britney Spears
Cruel Summer - Taylor Swift
Buttons - The Pussycat Dolls
Work it - Missy Elliot
Run the World - Beyonce
This Feeling - The Chainsmokers
Let me go - Hailee Steinfield, Alesso
Scared to be lonely - Martin Garrix
Call you mine - The Chainsmokers, Bebe Rexha
Fuck, I'm lonely - Lauv, Anne-Marie
Girl in the Mirror - Bebe Rexha
Head Underwater - Tom Walker
Most Girls - Hailee Steinfeld
Be mine - Kamrad
Jumpstart - A75
Power - Little Mix
Salt - Ava Max
End of the Road - Boyz II Men

Lena Knight

Someone Else - ClockClock
U + Ur Hand - Pink
Beautiful - Akon
Small Bump - Ed Sheeran

Prologue

Sabrina

There is nothing more liberating than taking control and destroying it.
And control I will take, control I will destroy!
Mark my words, I will burn it all to the ground!
So, sleep well, middle finger, we've got a long road ahead of us!

Summer of 2022

Five seconds. It took five seconds of falling to feel like I was flying into my freedom.

Time of death: 11:55.

My whole perspective regarding life changed. It was the first time I tasted liberation, and it forever altered my chemistry.

A version of me died today. The version that didn't know better. The polished, composed version that only knew how to color inside the lines.

There, in one of my favorite places on earth, everything I'd uncovered wanted to come out.

I clenched my phone, which had been receiving calls from an unknown number, calls I never picked up. That was until I got a text from that number. I stared at the words, reading them over and over.

Unknown: Can we meet? I think I'm your brother.

I tossed the phone, and it met the rock with a thwack. As I glanced past my cousin, all tall and skinny, like a stick man figure, I felt the breeze on my exposed skin. The Adriatic Sea below us, forming waves in lure—or invitation?

It was just a simple challenge, but I took it with a smile. And then I jumped.

That span of five seconds between my feet leaving the cliff and touching the salty water became the best seconds of my life. The fear, adrenaline, excitement…

My whole life flashed before my eyes, every lie, every secret playing out like the most vivid of dreams or nightmares. Everything I uncovered hit the center of my chest. But as the breeze hit my face, it was as if it erased it all, giving me a new purpose. It was unbelievable how so many emotions could go through a person in the span of a heartbeat. But the one that overpowered them all was freedom. I tasted it and wanted seconds.

My wings grew wider, and I stopped caring about the facade my mother made me wear. The obedient little doll was no more. I wanted to cut the strings and live.

Time of rebirth: 11:56.

Chapter 1

Sabrina

Kesha's voice shouted as my alarm woke me up, the lyrics of 'Tik Tok' reverberating. With eyes wide open, I leaped out of bed, threw on my clothes, and brushed my teeth. I descended the marble stairs of my prison to sneak out the back door before Rea, our maid, made her dusting rounds. I ran through the literal maze that was our backyard and shimmied myself through a small crack in the hedge until I was touching concrete. The moon was still at its peak as dawn began to fade. I got in my hidden Jeep and started the engine, setting the checklist on the passenger seat.

Our garage had over a dozen cars at my disposal, but every single one of them was unique and easy to spot. And for my task at hand, I had to be incognito.

This Jeep was mine, not theirs - my version of a getaway car. With the first address entered in my Google Maps app, I drove off into the literal sunrise coming up before me. Passing by the iron gate surrounding my prison, I cringed at the family crest in the center of it, and yes, we had one of those - a symbol that used to represent power. Now, all I could see were the lies associated with the name plastered above it.

The name itself - a deception. My parents were clever.

5

Well, my father was.

When they'd emigrated from Dubrovnik during the Croatian War of Independence, my father, being the respected man we all thought he was, used his connections and fled to the US, taking his newly wedded wife with him. They made a new life here with high expectations. Our original family name used to be Knezovic, meaning something akin to a title of a monarch's son, similar to a prince. My father wanted to keep the meaning, and he chose the German translation to mark the new beginning.

Drum roll, please…

The Family Furst was born, making it our new history.

By the time I'd arrived, they had already established their empire, hiding behind fake smiles to maintain the well-respected, rich, and famous act. The name meant something in this city. I was born into it, the title it came with, a silver spoon, and all.

Now, my billionaire parents owned more houses than they could count, as well as cars, boats, and planes… They practically owned the air we breathed, and once upon a time, I admired them for everything they had accomplished. My ignorant self didn't know better.

As I cranked up the stereo, one I had installed myself in this beat-up, sorry excuse of a car, a smile spread across my face. It was no ordinary smile, oh no. This one was special, one that I didn't have the luxury of producing much often. This particular smile had only one mission, one definition, and one meaning.

Vengeance!

The path I have chosen was not an easy one. Especially

for a 20-year-old, soon to be 21, who still lived with her parents in the castle they made to flaunt her away in. The Barbie doll, who's heard the saying 'smile for the camera' more than any other. The same girl who was her mommy and daddy's perfect little princess. So, why was I sneaking out of this so-called castle and driving a rust-infested Jeep, you ask? Well, it's a long story, and lucky for you, I like 'em long.

This one had started a year ago when I uncovered some disturbing facts regarding my father. It opened a can of worms, and my curiosity got the best of me, so I kept on digging. Behind my parents' backs, I did a complete 180 and switched my concentration to law. At the time, I was a 'proud' student of Harvard Business and Economics, while taking online courses at the Harvard Graduate School of Design. I had to keep it secret for two reasons. Reason numero uno: my mother. For her, the notion itself would be unacceptable, because God forbid her daughter did something meaningful. Nooooo. I had to be the mirror of society; our family name was at stake here. And reason number two, my father. To uncover all the dirt on him, I had to obtain a lot of legal files, and what better way to do it than to infiltrate myself in the circle. What I didn't realize at that time was how much I would love all the legal bullshit. Now, I could even picture myself in a courtroom defending the innocent. And on some weird level, I had my father to thank for that. Because if it weren't for his secrets, I would still live in the bubble, happy to do as I was told, and I would never have discovered myself.

The anchor keepsake dangled from the rearview mirror, the memory of the only place that shielded me from the flashes that my eyes had grown accustomed to by the age of one. I came out of my mother's womb a model, and I mean that literally. Two minutes old, that's how old I was when I got on the cover of Boston Common, cradled in the Amelie scarf. And yes, you guessed it - the empire was Fashion. I was born into that world and lived in the spotlight, where I learned how to do my makeup before I could walk. I never resented it or hated it much; it was simply all I knew. Thankfully, I wasn't world-renowned. My so-called fame stayed inside the city limits. I didn't do any modeling for anything other than promoting my family brand.

With the sight of a red light, I hit the brake and turned up the stereo, bobbing my head and letting Little Mix's 'Power' transform me into a tone-deaf siren.

Chapter 2

Mateo

The roar of my engine used to be my favorite sound. That first spot on the list was replaced by a voice coming from a shitty, barely functioning Jeep. My feet holding the balance, I found myself next to it at the red light and couldn't help but turn my attention to the beautiful creature entering another dimension. With her eyes closed, she belted out a song I've never heard before, but would surely Google later. Head banging in each direction, hands flying, and fingers wiggling - not a care in the world. My eyes traced the length of her braided hair, one loose strand dancing in the wind, dark, thick lashes, and when she opened her eyes, I forgot how to breathe. The most beautiful set of green eyes stared right at me, hitting me right in the middle of the chest. Those full, red lips pulled into a one-sided smile, and I flipped open my visor, but her focus went to my bike. With all her glory, she slowly raised those greens to meet my browns before giving me the middle finger salute, making my jaw drop, not that she could see it, but I was damn sure she could feel it.

The moment the light switched to green, her tires screeched, and she drove off. Without blinking, I shifted into gear and stayed behind her, never losing her out of sight until she finally parked in front of a small café. My spidey senses told me she knew I'd been following her all along and that I just took the bait. So without any hesitation, I parked next to her, took off my helmet, and tapped on her window. She rolled it down, the old-fashioned way, I might add, before she turned to me, revealing her smirk.

"Stalk much?" One cocked brow followed by crossing her hands over her chest. And yes, I paid very close attention to all the body language.

"I believe it's called serendipity," I said, giving my most innocent look.

"Uh, I love that movie, but I don't think that's it…"

Mental note: watch the movie Serendipity.

"And what do you think?" I asked, amused by her whole allure that wouldn't allow me to blink, let alone breathe. What the hell was this girl doing to me?

"There *is* this possibility of a certain motorcycle driver following me for the last…—" she checked her empty wrist— "I don't know, ten minutes."

I opened my mouth to play dumb, but she cut me off. "It's not like you kept a safe distance for me *not* to notice," she hissed, and I swallowed hard because I honestly thought I was being all smooth and inconspicuous.

"But I guess the joke's on you," she added, making me shift my weight from one side to the other.

"Meaning?" Narrowing my eyes, I tried to make my voice all husky, but it came out more stuttery than I'd anticipated.

"Meaning you're not so bad to look at." She finished it with a wink, the sight making my insides flutter. Crossing her hands over the window slot, she leaned over, slowly studying me from head to toe. I allowed it, doing the same as I placed both hands on the roof and bowed down to her eye level.

"So, what's a fancy girl like you doing driving a beat-up piece of shit like this?" I wondered, bewildered by the fact that she looked like someone who wouldn't want to be caught dead near the thing, let alone in it.

"Please don't insult Rusty." She stroked her hand over the steering wheel, shushing it, like I somehow offended the thing, then continued with an upbeat tone, "I have things to do, errands to run."

"Errands?" I pumped through a laugh. For some reason, this girl looked like she had never run an errand in her life, too polished, all the while giving off the opposite vibe. I wasn't sure which version was the right one, but I surely hoped the bad girl screaming out of her eyes was the real one.

"Yeah, just your regular side hustle." With a shrug, her chin found her forearm to lean on.

"Care to be more specific?"

"Not really." Another shrug. Guess she was determined to stay evasive, but I had to hand it to her, she was cute doing it.

"Fair enough." I let out a sigh, giving up, for now.

"So, Rusty, huh?"

"Suits him, doesn't it?"

Sure did by the amount of infestation.

"Oh, look, a coffee shop…" Her eyes flicked toward the terrace, her voice obvious with taunt. "I sure could use a cup of coffee, but damn..." One quick snap of her fingers. "I don't have any cash, and I don't see an ATM." She pretended to look around, not even trying to act subtle, biting on her lower lip. Her insinuation brought a new smile to my face, my response a grin.

"Darn."

She brought her eyes up to mine, flashing those thick lashes at full speed.

Hoping out loud, I played along. "I was about to go get a cup for myself, if you would like to join me."

"Well, if you insist." Nonchalance was this girl's forte, I was sure, but I saw the way she eagerly grabbed her bag. I opened her door, staring at her while she slid outside with elegance. Like a real gentleman, I let her lead, my gaze dropping to her swaying hips and that tight ass that begged to be looked at.

"Do you want me to slow down, give you a bit more time to stare before we sit down?"

Fuck. Was I really that obvious?

I dragged a hand down my jaw.

We found an empty table in the corner, and I slid a chair out for her. With a quick nod, she took a seat, and I followed, taking the chair right across from her. At the same time, two packs of smokes hit the table, gliding to meet in the middle. We both grinned, and she took one cigarette out and slowly brought it to her mouth. In a quick whoosh, I took out my Zippo and placed it at the tip.

"You sure you want to do that?"

I paused for a second, puzzled, but she didn't leave much time to mull it over.

"Where I come from, when you light someone's cigarette, you owe them seven years of pleasure." I didn't even flinch before I sparked my lighter, and she took it, dragging the poison in, curving those full lips.

"And where is that?"

"Somewhere far, far away." She gave me a side smile and more evasiveness. Lighting up my smoke next, I relaxed in the chair as the waitress took our orders - a double shot with cream and two sugars for The Vamp, and a plain black for me.

"So what's the deal?" I skimmed over her presence, taking note of the details of her appearance. Her whole graphic screamed designer. While my eyes roamed over her exterior, 'Miss Independent' played at the back of my mind.

From her knee-high black boots to her dark leggings, tucked in, and a black t-shirt, which covered her curves just right. Long, oval-shaped nails, not polished with color but shiny. Even her porcelain skin caught my attention. When my eyes rose, she smirked, green eyes slicing through me. Those naturally full, delicate lips and dimpled nose perfectly mirror the image, with one beauty mark on her left cheek disrupting the symmetry of her face. She was a fucking Goddess, Femme Fatale personified, sent from hell to torture any man in her vicinity. Her body: a weapon of mass destruction.

"Don't make me ruin this with a cliche." She couldn't hide her amusement.

"What? You'll have to kill me?" I quipped, and she let out a soft chuckle. Everything in me tingled at the sound.

"Something like that."

"How about a name?"

She gave me a look, a mix of intrigue, surprise, and a bit of relief. But then she puffed, "How 'bout no?"

Her tongue stuck out, slowly grazing over her upper

13

teeth, the sight of it sending an impulse thankfully hidden under the table. The more I looked at her, the more nervous she seemed, but something told me it had nothing to do with me. Maybe it had everything to do with the side hustle she was hinting at before.

She smiled and thanked the waitress who set our coffees on the table. Dragging another nicotine-infested breath, she eyeballed me, and I followed. The smoke we both exhaled collided in the center, as if our breaths had a mind of their own. My phone buzzed; I ignored it, knowing it was Ty calling to find out where the hell I was. I was determined to block out everything around this fucking enigma I desperately wanted to solve.

"You live around here?"

"No."

Well, she wasn't gonna make this easy.

"Got any brothers or sisters?"

She took a moment, contemplating, maybe. I couldn't get a good read.

"Nope," she popped the P, narrowing her eyes.

"Favorite color?"

"Seriously?"

Well, this was going nowhere.

Where the hell has my game gone? *And how do I get it back?*

The sound of her feet tapping was the only thing I could hear, and the more the seconds passed, the more she fidgeted. I tried my best to keep it cool, but the pumping in my chest wouldn't allow me.

When I opened my mouth to ask another question, she

looked at her nonexistent watch, then back at me, chugging down her coffee, mumbling out something I couldn't quite pick out, but it was definitely not English. She stood up, taking something out of her back pocket, husking, "Sorry to make this short, but I am on a tight schedule." A couple of bills flew to the table, and she turned to walk away.

No cash, my ass!

I jumped to my feet; the chair shrieked with the push.

"Can I have your number?" I could hear the desperation in my voice, but I didn't even want to hide it. I wanted to see her again, to get to know her, to kiss the hell out of her.

Not bothering to stop, she said over her shoulder, "I don't think so."

I ran around her and blocked her car door before she got to it.

"What can I do to change your mind?" I uttered, making her captivating eyes meet mine.

With confidence, she slowly took a step closer, grabbed the lapels of my leather jacket, pulling me to her, our mouths inches apart. I could feel her breath, the smell of nicotine, and temptation. Our lips met in a gentle peck, and she pulled away too quickly, finding my ear with a whisper, "Let's just leave it to serendipity."

Frozen in place, I watched her slip inside her car, my lips pulsing from the small contact. The exhaust popped when she turned the ignition, and a squeaking noise followed, making me turn. From the frame of her rolled-down window, she rasped, "Word of advice, grow out your hair a bit, give 'em something to pull on to."

In one blink, she was gone.

Fucking Vamp!

I got on my bike to follow her, but the vibration nudged me to answer my phone. "Be there in five, little brother; sorry."

Chapter 3

Mateo

When I finally pulled up in the school parking lot, I was welcomed by three of my brothers, cross-armed at the front door, making a barrier. Taking off my helmet, I yelled out a "Sorry" as I ran up the stairs. Luka, Mak, and Tristan moved to the side. "Oh, you finally decided to show. What the fuck, man? You made it just in time; she'll be here any second," Ty grunted out when I assumed my position next to him.

"Trust me, I had a damn good reason," I said, feeling my cheeks warm with redness as I pictured those captivating eyes.

"Fuck, man, are you blushing?" He wiggled his brows.

I shoved my younger brother aside. "Shut the fuck up!"

Eying the line made by students, faculty, and friends, my smile widened. This was our mother's last time walking into this school, her last day working here. Her class had the idea to acknowledge her with a round of applause. A high school teacher with a strong need to help and influence someone's life; she managed to do so for her pupils and us. Loved by an entire community, it was shown by the number of people forming a chain on both sides of the hallway. Even some of our neighbors were here. After today, she would officially be retired.

The sound of heels clanking up the stairs made all the Hart men turn to the door. The moment our Mama stepped through, tears immediately flooded her eyes, her hands covering her mouth in surprise at the sight before her. Warmth spread through me as I looked at the best woman I knew. She fostered us, taking us in when we were just kids; took care of the lost five boys all on her own while providing us with everything we needed. Despite being a petite woman, she was scary as hell. You wouldn't want to be near her when she unleashed her wrath. All the memories of me getting into trouble came flashing by. Every time I'd get caught, she would ground me, but I always ended up in her arms, with her words of reassurance and trust to ground me.

The moment the bell rang, we said our goodbyes and let our mom go to work.

When we stepped outside, Tyler jumped on my back. "So tell me, who is she?" Mak stepped on my other side, glaring. "There's a girl?"

We got to Luka's pickup, and they surrounded me. "Spill, bro!"

"There is no girl; now let's grab some breakfast, I am fucking hungry," I deflected, waving my hand.

"You can starve for all I care, and don't lie to us. Who is she?" Luka pointed his most serious stare, flexing his tattooed arm.

Hell.

"Fine. I saw her singing in her car and followed her like a crazy person, then invited her for coffee." I scanned their faces, all serious, their eyes wide open as if they were watching a suspenseful thriller.

Here we go.

"Hair?" Tristan asked, smirking.

"Charcoal black."

"Eyes?" Luka next, taking his signature stance with crossed arms locked under his armpits.

"Green."

"Mouth?" Mak to top it off.

Deadly.

"Full and so damn fuckable!"

"Nice," they all hissed simultaneously.

"Continue," Tyler demanded, fixing his hair in the side mirror.

"We had coffee, and I lit her smoke with my lighter. She implied that I owed her seven years of pleasure for doing that."

They all pulled their fists in front of their mouths, snaking out a "Daaaaamn."

"So what's her name?"

"She wouldn't give one," I admitted, only to get retaliated with four separate shoves to the chest.

"Did you at least get her number?" Ty squeezed my shoulder, as if the action would somehow snap some sense into me.

I shook my head in regret.

"Oh, Brother." Luka tapped on my back, giving me his most sincere *'shame on you'* head shake.

"I know." I dropped my head and slid into the back, Ty doing the same.

"So why don't you find her? It's not like you can't get all

the information with one click," Mak made his point, taking a seat next to Luka. Tristan got in last, slamming the door loud enough for Luka to growl. "Sorry," he told him, raising his hands in surrender.

"I don't have my laptop with me," I pointed out.

Technology was my thing, and I dabbled with some small, mostly legal, hacking.

Luka jumped in, "I could call Jimmy at the station?"

"Do it," Ty shouted, and Luka took out his phone, bringing the engine to life. My brother worked in construction, so he had a long list of connections, not to mention numerous favors he was owed. One minute of typing was heard on the speaker, and Jimmy finally spoke, "The car is registered to one Simon Gibson."

All eyes snapped to mine.

"Maybe it's her dad?" Tyler tried to keep my hopes up.

"The guy's 27," Jimmy cleared out.

The inside of Luka's pick-up got cold all of a sudden, and it wasn't the air conditioning.

Shit times three!

I knew it was too good to be true.

"Her brother, maybe?" Tyler gripped my shoulder.

"Yeah, maybe," I sighed, trying to unclench my fist.

Why the hell was I jealous?

Because you can still feel her touch creeping under your skin.

I brushed my inner self away, joining the silent drive, followed by a muted walk into our local diner. We sat down at our usual booth just as Chrissy yelled, "The usual?" and we all nodded in response.

"Come on, bro, chin up." Mak pushed me to the end of the booth, right by the window.

I couldn't figure out why a stranger's smirk had me so rattled, those green eyes promising trouble I couldn't resist. This kind of thing had never happened to me before. It was a weird, sensational feeling, one that made me itch to race home and dig up everything I could about her.

"It's fine," I lied, just as a familiar set of neon nails brought out our coffees. My brothers engaged in small talk with our favorite waitress, but the conversation was in the background. I was too focused on something else.

Since all of us took a day off—Tristan with a written note and Tyler coming home early for summer break—we took the time to reconnect. Breakfast turned into a darts championship in the back, and my brothers continued to mess with me during each throw. Much to their dismay, I hit the bull's-eye, not mentioning that I was imagining their faces on the board.

After consuming a whole gallon of coffee and being an overall darts winner, we headed back to pick Mama up from school. Since it was the last day, she had only two periods.

"Ready to relax?" Tristan tossed his arm around Mama's shoulder when she stepped outside, and she beamed at us. "I am ready to have fun with my boys."

With Luka's tailgate overloaded with all the necessities, we headed out to King's Beach. The summer officially started when we took our usual spot by the water. We stocked our hands and set up shop on the grass. Luka tied his hammock between two trees; Mama had her chair with a small sun protector so she could read. Tristan worked on blowing up his mattress, leaving Mak and me to spread out on the big blanket covering the ground. Luka guarded the blue cooler, placed under the tree trunk, as if it were a treasure chest. He tossed each a can of brew while Mama sipped on her wine from a tumbler, marking the beginning of the relaxing session.

Tristan played DJ, connecting his phone to a small Bluetooth speaker. We were all forced into Luka's musical taste, since he was the biggest out of the five of us and called dibs on the TV remote. His favorite channel was VH1, which got us into some old-school shit.

We played cards, swam, drank, and lost ourselves in each other, forgetting about the world around us. At least they did, my mind was still wrapped around a certain trouble-making vamp.

My, my, I was in so much trouble!

Chapter 4

Sabrina

When a person hears the word 'revenge', their mind usually associates it with The Count of Monte Cristo, but my mind goes to the one and only Emily Thorne. If you don't know who that is, you should be ashamed of yourself. But I will indulge you and explain a bit further.

Emily Thorne was an alias created by Amanda Clarke, the protagonist of a TV show called, you guessed it, 'Revenge'. Her father got framed for a crime he didn't commit and ended up being killed in prison. After years away, she came back with a new name and infiltrated the family responsible for her father's capture and death. She meticulously thought of everything, but love got in the way, as it always does.

That's why I didn't allow myself to go there, no matter how badly I wanted to.

Unlike Miss Thorn, I didn't have the opportunity to reinvent myself. I was the face, the name, and the fucking executioner aiming right at the judge.

My enemy? My own family.

So yeah, a new name was not going to cut it, at least not when it came to poking *that* particular bear.

My Jeep glove compartment had six fake IDs, two of

which had already been used on smaller fish. The trunk was filled with high-end wigs in a wide range of colors and styles, matching dresses, as well as a bag full of your regular sneak-around attire.

Over the years, I've built up so much muscle, thanks to my mother, of all people. To maintain the perfect body, she got me into Aikido at a young age, though she never set foot in the dojo where I trained. Javier, one of our drivers/valets, was the one who took me before I was old enough to take myself. He was there when I got my 2nd Dan black belt right after my eighteenth birthday.

Driving in my Jeep out of the Boston borders into the small town of Essex, I broke the double triangle button in an attempt to find one song that didn't remind me of the bike guy. I never should've kissed him. Fuck, I never should've smelled him. The nicotine and leather, the perfect deadly pair. I turned off the radio and switched to an audiobook. #BookTok ruined me, more like trapped me. All those snippets of narrators with their sexy voices compelled me into a new obsession. So thanks to Audible, I could 'read' a book while crossing off some faces—wink-wink!

Pressing play, I was instantly captivated by the voice that stated all the trigger warnings, and I entered my Mafia romance era, thanks to my friend Nala's recommendation.

Two chapters in, I parked around the corner from the location Simon provided. I opened the message thread on my encrypted phone and checked the last message.

S: *House empty, laptop should be in the study.*

My sidekick's Intel was gold.

Honestly, I don't know what I would've done without him. He was a legal investigator and so damn good at his job. He was the one who sought me out last year, revealing the secret his mother uncovered on her deathbed—a secret that bonded us forever. When we first met face to face, the congenital nevus under his left eye was the only proof I needed regarding his identity.

So, yeah, Simon was a byproduct of my father's misdemeanor; as in, his biological son, aka my half-brother.

I took a second to admire the huge gray stone townhouse of lies. The street was dark, so I easily blended in with my sneak-around attire, tiptoeing to the back. A master in the art of locksmithing, I navigated the bible (not the book, in case you were wondering), making the pin tumbler unlock with a click. Ok, so it was a brief YouTube tutorial, but let's not nitpick.

Inside, I closed the door behind me, finding my way to the study. Everywhere I looked, pictures of a perfect, happy family stared back at me. One of those smiles hid the truth - I knew better. Soon, everybody else would know all his darkest secrets. The three innocent souls in the photos would finally be free. Locking eyes on the laptop that held proof of Daddy's little helpers, I plugged in the cloning device and waited. My foot quietly tapped until the light blinked green. I took out the contraption and exited the way I got in, locking the door behind me like I was never even there.

On my drive back to the city, I continued listening to the audiobook and relaxed, forgetting everything else. The laptop's data burned in my pocket as I sped to the studio. I had a photo shoot today and was due for hair and makeup in thirty minutes. I managed to switch vehicles and got there with a minute to spare. After parking my Porsche in the garage, I took the elevator leading to the studio on the top floor. The door slid open with a ding, revealing a rush and hectic concept. Let me paint a picture: people running around, carrying clothes over their shoulders and props in their hands, spotlights making it look like an operating room rather than a chic studio, doing very little to hide the glitter covering the floor. None of the staff made any noise; only the soft music emanated from the ceiling speakers.

I took my seat in front of the lit-up mirror, surrounded by stacks of makeup and accessories. Simon's gadget stuck out of my purse, and I kicked it closed before my makeup artist could notice. Tina started working on my foundation, while Jenna, the styling guru, described what look they were going for.

An hour later, my hair was curled into beach waves, I was dressed in an orange bikini that barely covered my private parts, and my makeup was spot-on for a day at the beach, with my skin glowing from a fake tan. Thanking the girls who worked hard on me, I stood up to take my mark on the phony setup. Seeing the SPF poster reminded me of the new product my mother wanted to promote to the public. It was a commercial shoot for our new fragranced sunscreen.

Three muscled men entered the studio wearing nothing but tight Speedos and oiled skin. Ignoring everyone in the room, they strode right to me. One of them looked like a live version of Johnny Bravo, while the other two looked like twins, a mix of Tom Hardy and the guy from Upgrade. They introduced themselves, but the names evaporated from my memory in an instant. The snapping of Chris's fingers silenced the room as he glided to us wearing nothing but a silky robe—tied up—*thank God!*

"Sabby, darling," he said in his gentle British accent, planting an air kiss on each side of my cheeks. "You look marvelous."

Like always, his pointer tapped my nose, while his gray eyes gave me a once-over. After he hummed his approval, he explained the concept to the four of us and took my hand, guiding me to the fake setup. Being the obedient girl I was brought up to be, I took my mark, lying on the rock, owning it. Johnny Bravo waved a large leaf over me; twin number 1 held a cocktail out for me while twin number 2 rubbed the cream on my leg. The pitch was 'The FD30 not only protects; it also serves'. I had to give it to my mother; the pitch was rather clever.

The second Chris clapped to mark it was a wrap, I said goodbye to everyone and bolted to get dressed. Before I could reach the door, a firm hand gripped my wrist, spinning me around. I came face-to-face with Twin number 1, hovering over me. I shot him a look, lifting my head so he could see my unimpressed expression. He still dared to grumble, "How about seven minutes in heaven?"

The amount of restraint it took not to laugh at his face, not to mention keep my best retorts in check, was one for the record, because all I managed to say was, "No, thanks, got better things to do."

One of his over-thick eyebrows jolted upward, making a point of its own. He didn't expect it, and frankly, neither did I.

Fun fact: I had a reputation in the fashion circle. I'd christened way too many dressing rooms, so he had every right to assume I would spread my legs. So why the hell were my thighs clenched together, acting like a freaking chastity belt?

Shaking my head, I moved past him and entered the small boudoir, as my mother liked to call it, shutting the door behind me. My head slammed the surface with a thud, and I muttered to myself, "Koji Kurac?"

As if on cue, my closed lids turned to a screen, showing slides of brown eyes, a leather jacket, and a deadly smile. God, I could still smell him, feel him. Small bolts of lightning went up and down my bloodstream at the memory of his intense gaze. Yes, at first it was purely sexual from my side, but the more time passed, the more I felt a different kind of pull. The kind that wanted to discover everything he had to offer. He had a mystery about him, yet gave off an open-book vibe. I was intrigued, to say the least. I shook my head, putting on my t-shirt, trying my best to erase that entire day from my mind somehow.

Spoiler alert: I failed miserably.

On my way to my car, I tried my best to steady my breath, and when I got to the garage, I had to do an eye roll. You see, leaning on my hood, there was twin number 2.

"I don't have time for this. What do you want?" I sneered, uninterested, and walked around him to the driver's side.

"Oh, come on, you know you want a piece of this." To add to that statement, he flexed his biceps. Too bad the guy skipped leg day, because his thighs were smaller than mine. I practically gagged in my mouth, and without saying a word, I slid inside, reversing the car as he kissed his muscles.

Yuck!

Don't get me wrong, I had great people skills, but it was my tolerance for idiots that needed work.

Chapter 5

Sabrina

Commanding my dear old friend Bixby to call Aria, the dialing tone escaped the speaker. Before she even got the chance to answer, I straight out yelped, "I need alcohol, and I need it now!"

Understanding the urgency, she stated, "One hour, The Brick?

Confirming it with a "hell yes," I went to my house to change. One quick shower later, I was all dolled up in a black leather mini-skirt and a red top, slipping my feet into closed-toe high red heels. I left my hair down, the curls still intact. With full hair and makeup from the shoot, I headed to the club. Our mutual friend Nala worked there, and we were her most trusted regulars. Aria introduced us about a year ago, and we quickly bonded. We were an unusual trio, but we made it work. Aria and I grew up in the same circles, came out to society at the same débutante ball, and had mutual acquaintances. Nala was different, kind, untamed, and so fucking happy all the time. So much so that I resented her a bit for it. She and Aria attended the same business school and had their lives already figured out. I, on the other hand, always wanted to be something more, but was not allowed to. This Barbie doll was just supposed to sit still and look pretty, preferably with my mouth shut.

I met up with Aria at the back entrance of The Brick. She wore a simple yellow sundress, a pair of sparkling black stilettos, and her hair up in her signature tight bun. The line was so long, it stretched all the way around the corner. We got up front, winking at the tall bulk Vin Diesel wannabe. Recognizing us, the security guard let us in with a nod. Maneuvering through the crowd, we went straight to the bar and waved at a very busy Nala, who was navigating around a dozen shots placed in a line in front of some frat boys with their faces painted green.

One step away from barely touching the bar, two tall, dark-haired men intercepted us. The one on the left, wearing a green shirt and light jeans, eyed Aria, while the other one focused on me, barely keeping a size-too-small white shirt from ripping. His muscles were easily defined, and the moment he stepped into the light, so were his eyes. A shade darker than Aria's ocean blue came to light, hypnotizing me. They were framed with a natural, dark outline and long, dark lashes. His strong jaw framed that sexy square face. He was a walking dream, but nothing compared to the brown-eyed biker haunting my thoughts. The smell of his leather jacket, the fragrance of smoke and trouble, still lingered.

There I was, the center of 'Dream's' attention, and all I could do was think about another guy, a guy whose name I didn't even know. The club pulsed with neon lights, sweat, and desperation, but all I could see was his damn face.

Determined to let it all go, I engaged in an interaction. Two drinks in, we were grinding on the dance floor. His hands traced all the right spots, his body moved sensually, making every girl around us wet. And then there was me... Nothing! The only word to describe how my body reciprocated.... Spell it out with me: N-O-T-H-I-N-G, Nothing! And cue the pom poms.

Aria grabbed my wrist, her eyes narrowing like she'd caught me stealing her favorite heels. Leaving the two sizzling men confused on the floor, she pulled me outside. The moment the noise reduced, she screamed, "Ok, what gives? Spill!"

It was out of character for me not to enjoy the male attention. I liked the chase, exploring the lengths a man would go to have me, as well as the intensity of his appreciation when he finally had me. The game amused me, and I enjoyed it far too much, making her reaction valid, spot-on, even. Taking the fifth, I shrugged my shoulders, and per her usual, she read right through it.

"Oh my god," she shrieked, her brows arched upward, her eyes widened, and her jaw dropped as she stated the now very obvious, "You're hooked!"

I shook my head, but my mouth contradicted the action. "Worse, Aria, it's so much worse," I admitted.

"Let's go to Nala's place and talk. I'll text her to let her know," she said, taking a key out of her bag. I nodded, and we headed up the fire escape stairs. Nala snatched an apartment right across from the club—lucky bitch.

Aria unlocked the door, and we entered Nala's cozy abode. I took a seat on the couch while Aria ransacked Nala's fridge, mixing us some gin and tonic, holding the tonic. Handing me my glass, she took a seat next to me, giving me the go-ahead. I told her the story that I had been replaying in my head on repeat. She squealed when I finished talking, clapping her hands. "Oh my god, OMG, I am so happy right now! You have no idea! I never thought that this day would come. You like someone, and not only that - you didn't bone his ass! I am officially stunned." At least I got that going for me, because if there was one thing no one could do, it was make Aria stunned or speechless. So, yay for me.

"Wait, so he doesn't know who you are?"

"I don't think so."

I took a minute to let that sink in. Maybe that was the appeal, the reason why any interest existed on my part. I knew my name came first, my looks second, when it came to the opposite sex. So the fact that somebody took an interest in whatever was hidden behind the facade altered something in me.

"Why not look up his license plate? And don't even deny it, I know you memorized it, your photographic brain and all."

I liked to call it a character flaw because my brain was so adept at storing everything I saw or read that it was impossible to forget. It could bite me in the ass at the worst of times, much like the past twenty-four hours. The image of him was so clear that I would beat a sketch artist if I knew how to use a pencil. The model of his bike, the license plate, the tag on his bag, and the brand of his cigarettes... it was all permanently mapped into my brain cells, invading my every thought and making it hard to concentrate on anything else. It was starting to become a problem, interfering with my plans and actions.

Remembering that Nala was also a smoker, I took out my cigarettes and calmed myself down with one of my many vices.

"I can't afford a distraction," I said, my voice sharper than intended. "This plan is my shot at freedom, and I can't let some biker derail it."

My plans were not something I shared with anyone, well, except with Simon. There were some vague explanations as to why I was acting weird and had to bail on multiple invites. Thankfully, Aria understood, mostly.

"Oh god, I hate it when you get all cryptic." She waved her hands. "You do know that I am hella smart and that you can tell me the truth about what's really going on with this plan of yours," she croaked and patted my knee.

I pulled out the never-failing puppy eyes. "I told you, I don't want to get anybody involved, so be the best friend you are and don't make me feel worse."

"Fine, but you at least owe me a detailed description of the bike guy," she said, adding a more demanding note.

"That one I can do!" And so I did, from the tip of his hair down to his white New Balance sneakers; I portrayed him so thoroughly it felt like he was standing right in front of us.

Not long after, Nala came in, catching us red-handed in the middle of opening our second bottle of gin. She kicked off her boots, declaring, "If I'm drinking, we're doing this my way!" Then she explained the rules of her game, drinking three straight glasses of pure gin to even the playing field.

The game was simple: the person whose turn it was to drink had to say a number after the other person picked up a book from the shelf. The stated number indicated the page, and if it was a spicy one, the person holding the glass had to drink up. Luckily for us, the bartender liked her books spicy just as much as this girl (cue the pointing thumbs).

The night turned out just how I needed it to; hell, Aria needed it more. She was in the middle of another fight with her fiancé, Sebastian, aka Mr. So wrong for her. He never supported her, never truly accepted her for all of her awesomeness.

So we hid in our trio bubble, the only place the outside world could never break through. Well, except for a pair of brown eyes holding the power to crack even one of the strongest brick-ed walls.

Chapter 6

Sabrina

Waking up with back pain was not in my repertoire for today. I sat up on Nala's couch and looked around. First thing I spotted was Aria drooling on the floor, still deep in. When my head turned, there was Nala comatose in her bed. She left her bedroom door open, and I could see her feet dangling over. Dragging my body to the kitchen, I groaned at the incoming headache. The coffee machine hissed when I turned it on, and I shushed it like it would understand me. Knowing my way around Nala's place, I took three cups from the upper cabinet and placed them on the base. The downpour of brown liquid hypnotized me into a whole new state. Thankfully, a vibration from my purse intervened. I took out my phone, which had two unread messages, both from my sidekick.

S: *I cracked it*
S: *Call me when you can*

I snuck to the fire escape, the fresh air making me shiver, demanding a deep breath before I dialed back.

"What do you have?" I point-blank-ed the second he picked up, which made him snort.

"A lot. The idiot forgot to delete his cloud." His nerdy chuckle crackled through the line, as he lived for this spy shit.

"Perfect, back it up."

"Already done," Simon frisked.

"Good work. Any ties to *him*?"

There was no need to elaborate; he knew who I was talking about—the sole reason for this entire ordeal.

"No. Sorry, no luck there." I could hear the disappointment in his voice.

"Fuck... we just can't catch a break," I sighed, my stomach dropped at another dead end.

"We will, don't worry," he reassured, and my nerves instantly calmed. Simon had that power over me.

"Yeah, hope so."

We compiled a list of names that helped my father change his identity and start anew. Every new step took us two steps back. It was frustrating, and I was losing my patience, not to mention any hope for a smoking gun we desperately needed.

I hung up on a sigh, letting the freshness of the air hit me once more before I turned and walked back inside. Just as I closed the door behind me, Nala appeared, scratching the top of her head where her hair was tied in a messed-up ponytail. Yawning, she mouthed, "Headache, need killers!"

I laughed and slowly guided her to the barstool, trailing her cup in front of her.

"You are a godsend. Thank you," she heaved out the words, and I smiled back at her, sipping my coffee that burned just right. Aria soon joined us as we all drank, not talking, barely keeping our eyes open. It took us a whole hour to reach a point where we could pretend to be fine. You know that still alive, but barely breathing kind of fine.

After my second cup of coffee, I headed to wash my face. When I spotted an unfamiliar figure inside, I screamed. Aria and Nala appeared behind me so fast; Nala was even holding a baseball bat, and I burst out laughing. And it wasn't a normal laugh. Nope. It was hysterical. The flashback of last night started playing out. The three of us drunk, hitting a pharmacy and buying me a new hair color. My friends trying their best not to mess up Nala's bathroom with the dye, over a thousand selfies being taken. I stared at my reflection, admiring the look. You might think that dyeing my hair was just a regular thing, nothing special, but to me it was something big. Throughout my life, I never had any choices regarding my appearance; it was always chosen for me. So this little contrast was a small act of rebellion, and I loved it.

Checking my phone, it hit me.

Shit, today is Saturday, my doom day.

Damnit.

I got my shit together, sobering up with the apprehension. Every first Sunday of the month was family dinner night—two excruciating hours of mindless small talk, side-eye glances, and fine dining, followed by a private scrutiny. Each night ended with me sitting across from my father in his study, with a new list of the ways I had disrespected my last given name, and Daddy dearest cursing in Croatian. One fantastic aspect of the language was its profanity. Just last dinner, Dad went full native, threatening someone while on the phone. I hadn't caught the entire conversation, but I did hear him finishing off with the big guns in the form of a *'Mrš u pičku materinu'*, before he hung up, all the while Mom sipped her wine, unbothered. But I was determined to endure it all with grace and resilience.

For just a little while longer.

I said goodbye to my hangover friends and drove to my house, barely keeping my shit together. I turned up the radio to numb my mind from spiraling and to calm my nerves. It worked like a charm, and I floored my Porsche the moment I hit the interstate. I let the top down, air surfing to the beat, letting the wind brush away all of my worries.

When I reached the iron gate, I punched in the code, and the shrieking sound of the metal opening made my skin prickle with unease. On the other side, Derek, our security guard, waved at me, and I stopped for a quick chat like I always do. He showed me the newest pictures of his twin daughters, and I pointed out how cute they were before I continued the long drive to my prison.

It was an unexplainable sensation, hard to define, really. There was numbness, unease, anger, and a weird feeling of nostalgia.

The 1937 Georgian Revival estate looked like a place where dreams were made. It had ten bedrooms, twelve bathrooms, eight fireplaces, and plenty of space to entertain guests. A 19,000 square foot house overlooking a private beach was listed in Architectural Design as the top real estate of 2022.

It was beautiful, and there was no denying it, but it was way too big for a family of three. Come to think of it, with the size of my father's ego, it was probably not big enough.

Pulling up the paved driveway, Javier stepped out to

open my door. He helped me slide out before he took my place and drove my car into its parking spot. We had a 24/7 valet service; it was ridiculous, but at least someone got a full-time job out of it. Javier was one of my favorites. Although he looked like G.I. Joe, he was kind and funny, and didn't treat me like the rest of them, the ones who boxed me in the spoiled brat category.

I trudged past the marble foyer to my room, where even the walls screamed someone else's taste, further reinforcing my sense of alienation in my own house. Looking around my room, I thought about Nala's place. Her home was warm and personal, and you could sense her presence in every item inside. My room was chosen for me by the number one designer for my 18th birthday. It was pink, the color I hated most. A king-size canopy bed placed in the middle, accompanied by two sets of white antique nightstands on each side. No posters, no trophies, no books, nothing around that could show at least a bit of my personality. Thank God for Kindle, because God forbid I had an actual book on my shelves. *"Pretty girls don't read; they have stories written about them,"* my mother's words echoed, striking my already aching head.

My bed called for me, and I collapsed on it, setting my alarm to wake me on time before I dozed off.

The soft melody, followed by raindrops, woke me from a wet dream. The one place he had yet to impose was now breached. He managed to delve so deeply into my psyche that he now literally took over every part of it.

I jolted up and rushed to my bathroom. In the shower, I turned the water to ice cold; droplets made my body shiver, and yet my insides were boiling hot. And there I was thinking an ice bath would do the trick—no such luck. It wasn't until I couldn't feel my fingers or toes that I turned off the water and covered my skin with a towel. I stepped out, looking at the mirror and sighing at the dark circles I now needed to hide. I took extra time prettying up my face, then picked up the previously marked, appropriate attire for the torturous event and got dressed.

Taking slow steps down the spiral stairway, I dreaded more with each inch that got me closer to the dining hall. We had three different dining areas: one for entertaining a party, one for special family dinners, like on holidays, and the one I was now headed towards. Opening the sliding wooden door, I found it empty. A sigh of relief escaped me, and my shoulders relaxed a bit. The space was straight out of a designer's dream, featuring a personally designed, handcrafted masterpiece for a table. The base consisted of intertwining trunk roots, surrounded by six chairs, each covered in dark, jungle-green leather. A bouquet of fresh flowers stood in the center, and the place settings were carefully arranged to complement the interior's color scheme. The walls were painted in the same shade of green as the chairs, and the lower half of the wall was covered with wooden boards. A giant chandelier hung above the vase with deer antlers holding the small bulbs. A matching set of antlers was pinned on the wall right above my father's designated chair, and yes, daddy dearest shot that one. I'm ashamed to admit that one of the bullets came from my Remington, despite it not being the death shot. And yes, hunting was another thing I was 'forced' into.

The door slid open, and Dad's voice boomed before I could brace myself.

Chapter 7

Sabrina

The dinner turned into a shit show when my father revealed he had found out about my switch to law. My blood started to boil while my mother sipped her wine, ignoring the tension. This was going to ruin my whole timeline. And here I was thinking I'd hidden my tracks well.

Throughout the meal, my mother remained quiet while my father let out groans and disapproving sighs. Each pointed at me. Usually, our dinner time was not reserved for such conversations, but I guess tonight was the exception.

I feigned indifference, saying I wanted to follow in my father's footsteps while pointing out that I was still taking online fashion classes. That settled the tension enough to get us through the dessert.

Glaring at the ticking Koo Koo clock in the corner of the room, I waited for the 8 o'clock chime marking the end of dinner, preparing myself for the study session, pun intended.

Two more minutes left, I counted each movement of the biggest hand, clocking the seconds. At the sound of a bird shrieking as it flew out of the house, we all stood up, bowed our heads, and went our separate ways.

Trudging past the empty dining hall, the chime's echo chased me to his study. Once inside, I got comfortable in my chair, and yes, I had a designated chair for the scorning.

His mobster-chic study exuded power, with bookshelves filled with dictionaries and a Rakija bottle gleaming in the corner. An entire wall was covered with framed headlines worshiping the family Furst. His Boston University diploma had the tackiest frame, drawing all the attention to his law degree. Oh, I haven't mentioned that detail. Sorry. Yes, my father had pulled a Mike Ross and obtained a fake law degree, not to mention a throne in the courtroom. Okay, full disclosure, it was all speculation, due to my distrust of anything my father had accomplished. For dramatic purposes, let's pretend there's a *'dun dun dun'* here...

Jakob Furst was a state judge, a respected one at that. Aside from all the praises pinned to the wall, there was only one picture in the entire room, and it was of my father shaking hands with the governor. Our not-so-much-of-a-home had a gallery with framed posters from every commercial I've ever made for FD, which stood for Furst Design, or how I liked to call it: Fucking Dicks. There were no family portraits, no photos of my first steps, no family dinners—nothing that would indicate a family even lived here. Come to think of it, I didn't have any pictures of myself growing up, which would be considered a sad thing, right?

I knew that the way I was brought up was the reason I had never known love. I never felt it from the only people who were supposed to introduce me to it. Sure, I saw it on the screens and read about it in books, but it was fictional, in every sense of the word, at least to me. That's why I had a phase of searching for it in all the wrong places. Frankly, it was a phase I never outgrew. Though my body was thankful

44

for all the exploring I had done, my heart felt ever more empty.

The cracking of the door straightened my posture when the all-mighty Jakov Knezovic (now known as Jacob Furst) stepped up to his desk. He slid into his chair like a king addressing his kingdom.

"Why didn't you tell us you wanted to make such a switch?"

"I guess it slipped my mind."

Since my eighteenth birthday, I've practiced a so-called 'Do first, deal with the consequences later' motto.

A soft hum vibrated in the back of his throat, and he fought the urge to smirk.

That was when he tossed a newspaper in front of me with a thwack. My fingers twitched as I grabbed the paper, heat creeping up my neck. The headline, saying '*Another night on the town with Boston's finest*', made me cringe while the picture of me with two men licking my neck made me wanna gag.

Great, here comes the reproof!

"I am very disappointed, Sabrina." His tone was indifferent, cold. "You could have at least fornicated with a name, not some unknown lowlife."

Of course, he would go there. He wasn't angry that a stranger took advantage of me, pinned me to the couch, and forced his tongue on me. What upset him was that the tongue had no title; the audacity, the shame. Sure, I shoved my knee in the guy's crotch, but still... I swallowed the words that I was in desperate need of saying. I needed to keep up the obedient Barbie-doll act for three more months, and then it

45

would all be over. Ninety days to topple his empire—or lose everything. So I had to keep it together, fake it till I make it!

Motivation was a driven bitch, making no room for error or fear, but it made a hell of a good company. Mine was leveling over common sense and any shred of doubt, giving me the confidence and stride much needed to make the biggest of moves.

I adjusted in my chair, glancing at the wooden board in the corner. My father taught me the game of chess when I was eight years old. First, he'd started with the basics, then gave me a book on the history of chess to learn more. My photographic memory had already been evident when I started first grade, so I was able to devour the book in a day. I'd checked out other books about chess from the school library to learn as much as I could about the game. By the age of nine, I was the in-house champion. A mistake had been made on his part—he'd underestimated me. Ego was my father's only weakness, and it would cost him everything.

He will see it coming; he just won't know who hit him.

Sitting across from the egomaniac, I bit my inner cheeks in protest of the grin that was so desperate for attention, needing to be shown.

You have no idea what's in store!

Chapter 8

Sabrina

"I got the photos from the shoot. Want to see them?" My mother entered my room without knocking, per usual.

"Not really," I deadpanned.

"You could at least act interested."

"Now, why would I do that, mother? It's not like you care about my opinion."

"Well, you sure don't care about mine, since you chose that of all colors." She swayed her hand over my hair, elegantly so. I wanted to go full red, but I'd fallen in love with the box with the number 69 on it. I wasn't sure whether I'd picked it because of the number, the alcohol, or the color, but I didn't care. It helped that it turned out great and made me look deadly.

The only positive aspect of living in the spotlight was the boost in confidence it provided. I never had trouble feeling comfortable in my skin, and I had no problem using my body to prove a point.

The fact that my mother hated the color made me love it that much more.

"What? You don't think it makes my eyes pop?" I said in a mocking tone, even though it was true. The Cherry Coke did make my eyes look greener as opposed to my natural black.

"Sabrina, that tone is not welcome, so please restrain yourself from using it," she exasperated, nostrils starting to flare.

"Wow, you used the word please. I am shocked." I acted it out too, hand on my chest and everything.

"Sabrina!" she shrieked.

Sranje! She'd probably tattle to Daddy dearest, setting up another study session.

Time to put on the act.

"Sorry, mother." I lowered my head. Unfortunately, I knew better. My mouth needed to stay put and away from trouble, at least while under this roof.

I can't wait to leave this place in the dust.

It was a good thing I had a hell of a poker face, which I had undergone extensive training to develop. I was ten when my lessons started; my mother—my teacher. It had been a month of quality time spent. The lessons in question had consisted of videos on various themes, ranging from birthday parties to sex scenes, fights, and even some magic tricks. During each video, I had to stay immobile and remain emotionless. For every flinch, every unnatural blink, I'd get belittled. My mother loved using her words to hurt me, and she was good at it. She knew exactly where to hit.

I almost laughed, remembering how she had thought her insults were Shakespearean. I could practically hear her '*useless*' cutting through me like glass.

The advanced lessons were more on a happier note, as in, I had to smile while I got yelled at—no, screamed at. Oh, and let's not forget how I had to thank her every time she'd insulted me. That was a month. And yes, it is sarcasm you're sensing here.

Another positive aspect of my upbringing was that I was a quick learner. I excelled at every task at hand. Sometimes I got punished for that too, with words, to clarify. Always with words.

When my body had begun to reveal to everyone that I was growing into a woman, my father had stepped in with his lesson plan. He'd taught me how to get what I wanted out of a man.

How sick was that?

Don't answer that.

I should thank him, though, since I used all his lessons to gather the evidence I needed to take him down. Call it poetic justice.

The clicking of my mother's heels echoed like a countdown as she stormed out.

In my entire twenty years on this earth, my mother and I have never had a meaningful conversation. I spoke to my father even less, if we were to exclude the study sessions, regarding how big a disappointment I was. Don't get me wrong, there was a time when I'd loved them, blood and all that shit. But the more of their secrets came to light, the more my love turned to hatred.

I thought my father built this extraordinary life with his hard work, with my mother by his side. And for a long time, I admired them for everything they had accomplished.

Now? Well, there was only disgust. They lied, cheated the system, used people, and discarded others to get to the top. And even though my father held most of the responsibility for their actions, my mother condoned it.

I slumped on my bed, the memory that started it all playing like a movie in my head.

"Hi." A tall, blond version of me stepped closer to me. I blinked, trying to absorb his presence.

"Hi," I said shyly, despite not having a shy bone in my body.

"I'm Simon, nice to meet you."

"I'm Sabrina."

I didn't say it was nice to meet him because I didn't know his motives for this meet-up. Was he after money? Or was he in search of a family?

Whatever the reason, he'd set himself up for disappointment.

"So…" I said at the same time he started with "Anyway."

"You go." I motioned with my hand to him.

He cleared his throat and took a deep breath while I prepared myself for the big reveal.

"My mother got sick three months ago…" he started, and my heart instantly sank. "Before she took her last breath, she finally told me who my father was after keeping it from me my entire life. He left her in the middle of the war for another woman, and fled the country, while she was eight months pregnant with me."

I didn't know which feeling was stronger, the guilt or the pity.

"She gave me a picture and his name." He took out a photo of a young couple smiling: a beautiful blond girl, sporting a big belly, and a man I instantly recognized as a younger version of my father, standing next to her, his arm

around her shoulders. My mouth went dry, and my heart started pounding.

"I looked the name up…" he didn't finish, watching me closely, almost as if he was trying to read whether I knew the rest. I didn't.

"I got his death certificate as a result."

My mouth dropped.

"I don't understand," I gasped in disbelief.

Without any emotions on his face, almost robotically, he continued. "I scanned the photo using the aging app and ran the face through a program that linked me with a personal page of a state judge."

Have you ever felt a sense of crumbling, as if your body were embodying the impact of a life unraveling? Well, that was happening inside of me while I took his words in.

"So, I moved to Boston with every intent to confront him, until I saw a poster on the bus stop."

Oh great. I wondered which one it was.

"I noticed the name first. Then the mark we all shared, and decided to seek you out instead."

I didn't know whether to feel honored or scared; I chose the former.

"I'm sorry," was the first thing that came to mind. "I had no idea."

"I figured."

"Wait, you mentioned a death certificate."

He nodded, taking out a manila envelope from his bag and handing it to me.

"It's everything I dug up. I'm sorry, Sabrina, but your father is not who he seems."

Blinking the memory away, I pinched the bridge of my nose and sighed. My mind flipped through every page from that envelope, from the fake death certificate to the last case he overruled.

I closed my eyes, thinking over the plan that Simon and I had devised.

Chapter 9

Sabrina

"So what do you have?" Carl, my boss, asked as soon as I got to the clinic. At the beginning of the year, after we had established a professional relationship, I'd decided to let him in on the plans, and he'd generously provided me with all the necessary resources.

"Not much," I told him, taking an envelope from my bag.

"These are all the emails we retrieved, bank statements, and dates that we need to cross-check."

"Not much, huh?"

Carl was in his late forties, but had the soul of a young daredevil. Solely by his looks, you would've never guessed he was a lawyer, more like some con artist. He reminded me of Matt Bomer's character in 'White Collar', charismatic and charming. His looks were not so far off, come to think of it, except for the ginger hair. He came from a wealthy background, so he always wore fancy suits, but kept the clinic strictly pro bono. And despite all the money and connections, he was a kind-hearted, down-to-earth person I learned to admire over time.

"He's waiting for you in the conference room," he revealed with a smile. I went straight to the separate room, the door creaking as I opened it. The room was too small to be called a conference room, mainly since it was used for other purposes. Currently, it has been converted into a storage room, serving for inventory. Three tables were pushed together, surrounded by nine chairs. Stacks and stacks of papers hid the color of the wood, and boxes filled up the entire wall in the corner. I found Simon in the middle, dabbling on the laptop spread across his lap.

"Hi," I whispered, and he turned to face me before standing up to greet me. We were still more business than friendly, so he just stretched out his hand, and I shook it.

"Jet lag?"

Excellent, so my attempt to hide the circles under my eyes was for nothing.

"Yeah, I need my shot of coffee," I admitted and took a seat across from him.

"So, was your summer productive?"

"It didn't turn out to be a total waste." I shrugged.

It had been a blissful end-of-summer week spent by the coast, lying on the beach, tanning, drinking, and mingling with my cousins. Ana was my age, a blonde, driven pharmaceutical saleswoman. Her younger brother, Zvone, was a Kinesiology student at the top of his class. For most of our time together, Ana had teased me about my accent, her saleswoman's charm relentless. Zvone had bulked up over the years, far from a stick figure, making it hard for me to poke at him. Their free spirits had made our time together enjoyable, mostly filling it with laughter. My time in Croatia always had a rejuvenating effect on me.

"I got you this." I took the magnet out of my bag and handed it over. He eyed it, holding it carefully like it would break.

"Thank you; Greg will love this."

Greg was the love of Simon's life. I'd met him a couple of months ago, and we clicked right away, something that came easily due to his kind-hearted soul. Greg was a poet who had a couple of published collections of poems. I had every copy in my secret hiding place.

"So, did you follow the trail?"

"You're never gonna believe this…" Simon's eyes widened when he turned the screen so I could see. My jaw dropped. We now had five new names on the list. We worked hard this entire summer. I was focused on the cases, and Simon was focused on the people who helped our father get to the top. By the looks of it, he found them all.

"And Mr. Darcy's phone, do you have a plan?"

"Yup," he popped the P, bringing his glasses to the bridge of his nose. He handed me a device, and I examined it before putting it in my bag. How he got these things was beyond me, but I was not one to look a gift horse in the mouth.

"Just stay close enough until it vibrates," Simon explained, grinning.

"That's it?"

He nodded, but his expression turned into something I had trouble figuring out. Maybe it was worry?

"You sure you don't want me to do it?"

"No, I got it. You focus on finding out when he goes to the club, and I'll do the rest."

"Suit yourself." He gave me a disapproving shake, but he knew it was pointless.

"And you're sure his phone will have it all?"

"Colonel Brandon and Mr. Tinley were both on his call logs, so I am pretty sure."

Ok, so don't go hating on me for giving them code names from Jane Austen's novels, but I had good reasons. I couldn't go around with the words 'Devil' or 'Lucifer'; it would be too obvious. Additionally, the names I had chosen helped keep my anger in check.

"Great, and after that, we can start with phase two?"

He gave me another nod. "Do you want me to put it all together?"

"No," I shook my head, "I have more motivation."

He arched a brow, trying to read me. He was getting better at it, or maybe it was me who couldn't hold it up any longer.

"And the other thing?"

He referred to the pattern we've figured out while going through Jacob's cases.

"Carl got over all the cases I've dug up before my trip, and with all the intel you provided, we're set to set it in motion," I concluded. Simon gave me a knowing look, one sparkling with pride. His stare felt like a warm hug, and I suddenly wanted to see how a real one of his felt. We never crossed that line. Mostly because I didn't know how to act, he knew how I was brought up, knew my story, and I knew his. And he never pushed for a deeper connection. Just as I was about to step closer, a knock on the door made us both turn to find Carl with a mug in hand, and not just any mug, my mug. Yup, in the clinic, all the employees and volunteers had a personalized one, courtesy of the man who owned the place. All were the same, a name on one side and a legal pun on the other. But mine had something extra on it—a graffiti of a crumbling Lady Justice statue, wearing a motorcycle helmet.

"You are the best boss ever," I praised while I strode to him to grab my coffee.

"Doing my best to get in your good graces, taking into account that one day you will be running this place." He winked and eyed the stacked pile of junk.

Flashbacks of my first day working with him came to light, how he'd told me my mind was wasted on the wrong stuff, and how he could see me somewhere high up, running the show. I smiled it away, cuz at the time I only wanted the job for the information. He helped me see things from a different perspective and showed me how to leverage my potential to benefit others. I got addicted to it quickly and never wanted to go back.

Tom, or Tim, or whatever his name was, stormed in with his resting bitch face. The tension between us was palpable. He had some problem with me since day one, and I couldn't figure out what it was, not that I wanted to anyway.

"Princess, nice of you to grace us with your presence. What, you got tired of the Cosmo's by the beach?"

"Thinking about me in my bikini? You know, there are posters all over the city where you can enjoy the view all blown up for your pleasure."

Our boss choked on his coffee, and Simon snickered from behind me. Tom, or Tim, got red-faced.

"What, cat got your tongue?"

He swallowed and disappeared from my sight. Carl gave me a nod before he too left.

I gulped my coffee, my body coming back to life when my phone buzzed.

Aria: *Dinner tonight?*

Me: *Sounds great, 8, the usual spot?*

Aria: *See you then*

Chapter 10

Mateo

Sweat stung my eyes on the construction site, but every penny saved was worth it. Luka came to my side, acting like the boss he was, giving me a wink just as he lifted his watch for me to see the time, marking the end of my torture. Full disclosure: working for my brother this summer hasn't been as bad, but I certainly wasn't going to tell him that. Frankly, spending more time with him made me look at him in a different light. He was a good boss, friendly with the workers, making them his equals. Luka was a provider and our protector, always guiding us. But on the site, he was in his element, more open and relaxed.

We arrived at his pickup, the tailgate filled with our beach gear. During the summer, I'd worked every day of the week, except Sundays, which were spent on the beach with the rest of our family. I'd managed to save some money in the process, and it felt good. Tired and sore as hell, I leaned in the passenger seat, happy it was my last day. Come Monday, I was back to class, and I could hardly wait. I would still be willing to work when needed, but was happy to retire the gloves. After a hard day's work, all I needed was quality time with the fam and the anticipation of making Mama happy.

After a grueling week, Mama's birthday dinner felt like a reward. For her special day, we wanted to surprise her by taking her to a fancy restaurant.

"Kids, no, this is too much, we can't afford this," she gasped, stopping at the entrance.

"Don't worry, Mama—" Tristan wrapped a hand around her shoulders "—we got this!"

We all saved up for the entire month so that we could all eat whatever we wanted from the menu. She once mentioned that she'd traveled to Greece before college, falling in love with the food, so it was a no-brainer when we settled on a Greek Michelin-star restaurant. All dressed up, we made our way through the place. The Apollo was out of our league, but we managed to blend in by trying to hide our impressed faces at the surroundings themed around Greek mythology. The interior walls were adorned with artwork from the era and various monuments. It only got better when we got to the terrace, which was like an ode to ancient folklore, featuring standing sculptures of famous heroes, gods, and creatures, down to the snakes dancing around Medusa's head. A young-looking waiter with high cheekbones took us to our seats when a familiar laugh echoed, tingling my ear.

I snapped, turning around only to see the back of her head slightly tilted, her shoulder shaking. At first, I thought it wasn't The Vamp, since her hair was different, and I couldn't see her face, but I felt with every fiber of my body that it was her. The hair color matched the wine in her glass. She was sitting across a cute blonde who was facing me, but my eyes were focused on the strands falling down her companion's hips. The wine glass moved in the air, getting closer to her mouth. I watched as she slightly turned, revealing her profile, and my heart stopped.

"Is that her?" my mother asked, and all eyes at the table immediately switched on to me. I nodded and turned my attention back to the Vamp.

"Oh shit," Tristan whisper-yelled.

My thoughts exactly.

What are the odds? And what do I do to keep them?

Everything around me dulled away, only her in focus. She looked like she belonged here. By the way the servers were catering on their hands and feet, you'd think they were royalty or something, a complete contrast to the girl I saw driving a piece of nothing Jeep.

She took out a box of cigarettes, and I rushed over to her without thinking or fucking blinking. Taking out my Zippo from my back pocket, I flipped it open and lit it in front of her mouth. She gradually guided her eyes upward while curving her mouth into a side smile, and drew in the moment our eyes locked. I broke the contact, focusing on the red dress barely covering her chest, the outline of her breasts, all the way down to her knees. Her naked calves showed off a tattoo that looked like shackles around her ankle, but I couldn't see the

61

details due to the shadows forming around her legs.

What do they mean?

My eyes focused back on hers, and I noticed they were greener, somehow.

"Serendipity, huh?" she gasped, and all I could do was nod before I turned to her friend; jaw dropped, brows high, and forehead wrinkled. Rotating to the table next to them, I asked to borrow a free chair, slid it around, straddled it, and placed myself between the two dames. I took out a cigarette from her pack and trailed it to my mouth, giving it a gentle lick down the side, and waited. As if reading my mind, she grabbed the Zippo from my hand and lit it. The brush of her fingers made my body go still. I took a drag, the air around us smoked with our exhales, emphasizing the tension.

That makes 21.

The blonde coughed, and our gazes separated.

"So I see none of you have any manners, but I will bypass it… I am Aria," she held out her hand, "you must be the motorcycle guy." I took her hand and gently shook it.

"I am Mateo, the guy who owes her fourteen years of pleasure, and I believe now she owes me seven more." My head tilted so I could face the object of my obsession, noticing her *'I'm going to kill you'* look pointed at both of us.

I raised one brow, whispering, "So you've been talking about me?"

Giving me a grin, she uttered, "Don't get full of yourself; I might've mentioned some guy stalking me."

I laughed, stretching out the word, "Riiight."

Taking another drag, I took my time staring into those spellbinding eyes. "So are you going to give your name, manners, and all that, or am I going to have to keep calling you Vamp?"

She blew out a cloud of smoke, her greens disappearing behind, but it didn't hide her little head shake.

"It's Sabrina, but she goes by Sab; thought Vamp suits her, so kudos for that one," her friend revealed. She took a sip of her wine and continued playfully, "Fun facts: She's smart, funny, Scorpio, loves sunsets, goes to Harvard Law, usually sits by the tree on the west side of the Radcliffe quad... But do be advised, she is a heart-breaker." Aria finished in a high-pitched, amusing voice, making Sabrina's death stare more potent.

Harvard Law? And yet, she moved like she owned the underworld.

"Well, thank you, Aria, very much, and believe me when I say that she has already stolen my heart, might as well break it in the process!"

Aria choked on her wine, but all I could do was stare at Sab's chest as it rose with her breath. She swallowed hard, looking straight into my eyes, slightly parting her lips. Her breath shallowed, mine matching hers. Snapping out of this fucking spell she had over me, I asked, trying to keep my cool, "So Aria, tell me. What's a guy gotta do to get this one's number?" I turned my gaze to Aria, pointing to the siren in a red dress. Aria's shoulders shook as a loud laugh escaped her. "Sorry, Mateo, but that's pushing it. I gave you enough information; the rest is up to you."

"Fair enough. And it's O," I drawled, switching my looks from one to another, both with confused looks on their faces. I bowed down to Sabrina's ear, purring, "As in how your mouth would form before screaming in pleasure!"

Preferably with my fingers inside you.

Goosebumps erupted over exposed skin, and my dick hardened at the sight. Straightening up, I said, "Now, ladies, I have to get back to my family, but it was a pleasure." Turning around, I returned the chair and walked back to my table, feeling her stare follow me.

Chapter 11

Sabrina

"You are so screwed," Aria ribbed.

"I know. Trust me, I know." My head fell into my open palms, elbows plastered on the table, holding me afloat. Shaking my head in hopes of stopping the storm from brewing, I put out my cigarette, immediately lighting up a new one. Nerves overwhelmed me, feeling his stare, while my whole body fought the urge to turn around.

"Sab, he's gorgeous, charismatic, and his family's a whole vibe," she thundered.

Point taken.

Fuck me, he looked yummy in black suit pants forming tightly around his legs and plump ass, paired with a white dress shirt featuring black buttons that couldn't hide the definition of his muscles. He was athletically built, tall and strong, with black ink barely visible on the right side of his collar, resembling the end of a flame. I wanted to rip his shirt off so badly to see it, to see it all.

But his face, his fucking face, now that was a work of art. The possession of a distinctive and charismatic appearance was dominant. The strong face with a chiseled jawline, full lips, and expressive almond-shaped brown eyes hidden under even darker straight, thick-lined eyebrows. One sexy-ass scar cut right over the middle of his right brow, adding to his bad boy vibe. And that pierced ear of his, damn—it did something to me. His bare skin was now covered with a short, trimmed stubble that suited his facial features perfectly, accentuating his prominent chin. All of it complemented by his brown hair, sporting a slick, high fade, replacing the previous crew cut.

Did he grow it out for me?

His olive-like complexion, warm and toned, skin glowing almost as if covered in oil, so smooth, but his fingers were rougher. When I grabbed his Zippo from his hand, I felt the hardness of his skin, knowing he had working hands, which only made me want him even more.

Aria spent the rest of the dinner telling me how he had four more men at his table and an older woman. One guy looked like he was in high school, semi-bold, athletic, and tall, with chocolate skin. The one next to him was described as huge, with dark hair and olive skin, resembling the Hulk. One was a younger version of Mateo, and the fourth was a Filipino-looking individual, shorter than the others, with curled hair and glasses. She said the woman was beautiful but old, probably in her sixties, comparing her to Mandy Moore in 'This is Us', but with darker gray hair.

I kept fighting off every urge to look at him, to stand up and join them. My heart was racing at an alarming rate.

"I don't get it." Aria's voice snapped me out of it. "I mean the effect he has on you, damn girl. And I still can't believe he didn't recognize you!"

"Not everyone knows who I am."

"But most men do," she stated.

Another point for Aria.

If I got a penny for each time a prick came up to me saying they jerked off to my photos, I would have another million on me.

"Why don't you just give him your number?"

I shook my head. "I can't go there right now, I need my full focus on the plan. I can't afford a distraction, and you know that." I played with my fingers on my lap, then took another cigarette, praying his Zippo would light the fire. Disappointment crept up when it didn't come, so I lit it myself.

"When are you going to fill me in on all this sneaking you have been doing? You're getting me worried." A concerned look appeared on Aria's face, causing warmth to spread through me.

"I can't say anything, and you know that. It's not safe. Simon is the only one who knows, and even that's pushing the limit on the people involved," I said in a firm tone. To keep him sheltered, I had not shared the information that Simon was my brother. Aria only knew he worked with me, and that was that.

"You don't have to do it all on your own; you know that, right?"

She took my shaking hand, softening her gaze, but it did nothing to calm me down. I was on the verge of spiraling. The guilt, the plan... It was all too much.

"I'm not doing it alone." I took another drag and removed my hand from her, not ready for her to feel my nerves. The wheels in my head started spinning as I tried to bypass these growing feelings. This was the worst possible time for something like this to be happening. And I couldn't afford to be selfish right now, but I wanted to; more than anything—I wanted him.

The worst part was that I had never wanted anything more in my entire life, and that bothered me the most. Men had never had that effect on me before.

Mateo was the first.

I shook it all off because I damn well knew I couldn't allow it. A plan was set into motion and needed to be executed; a ticking clock in the works.

Aria broke the silence, mumbling, "They're all standing up."

I turned around so fast my head protested with a start of a headache. Mateo offered the woman her shawl, helping her put it on, and it was the sweetest, sexiest thing to witness. Four out of five men gave me a wave, and I could feel the blush forming on my cheeks. The woman gave me a nice, warm smile, and my heart fluttered. Hulk's eyes flicked to Mateo, protective, like I was a threat. The tall, athletic one revealed a grin, mimicking Mateo's, easing the tension that was building. As his family left, I stood up, and before I took the first step, a shadow loomed over me.

"Don't!" A harsh, deep voice sent chills down my spine. I looked up at the 7-foot Shrek.

"Stay away from him, you will only hurt him."

A part of me wanted to counterattack, to tell him he didn't know me, but I stayed quiet because he was right. I would only hurt him; it was all I'd ever known. Frozen in my spot, I just stood there, not able to move as I tried to steady my breath.

"Shit, Sab. You're white as a sheet."

I loved how worried and protective Aria was over me. I loved even more how she accepted me, and despite all my darkness, she chose to stay by my side.

Taking the weight off my wobbly feet, I sat down with a deep breath, blinking away the tears forming in the corners of my eyes.

You don't cry, remember?

My pep talk worked, and I finished my glass of wine, pouring another one and topping off Aria's.

"You got it bad, don't you?" she wailed, and her blue eyes glowed in the moonlight.

"I can't even explain it. It's like a pull of some kind, like a force that draws me to him. And his eyes," I groaned, letting out a frustrated laugh. "Do you understand that his eyes are brown? The most common of eye colors. And somehow I find them intriguing."

Aria snorted, and I shot her a glare.

"This is not the time to mock me!" I exclaimed.

"I am not, it's just all so…" she hesitated, "new. I've never seen you like this."

"Like what?" I prowled, curious, desperate for insight I couldn't figure out by myself.

"Soft."

"Soft?"

"Yeah, you're all mushy."

"Mushy? You're calling me mushy?"

"I say it as I see it. You better be careful, Sabrina; your heart is showing."

A lump formed in my throat so big I couldn't swallow it. I peered at my friend blankly, unable to utter a single word -

her words repeating over and over in my mind.

The ringtone specifically set for Simon's calls intercepted my thoughts, and I answered, stepping away from the tables and ears.

"He's at the place," he whispered on the other end of the line.

Sranje!

"The guy has the worst timing," I sighed, "I'll handle it."

He hung up, and I returned to my seat. My heart sank; Mateo's eyes still burned in my mind, but the plan couldn't wait.

"Damn girl, every time you sit down, you get paler." She shook her head disapprovingly, and I shrugged in response.

"How much will you hate me if I call it a night? Something came up, and I have to go," I kept my tone steady and apologetic.

"You know I could never hate you. Call me if you need me to help bury a body," she ended with a chuckle.

My best friend, ladies and gentlemen.

"Means a lot." I kissed her on the cheek and bolted, Simon's words echoing.

Time to hustle.

Chapter 12

Sabrina

The drive to the Underground was short. I parked my Porsche in the garage and took the elevator down to the ground level. The Underground was a 'secret' club two stories below the city. The best-kept legally illegal secret in town. It was for the elites and elites alone. Even the servers had to be vetted meticulously. Despite being a member, the fine establishment was rarely graced with my presence. I quickly worked around my appearance: I'd used colored lenses to make my eyes blue, put on a blonde wig, and concealed my beauty mark. I pulled my dress up to the middle of my thighs and stepped inside. The security guard winked at me, whispering "The red VIP" in my ear, so I nodded and continued my stride to the designated area.

Full disclosure, the guy may or may not have thought I was an escort. So, let's just keep it between us.

The club was high-end, featuring five separate chambers, each in a different color and music style. For example, the blue room was also the blues room. Every piece of furniture matched the color, down to the carpet. Each space had its own bar and staff, and, yes, the staff wore uniforms matching the color theme. Apart from the color and music style, all rooms were identical, down to the VIP areas. Leather bar stools around the standing tables, couches, and lounge chairs on the sides, with a small dance floor in the middle. Mirrors of various sizes and shapes covered the walls above the couches, giving the space a unique yet intimate feel. Each corner sported a platform where dancers moved sensually, showing just the right amount of skin.

Eying the red curtain, I called a waitress for a glass of vodka. Two minutes later, I had it in my hand, and I took a mouthful, mixing the liquid around my cavity before swallowing. Pouring some on my hand, I drew it around my neck. Taking a deep breath, I started my act, stumbling through the curtain, pretending to lose my balance. Code name Mr. Darcy sized me up, then stood, grabbed me by the waist, and ordered the woman he was with to leave. Mr. Darcy was a 46-year-old district attorney with his mind set on a Senate candidacy. Even his cologne reeked of old money. He was also very violent to his, to be polite, dates. I grabbed his hand, mouthing a "Tken me," in fake gibberish, allowing him to set me down. His hand immediately lifted my dress, his mouth creeping to my neck.

The bastard!

His touch made my skin crawl, but I hid my disgust, knowing I would ruin him.

The fact that I was perceived as beautiful came in handy for the purpose I had set out for myself. It was easy for me to get what I wanted from men, to manipulate them. The fact that I was smart and too cocky for my own good was the reason I knew I could do it all on my own.

Not once looking at my face, he grazed his hand over the inside of my thighs when I pushed them together, trapping his palm. I pulled his hair, causing his head to lean back to ease the pain. His eyes fired up, and yup, the jerk was into the whole Dom thing, but I just needed two more minutes of his attention; two minutes till this thing in my purse cloned his phone; 120 seconds of holding back... but if anyone could pretend, it was surely me. After a brief vibration confirmed the task was complete, I released his hand and pushed him down onto the red carpet. I dug my heel into his crotch, and he screamed like an opera singer. Taking out my phone, I gave my heel a little twirl, then took a picture with the light flashing. Turning around, not saying a word, I moved the curtain to the sides as a voice yelled behind me, "You will pay for this." The smile, the one described at the beginning of the story, felt so good as I curved my lips into it. The threat made it even better. If I were a man, I'd be hard right now.

Back in the garage, I ditched the wig and the lenses in my car, removed the makeup from my cheek, craving the gold room's chaos to drown my thoughts. I could use some alcohol mixed with dance therapy, maybe indulge in some heavy groping. My mind needed to be cleared, desperate for a moment of rest from overthinking. That was how I found myself in the middle of the dance floor, pressed to a hard chest, not to mention something else. One good thing about this place was the no-paparazzi rule, which happened to be my favorite. One that meant I could dry hump this guy, whose name I had forgotten, in the middle of the dance floor, and there would be no proof of it anywhere. There was also an unspoken rule, somewhat akin to 'what happens in The Underground, stays in The Underground', making it the perfect place to lose myself.

Two, maybe three songs later, we were in the Separee, yours truly riding the lap of a cute stranger. His athlete's grin screamed rookie fame. Hockey player, I thought, but wasn't sure. All I knew was that he was rock hard, giving me exactly what I needed.

His kissing was a bit sloppy, but his hair was perfect to twine my fingers in to pull on hard. A bad thought crossed my mind, a truly terrible one. My heart reacted, pumping fast while my greedy fingers retreated, wishing they were wrapped in someone else's hair.

Fuck!

With both of his hands groping my tits, ignoring the nipples that were begging for attention, the horny side of me died. His hands felt all wrong; Mateo's would've felt right. Standing up, I got out of a cold shower and mumbled out an excuse. There was a gruff protest, and I could hear him yell from behind me, 'Can I at least have your number?' before I disappeared.

Stupid Mateo and his hair that he grew out over the summer.

Stupid, stupid, stupid! Him, me, both of us, all of it—just… *Stupid*!

Storming out, his damn hair haunted me as I floored the Porsche. My phone lit up; Simon's text flashed: 'Did you get it?'

Chapter 13

Mateo

What was it about this woman that I couldn't get out of my head? I spent the whole night tossing and turning, trying to erase the picture of her that now permanently resided in my brain cells. She was still the same, except for the new color and bangs spreading from the center to her sides, following the lines of her heart-shaped face. Her berry-like scent, with a hint of tobacco, overwhelmed my senses, almost making me taste her aromatic fragrance. The spark I felt all over my body when she touched my hand, taking my lighter, finding new places inside of me to light up. I was a goner, officially and unrecoverably a fucking goner. And I now knew her name. My willpower was at its finest, not allowing me to fucking Google the hell out of her. I stopped the alarm before it went off and jumped down from the upper bed.

With an early class ahead, I grabbed my jacket, gloves, and helmet before riding down to campus. I was in my third year at Boston University, studying engineering and computer science, a full ride thanks to my mother pushing the smarts out of me. Mak was in the middle of his residency, and Luka landed a job in a construction company, slowly rising to an overseeing position. Tristan was still in high school, making his mark on the football field with a bright future ahead of him. Ty left yesterday to start his first year at the University of Tennessee, where he'd be the starting shooting guard for the Volunteers. I, on the other hand, had a knack for building things, with a shelf full of trophies to prove it. That's why BU was a perfect fit.

The auditorium was packed, but since the seats were assigned, I quickly checked the list and confirmed I was in the third row. I claimed my seat and opened the laptop, opening a fresh document. My informatics teacher in high school had been a godsend, teaching us fast, blind typing, which came in handy in all my classes, allowing me to transcribe every word said aloud. She was also the reason I took a more intense approach to everything computer-related.

At the end of a very long monologue coming from the front, the girl next to me spoke out, "Could you send me the notes? I barely managed to write a third of it." I gave her a polite smile, accompanied by a nod. "Sure, write down your email." She handed me a torn piece of paper with her name, Piper, her email address, and her phone number written on it. Her nervous giggle did nothing to spark any interest.

The dismissal of the class nudged the crowd to their feet for the exit, as I waited for the rush to pass. The professor called me down, "Mr. Hart, a word?" I nodded and descended the stairs, meeting him at his desk. "Your paper blew me away, Hart. Mind if I send it to ENOVA? They'd love you for their internship."

ENOVA was a high-end mechanical engineering company specializing in building projects for hospitals and the development of therapeutic equipment. I nodded, losing all words in my confusion.

"I need verbal consent, Mateo," he said through a slight laugh.

"Of course, sir, you are most definitely permitted to do so."

"Good. I think you'll be a good fit there."

My eyes widened, and excitement flooded me. "Thank you, sir; it is much appreciated."

"Don't thank me yet. Now, I have the next class coming and need to prepare, but I will keep you updated."

I pushed my laptop into my rucksack and enthusiastically said, "Of course, sir, see you next week. Have a nice rest of your day." Waving goodbye, I exited, leaving the door open as a new rush of fresh meat entered the room.

With my classes done, her name burned in my head, so I hurried to Harvard's quad. The drive took less than 5 minutes with my bike, and the fact that we've been so close all this time unnerved me.

Scanning all the trees around the rectangular square, I picked the one farthest away, slightly separated from the others, with minimal foot traffic, which I thought would be her favorite. I sat down, leaning my back against the trunk, and took out a copy of 'Brave New World' by A. Huxley. Our mother got us into reading and even formed a family book club.

"Trying to look smart now, are we?" The sexiest voice made every hair on my body stand on end in excitement. There she was, the sun behind her, showing nothing but her silhouette; the light illuminated around her. I could almost hear the angels singing the high-pitched 'Aaaaaaaa'.

I closed my book with a thud and stood up to face her. She was wearing a white shirt tucked into high-waisted dark jeans; a brown belt kept them in place, and a pair of white Birkenstocks covered her feet. She looked so different from the girl I saw the other night, with her hair tied in a high ponytail and her makeup on the more natural side. Her eyes had that twinkle that was specifically loud for me, crossed arms on her chest, and all.

"A guy's got to do what a guy's gotta do," I said while smirking. "Hello, Vamp, fancy meeting you here."

"Sticking with that one, I see." She uncrossed her hands, giving me my opening, so I grabbed her hand and pulled her down, but she resisted. Before I could protest, her hand took out a blanket from her briefcase-looking bag, and I watched her swing it in the air and spread it on the ground. On her way down, she grabbed my hand and pulled me to sit next to her. I would be lying if I said my heart didn't jump at the gesture. She grabbed the book from my grip and switched her focus to the cover.

"It's for our book club. We are doing a compare and contrast month," I mumbled, making her gaze snap to mine.

She took her time scanning me, trying hard not to laugh in my face before she decided I was serious, then she started humming… "Fahrenheit 451, 1984, and…" She tapped her finger to the side of her mouth, eyes looking to her upper right corner. "Animal Farm?"

Fuck me!

Speechless, she left me utterly speechless. Afraid to say something stupid, I sat there in mute awe of her.

"I'll take that as a yes." She swallowed and enthusiastically continued, "I would strongly recommend the Ravenhood series. It is somewhat of an answer to those books. Set in today's world, it's kind of a take on Robin Hood with a lot of spice." She smacked her mouth with a twack. "Shit. Sorry. I don't know who is in your book club, but the female portion would surely appreciate the smut."

I let out a laugh, not able to stop it as she joined me with hers. The sound of her chuckle was a drug I couldn't quit. The roar of my engine had just been demoted to third place.

"So you like spicy?" I struck a serious, somewhat seductive tone.

"Hey, what can I say? I don't watch porn, I read it like a fucking lady!" She exclaimed; another laugh burst out, and I was officially obsessed; so was my hardened cock.

"Are the Ravenhood series your favorite?" Our eyes met at my question.

"The audiobooks are amazing, and I am not one bit ashamed to say I've listened to them far too many times to count." Her cheeks turned red, and I took a mental picture of the sight, disregarding her ability to avoid a question, and also putting a mental note to read these books.

Mama would've loved her book talk.

"Are you free today?" I asked, flushing the redness away.

"I have time until 2 o'clock."

Checking my watch, noting we had three hours.

Good enough.

I stood up and pulled out my hand in front of her, opening my palm. She took a couple of seconds longer than necessary, and I started to sweat, begging every power that existed for her not to reject me. If I'd blinked, I would've missed the decision softening her gaze. Her hand fit perfectly in mine as I pulled her up. I picked up the blanket, shook it clean, then neatly folded it. Her warm gaze was on me when I handed it back to her before she tugged it back into her bag. We walked side by side to my bike, and I stopped, realizing I had no idea where to take her. Panic engulfed me as my head started spinning with ideas, none of which were good enough. I scratched the back of my neck, and as if she read my mind, she said with a laugh, "I know a place where we could kill some time."

A sigh of relief calmed me down, but panic rose with her words, "But only if I drive!"

My eyes narrowed at her request, and she rolled hers. Sighing, she took something out of her bag and lifted it for me to see. I read her license, stating she had a Class M permit.

Oh, Hell!

One second, she was a Harvard scholar, a troublemaker the next—how did she switch so fast? I took out the spare helmet, covered her tiny head, and fastened the clip. I held the bike straight so she could saddle it before I took my place behind her.

The whirring sound of the motor gruffed while I contemplated where to put my hands. The decision was made for me, and it played out in slow motion: my hands were captured by soft fingers and placed on each side of her waist, low enough to make me swallow. She took a route between buildings, owning my Royal Bullet 350, downshifting ahead of a sharp corner. During the drive, Sabrina handled my bike like she had been riding it her whole life, and I enjoyed every second of it. When we got to the open road, her right hand on the gas, her left arm reached behind, giving the outside of my thigh a gentle squeeze, striking me stupid. The caress made my dick hard, and my stomach fluttered. Some inside part of me giggled because the Vamp stole my move right out from under me, striking every nerve in my body, leaving me utterly breathless. And even though I couldn't see her, I knew she had the biggest smirk on that beautiful face of hers.

A ten-minute blissful drive of my hands wrapped around her, her foot switching gears as she took in every curve, leaning us to the sides, ended when we parked in front of a bar straight out of a cowboy movie. Like a true gentleman, I got down first, holding the bike for her descent. Leaving our helmets hanging over the mirrors, we strode inside, swinging the batwing door open. All I could think was that we had stepped into the Twilight Zone. Inside, the bar looked nothing like the saloon on the outside. It was dark, with green and red spotlights dancing in circles from each corner of the ceiling. The bar was lit with neon yellow lights, some dance song blaring, but it was practically empty, with one guy sitting in the corner. She waved at the bartender, making the peace sign, and continued walking, leading us to a separate room with a pool table.

She turned her head. "You play?" I nodded whimsically. "Sure."

She started to arrange the balls, spinning the eight ball, smirking as if she already owned me. The bartender brought two beers, and that's when I realized how stupid I was for thinking she had given him the peace sign.

Chapter 14

Sabrina

I gave him the opportunity to break, but, as if mapped in his male brain, he let the girl, who in his mind probably didn't stand a chance, get the upper hand. Three moves in, I had four balls in the pockets, claiming the solids as mine. Impressed and sexy about it, he grabbed his stick and gently struck the cue ball, allowing the yellow stripe to fall into the side pocket. With a grin, he continued, showing off and letting me know he was, in fact, a worthy opponent. Though the first round was tight, I was the one who sent the black one in first, taking the lead.

He set up the balls before he started walking toward me with a confident stride and his signature grin, which affected my already damp underwear.

"What are we playing for?" Mateo taunted, and I acted offended, hand on my chest with a pout I damn well knew was cute as hell. "What, my company is not good enough?" I teased, batting my long lashes, happy that I had put in extra effort.

"It's more than enough, but I wouldn't mind some heavy getting to know each other in the mix!"

"So you want to play for information?"

"Yup," he popped the P. "Each ball in for a question."

"Fine," I agreed and broke. Without any hits, he took his stance, shoving the striped green one into the middle-left pocket.

"What's your favorite book?"

"Heavy start and a hard question. Gun to the head, I would have to say 'The Black Tulip.'"

There was a slight drop of his jaw; his damned sexy, freshly shaved jaw. Observing him more, I felt a slight admiration, maybe? I couldn't really tell, but I sure hoped to be right.

"No need for guns, Vamp, we're just talking."

"Whatever," I feigned indifference, but desperately wanted to keep it going. He rounded the table and hit the red one, sending it across in the corner pocket, smirking.

Stupid, smug, hot face!

"Favorite song?"

"Blackbird, by the Beatles," I answered easily.

He paused for a moment, and dare I say, looked impressed.

"I just got a new nickname for you." He raised his brows, revealing another smirk.

The bastard managed to split the yellow one and the maroon to the sides, both getting in.

"That gives me two... let's think..." he hummed, "If you could be any animal, which would it be and why?"

"Going philosophical on me? K, I'll bite." I took a minute to pretend it wasn't something I thought about often. "A harpy eagle. It's the strongest of birds; the female is stronger than the male. And I like birds in general, the freedom they represent."

That earned me an approving nod, as if I needed it or something. I dismissed it with a *middle-to-silent "Pft."*

He finally missed his shot, and I was determined not to allow him another. Number four went in, easing the anxiety.

"Come on, Blackbird, shoot."

"Didn't bring my gun with me," I singsonged.

That got him to chuckle, and his eyes fired some heavy flames at me, sending mixed signals. I swallowed whatever lump was causing my brain to short-circuit.

"What do you do? For work, I mean?"

"What makes you think I work?"

"I'm the one asking questions," I pointed out.

"I worked in construction during summer break."

Hm...

I thought, thinking about his rugged hands that I imagined all over me... Blue number two went in next. The balls seemed to align perfectly with each shot, making it way too easy for me, but hey, a win's a win.

Considering the limited number of questions, I had to phrase the next one very carefully. I ended up pleased with the way I formed it. "What were you taking the summer break from?"

There was a curve on his lips, obviously amused by the way I got to that in one swoop.

"School."

When he winked, I felt something sizzle inside of me. I was doomed—doomed I tell ya!

I missed a shot daydreaming about him, while right there next to him. He made his easily, putting the purple in.

"Your favorite book boyfriend?"

"Ryke Meadows," I answered swiftly, impressed by the question.

Over the years, I had imagined doing unspeakable things with a lot of fictional characters, but Ryke was the one I always went back to. He fell in love with a supermodel who had a life similar to mine. He was her cure and her escape from it all. He also rode a bike, just like my man did.

Mine?

What the hell just ran through my head?

No mind, we're not going there. No claiming whatsoever!

He miscalculated, and the white ball hit my lucky number 3, turning it all around. I couldn't help but laugh, mocking, "Thanks for that."

Giving a simple shrug of his shoulder, he stepped back to the table, taking a sip of his beer. The way his lips formed before they touched the mouth of the bottle made my jaw tick. I was fucking jealous of a beer bottle... What the hell was wrong with me?

"You're not going to ask me what my favorite song is?" There was obvious amusement in his voice, with a side of curiosity.

"I have a feeling you do not have one."

He hummed, letting me know my assumption was spot-on.

"What do you study?"

"Engineering and computer science. I just applied for a summer internship at ENOVA."

Trying to act unfazed while dying to put on a bit of a show, I bent over in front of him, taking on a harder shot, as opposed to the number 6 hovering over the hole, screaming at me. He cleared his throat, and I gave myself a mental pat on the back before I made the impossible shot, sending the yellow number 1 into the middle pocket.

I leaned on the table, catching my breath—his grin too damn distracting.

"Tell me about your family," I prompted.

"What do you want to know?"

Everything.

When nothing came out of my mouth, he shared, "We're messy, loud, and very close."

Must be nice.

My lips tightened, holding me back.

Refocusing on the game, I walked around the table, scanning the setup. No. Six went in next, and I had trouble thinking of the next question, but it soon hit me. The game slowed somehow, his eyes daring me to dig deeper.

There's one question I've been dying to ask.

"So, about that book club of yours, can you shed some light?"

"I was wondering when you would get to that one," he confessed, then smirked, taking another sip of his beer.

"It's a family book club. Our Mama created it to get us to read. It turned into a weekly thing, and we all love it."

God, his voice was so smooth—pure trouble.

"Wait. So, you read one book a week?"

Where do you find the time? I wanted to add, but chose not to.

"That's the requirement, though we do our own reading on the side," he answered, despite no balls hitting any pockets.

"Wow, I barely have time to listen to one book a week, let alone read it." I shook my head at him.

"What consumes your time?"

"Hey, it's my turn," I squeaked.

"Hey, back," he grinned, "I gave you more than one answer, plus we're kind of on a roll here."

Which was a first for me. I usually get in, get naked, and get out. No small talk, no talk whatsoever for that matter.

"School, family obligations, and a job on the side."

"The secret side hustle?"

His questions were edging too close for comfort. Jacob's downfall couldn't afford this, no matter how much Mateo's voice tingled all the right spots.

"Yeah, and please don't ask about it or you'll ruin this whole thing."

"I wasn't planning on it."

And I believed him. Despite his obvious bad-boy image, he came across as trustworthy. And it made me feel all the guiltier for hiding so much from him.

"I have to ask..." He took my hand and pulled it between us. "What does this mean?" His eyes shot to the tattoo on my ring finger. It was just an X, repeated multiple times to form a ring.

"That..." I hesitated. "Is a simple gesture of full disclosure."

"Okeeey?" His brows furrowed in question.

"I don't believe in marriage and have no plans to get tied down," I revealed.

"Noted, how 'bout tied up?"

His husky voice hid a hunger that matched mine.

"Though my heart can't be tamed, bondage is not off the table." I lifted one brow in challenge.

"Thank you for the visual."

I pinched the hem of an imaginary dress and curtseyed. "You're welcome."

There was a beat, a moment when both our minds went to a place, and by the bulge forming in his tight jeans, his thoughts went in the same direction as mine.

My bag vibrated, but I ignored it, knowing it was probably Simon. I just hoped my current distraction didn't notice the slight flinch.

Chapter 15

Sabrina

Ava Max's 'Salt' started playing, and my legs automatically began to move to the beat. Sizing me up, Mateo parted his lips, slowly sliding his tongue over the lower one. I could feel his eyes on me the entire time, a silent dare I couldn't ignore. His cologne hit me, sharp and warm, pulling me closer.

Another 'pool' appeared down south, and after mentally saying 'screw it', I took three steps separating us, grabbed his shirt, and took his mouth.

His stick hit the floor at the exact moment our tongues collided, giving the explosion a corresponding sound. He tasted like perfection, and I wanted to suck all of his everything. His hair was long enough for me to drag my finger through, but lacked another inch for the full grab in my desperate need to get him closer.

His hand wrapped around the back of my neck, and I tilted my head, allowing him more access. In one effortless swoop, I was up, my ass situated on the table with him filling the space between my spread-out thighs. I could feel the rock-solid pressure of his arousal, and I snapped. Forgetting any rationalization roaming my messed-up head, I took charge, unbuttoning his jeans. He slapped my craving hand away, pulling from my hungry mouth, leaving my lips swollen with unsated desire. His eyes were reading me with a serious focus, slowly descending to watch my chest rise and fall with each sharp breath I took.

He stood there, staring at me, reaching the deepest parts of my soul, and all I could do was focus on the golden specks around his iris, if only to keep my mind from overthinking.

Clenching my fist around the fabric of his shirt, I pulled him toward me, claiming his mouth, biting the lip he had licked a few minutes ago. Feeling the metallic taste on my tongue, I took it down a notch.

He pressed his rock-hardness on me, and sparks started to fly. Finishing my act from earlier, I freed his cock and stroked it with my firm hand, swiping away the pre-cum. Without looking, he worked my belt, then the button. I could hear the zipper of my jeans—the sound of pure anticipation. He slid them down to my knees, making sure to graze my skin on the route. He stepped over them, desperation mixed with craving evident. I pulled my legs over his hips, locking him in with my jeans now around my ankles. Slowly, my tongue covered his skin from his throat to his ear, a quiet 'Hell' escaping his mouth. Taking it as an encouraging moan, I attacked his neck. He froze, his breath hitching, and I knew something was off before he spoke, "No condom."

My heart tripped, and his eyes bored into mine.

Sranje.

Does that mean sex was not his endgame here? Was it mine? I couldn't think straight. No one had ever wanted anything more than to fill the space between my legs.

My pulse raced; a part of me wanted to risk it, to feel him

with nothing between us, but I wasn't that reckless. Was I?

I eyed my bag, sitting on the floor next to the door.

"In my bag, I have a couple," I said in one breath.

His eyes darkened before he slowly stepped out of my ankle lock. He reached the door, placing a chair under the knob to block it, then rummaged through my bag. When he found what he was looking for, he got back to me, placing his hands on my waist. His fingers lingered, like he'd been waiting for this forever. The guy who invaded every thought for the entire summer was finally in my reach. Knowing it was a mistake, I no longer cared. As if reading my thoughts, he went down on his knees, removed my jeans and underpants, and introduced himself to my soaking pussy. His tongue worked wonders, making me unbearably frantic.

I had a hard-to-please clit, but somehow his tongue knew precisely how to work it. I wanted to scream at the feeling that was starting to erupt within me. He slid two fingers inside, curling at the spot where it was needed most. The pressure was just right, the rhythm musical as he artistically led me to a big ass O in record time. But he wasn't done—no—he pumped until I rode the whole thing out. Catching a steady breath was impossible, and I couldn't stop staring at him as he brought his fingers to his mouth and sucked them dry. Now it was my turn for action, my hand doing the work of grabbing his dick to cover it, before I guided it to its rightful place.

A blissful torture. That's what he did by gradually pushing himself inside. I stretched out, welcoming his length as he filled every inch of me.

"Damn, what are you doing to me?" His husky voice sent

shivers up my spine, meeting all my needs.

My hands grabbed his soft ass just as my thighs tightened around his hips, making him speed up his pace. Thrusting in with his full power, I clenched around his thickness when his thumb found my clit. The circular motion mixed with the filling rhythm of his cock was too much; another orgasm already forming. He claimed my mouth and continued his torment with precision. Out of it, I never even noticed I was still in my shirt, so I swooped it off, and he pulled down my bra, wrapping my nipple around his wet lips. His hand went straight to tease my other breast, and I heard him mumble another *fuck*. Taking his tongue to my neck, he growled out, "You're too damn much, Blackbird."

Damn that nickname for making me moan.

His eyes found mine, holding something I'd been chasing my entire life, and with one quick flick of my clit, I showered him with my orgasmic bliss, which only made him groan harder. Three thrusts later, I felt the warmth inside me with his chin pressed to my shoulder, biting down with his release. I felt the rapid beating of his heart on my chest. His body temperature was so high, like a fireball, and I reveled in it.

I had mind-blowing sex before, and I did stuff with my vibrator that would put the devil himself to shame, but nothing—and I mean nothing—had ever felt like this.

Only when he softened did he pull out, but his hands stayed wrapped around me. The hug was gentle yet powerful, and life, as I knew it, the world, everything, was forever changed.

He pulled away, then disposed of the used condom in the trash can hidden in the corner next to the door. The next thing he did was the one to ruin me, because before I knew it, he grabbed his boxers, used them to wipe the area between my thighs with the fabric in a gentle caress. I grabbed my shirt and put it on, eying him as he took my underwear and slid my legs into the designated holes. He did the same with my jeans, clothing me. Without a single blink, I watched him take off my hair tie, felt his fingers comb my hair to tug and tie it up in a high ponytail.

Everything in me went numb, and I felt a compulsion to cry.

Why the hell did I want to cry?

I frowned when he covered his nakedness with his pants, and he took my lower lip between two fingers. I stood up, knees buckling, and I reached for my jeans, only for him to beat me to the punch. He deliberately dragged them up, worked the button, and tied the buckle around my waist.

Something heavy pressed onto my chest; air was nowhere to be found.

His palm covered my face, thumb grazing my dry lips. I met his gaze, lingering there before he gave me a soft, reassuring peck.

It was him seeing me, broken parts and all, and still somehow choosing me. And I could see it in his eyes; I could feel it in his touch—it was everything.

Chapter 16

Mateo

Checking my watch, I felt the sting of disappointment with the notion that we had precisely 15 minutes left. Ten of those minutes were needed to get her back to campus, which left us with five, and I would make every second count. With the need to freeze time, I cupped her face, my thumbs tracing her jawline, committing it to memory. I pressed our lips together, hers so soft I could easily lose myself in them—in her. I craved to explore her more, to be the fucking Marco Polo of everything that was Sabrina. My hands dropped to hers, fingers grazing in invitation, and when her palms turned outward, a sense of triumph flooded me. I locked my fingers around hers, the tip of my digit hovering over her warning tattoo, trying its best not to wipe over it in an attempt to erase the damned thing.

Separating us, she gave me the look that perfectly captured my exact feelings. She grabbed her bag and pushed away the chair I had placed to block the door. She beelined to the bar, pulling bills out of her back pocket, and lifted her hand in warning, knowing I was about to protest. I zeroed in on the Franklins, wondering why on earth she carried that much cash.

Stepping outside, it took me a minute for my eyes to adjust to the light. We got to the bike, and I handed her the helmet I was, as of now, calling hers.

"You drive, I want to hold on to you this time." Those words, mixed with the rasp in her voice, unleashed a storm in the center of my chest.

Hell!

The smile beaming used up all my long-forgotten muscles. She took her place behind me and tightly gripped me, leaning her weight against my back. It took everything in me to fight away the demons compelling me to disappear somewhere far away with her. Instead, I drove to the tree under which she found me. The second she stepped down, the bike felt lighter, and the sensation was pure torture.

I felt the desperation in my voice when I said, "I need to see you again!"

Her greens met mine, and without hesitation, she unfolded, "I am free after; we can meet up at the World's End, 6.30?"

My heart skipped a beat—no, it jumped a beat.

"See you then."

She looked down at her watch and waved at me before she started running. I snorted at her clumsy run, which somehow made her more human, since I already thought she couldn't be real.

My ride home was too short, her warmth fading from my back as I pulled into the empty driveway. I got inside and heard the TV going in the living room. My mother sat on the couch watching a soap opera when I spoke out, "Hi, Mama. You good?"

She lifted her head to look at me and stared, saying nothing. Perceptive as always, she said, "You were with her?"

I nodded, and she tapped the spot next to her, inviting me to join. Pausing the TV, she turned to face me. "You look happy."

I couldn't help but smile. "I am Mama, so happy." She placed her warm palm on my cheek, and I leaned into her touch. Giving me a beaming smile, she whispered, "You deserve to be happy; just make sure you keep it real."

Mama always said how important it was to be and stay true to oneself, and I lived by that notion most of my life. The problem here was that I wasn't sure if Sabrina was doing the same. She was a puzzle I couldn't solve, but desperately wanted to.

I pulled my mother into my arms with a soft, "I love you, Mama."

"Same, my little rider, same," she added with a couple of gentle pats on my back before I pulled away and dragged myself upstairs. I took a long shower, the cold water doing nothing to ease the jitters, if only for a moment. The anticipation of seeing her again played with my head, and I could feel the stupid butterflies every girl talked about flying around in my stomach. It was as if I were under her spell, bewitched, making me a total fool for her.

All dried up, I put some extra effort into my appearance, wanting to make a good impression. Looking in the mirror for final approval, I nodded at the dark jeans and t-shirt with the New York skyline combo. The stairs creaked with each step down, and when I hit the last one, the front door swung open.

"Honey, I'm home!" Luka's voice echoed throughout the

house right before the thudding sounds of his boots hitting the hardwood.

"You're late," I mocked, "lunch is all cold now."

With a grunt, he stepped into the living room, kissing Mama on the cheek before he went upstairs. I took it upon myself to heat up lunch for both of us and get everything ready by the time he finished his after-work routine.

My big brother joined me soon after, and we ate while he talked about his new hotel project. I tried to focus, honestly, but all I kept on doing was watching the time, how slowly it passed. To keep myself busy, I washed the dishes, hoping the seconds would tick faster, but no such luck. Without any other ideas, I joined Mama, who was watching a couple fight in Spanish. I never understood the bullshit she watched, but she seemed to enjoy it, so what was I to say?

When the clock struck quarter to six, I kissed Mama goodbye and, on my way out, bumped into Luka's chest. His heavy foot tapped the floor, arms locked under his pits, and yup, he was in one of his moods. He glared down at me, harshening out, "Where do you think you're going?"

I straightened up, confused by his reaction. "Out," I said matter-of-factly.

"Who with?"

"None of your business." Feeling like I needed to defend something, it came out harsher than intended. Luka had that resting serious prick face as a way to distract people from his inner softness, but the look in his eye matched the expression. He had five inches on me, but with the angry look on his face, it felt like he had a whole foot.

"She is not who you think she is." His tone was low and

serious. I narrowed my eyes, "What's that supposed to mean?"

He turned around, grabbed something, then came back to me, snapping a magazine onto my chest. The moment I saw the cover, I was transported to hell, but this kind of hell was freezing over. Sabrina, half-naked, lying down on a fluffy carpet with two bare-chested men licking her sides. The headline 'Sabrina Furst - the next best thing in fashion' splattered in bold.

"She's a Furst, man; those people play games we can't win," he said through gritted teeth, but I felt he was holding something back.

I reached into my pocket and grabbed my phone, typing her name in the Google search bar and pressing the arrow. Articles going on for days started to hurt my eyes.

-Sabrina's new boy toy

-Sabrina on the night out

-Sabrina using her stomach as a drinking tray

-Sabrina turned down a Milan fashion show

-Sabrina, the new face of the family beauty product

-How to emphasize your eyes with Sabrina's technique

She had a Wikipedia page for fuck's sake.

I scanned it closely and read aloud, "Sabrina Pearl Furst, heiress to the Furst fashion line. She's a model, entrepreneur, and designer. Currently, she's a business and economics student at Harvard University. She's 20 years old, born on October 23, 2002."

Business and Economics? The hell?

I felt like the biggest fool. She played me, but I couldn't figure out why. What would she have to gain from lying to me? A part of me wanted to ditch her, but those green eyes haunted me, and I wanted answers. I gripped the magazine, her face on the cover tempting me to tear it apart.

Completely phantomed, I stormed out. The crisp air felt refreshing after the heat wave we endured the past couple of days, but it did nothing to cool me off. Neither did the short ride. Ever since I got my first bike, riding felt calming, and she managed to ruin that for me

I parked in front of the sign that said 'Public Welcome World's End,' and took a seat on the wooden rail, awaiting her arrival. Expecting a Jeep—I now realize was a facade—I was surprised when I saw a woman on a motorcycle approaching. Straddling the newest black Honda NCS750s with red rims and a matching seat, I could sense it was her. If I hadn't learned about her deception, this would have been the most beautiful sight to witness. Her red helmet gleamed, but all I could see was the lie.

Chapter 17

Sabrina

His intense gaze bore into me, stirring a discomfort I couldn't shake.

Sranje! He knows.

Stepping off my Honda, I turned away from him to gather myself. I took off my helmet, my fingers trembling, like they always did when the mask started to slip. With a deep breath, I gave myself a pep talk...

You got this!

Closing in on him, I noticed the magazine rolled up in his hand. That glossy lie threatened to ruin the only real thing that made me feel. I quickly rehashed all the covers I had done, thinking of the worst one, but in all truth, they were all terrible—with me half-naked—mother's choice, not mine.

I gathered all the strength I had and pulled my eyes up to his. His dark brown irises now looked pitch black, matching the shade of his pupils, causing my vision to blur.

Oh God, not now, please not now.

I fought back the tears, an instinct that was drilled into me since my fifth birthday party. *"Fursts don't cry, they only show their teeth, not tears!"* My mother's mantra echoed in my head, but it was Mateo's voice, rough and demanding, that cut through the air—"Explain!"

"Please," I implored, "before I reveal everything, I need to show you something." My voice quivered with desperation, and he relented, nodding slowly.

If I could show him my cabin, my safe space, maybe he'd see past the lies.

"Follow me?" I asked in a whisper, and he gave me another nod before putting on his helmet. Covering my face with the protective shield, I turned on my bike and began the drive. Seeing him tailing me in my mirrors gave me a sense of comfort, even knowing it would all be over soon. We drove about five miles outside the city limits, leaving the main road to take an earthen path. The air got fresher the deeper we went into the woods.

My cabin in full view, I pull to a stop, unease settling. I turned off the engine, stepped off my road pet, and with my helmet in hand, I got inside. Mateo followed suit.

It was small, cozy, but also mine. Okay, technically, it was listed under a fake name, but it was mine nonetheless. My favorite part was the fireplace in the middle, with a small coffee table from Ikea across from it and a brown sofa bed facing it. No TV, no electricity, just a wall filled with stacked books and a large number of pillows. There were a couple of solar panels to charge my phone and laptop. There was also a well out back giving me access to fresh water. Before seeing the look on his face, I had a plan to spend the whole night with him here, lying in front of the fireplace, fucking, talking, and fucking some more.

Now, looking around my sanctuary, I realized it had turned into my asylum. Not ready to face him yet, I took off my jacket and headed to the small kitchen in the corner, and by kitchen, I meant a small fridge, a table with a coffee machine, and a large bowl pretending to be a sink. The coffee maker sparked to life, and with my back to him, I asked, "You want some coffee?" Without his answer to my question, I put out two mugs and watched the steam fly around them. My arsenal in hand, I turned to find him squatting down, getting the fire started. It was a hot September day, but out here the air was crisper. His fingers fumbled with the matches, like he was holding back a storm.

I slowly walked to him, pulling down my hand to offer him his cup. He took it without saying a word and lit up the newspaper he had previously laid down for the base. I kicked off my boots and sat at the corner of the sofa, my feet snuggled under me, and I took a sip, savoring the hot taste. When the fire started to light up the room, he stepped away, taking a seat on the couch as far away from me as possible. The cracking of the wood worked like a charm in relaxing me; the sound of it always brought calm.

I swallowed hard, feeling his gaze pierce through me, stripping away every lie I'd told. I was frozen, my heart pounding with the fear of rejection.

"I'm sorry," I started apologetically, "when you didn't know who I was, it felt different, nice, and I wanted to keep it that way for as long as possible." I clenched my jaw, forcing the tears back like I'd done my whole life. He had his elbows on his knees, his hands connected over the cup, and his focus was now on the brown liquid. Somehow, I appreciated him not looking at me, knowing I wouldn't make it if met by his gaze.

"That is not who I am, that person on the cover," I

clarified, "it is what everyone wants me to be, but it's not me."

Reading his body language, all I could focus on was his thumb circling the cup's handle.

"So it's all a lie," he croaked, and I shook my head.

"Everything the public sees, yes," I gasped, tears breaking through all barriers. "But everything you saw and felt, that was real."

A slight bob of his throat sparked some hope that he might understand.

"I'm having trouble grasping. According to your Wikipedia page, you study business and economics?" It came out more like a question, and I opened my mouth to clarify, but then he whispered, "And I don't think I can even think about all the articles."

I swallowed a lump; anger, mixed with shame, took the front seat. I was stamped with the slut label, and though it was an accurate assumption, coming from him, it hurt a lot more than I liked.

"Don't trust everything you read," I snarled, "I switched to law this semester."

When he finally turned to face me, the area around his eyes softened, and he tilted his head, like he was trying to see me for the first time. "Why law?"

"I want to change the justice system," I replied evasively, though the fact held some truth.

"Mighty ambitious of you," he stated.

"You sound surprised?" I phrased it like a question, having trouble reading his expression.

He smirked, and I knew he would avoid answering me.

"What's with the Jeep?"

I averted my gaze, focusing on my fingers playing with each other in my lap, shaking my head. "That I can't tell you."

He huffed out a laugh. "Can't or won't?"

Feeling the tension rising in him, he turned away to the fire. I examined his profile, watching the flames form shadows on his cheek.

A tight knot formed in the pit of my stomach, my chest drowning in nothing. I hated this, and I didn't even know why. For a split second, I wanted to come clean. The smart me took the reins and chose to keep it locked.

My heart protested.

A tear finally escaped, marking the end of the ongoing battle.

"Both," I said under my breath, catching the drop with my finger to feel it with my thumb for confirmation.

I was leaking, and I hated it.

Ten years. That's how long it has been since the last time I cried. It was when Lucky, my horse, had died. He was sick and in a lot of pain, so we had to put him down. I was ten years old, all alone, with no one holding my hand as I said goodbye to both my friend and my eye water.

Another one followed, and I sprang up to my feet and tore outside. No one could witness it; I wouldn't allow it. The ache made my heartbeat race, matching the pace of my running feet as I met the rocks that circled the deepened water. I fell to my knees, welcoming the waterfall, releasing it all. Now aware of everything I've been carrying for the better part of my life, I mollified my scream. My tears were racing down my face, and my breathing turned on full speed, making me lightheaded. Honestly, I didn't even know why I was crying, let alone having a full-on meltdown, but it was happening and couldn't be stopped.

Strong arms lifted me into the air, shuffling me into a cradling position.

My hands flew around Mateo's neck, and I buried my face in its crook, smelling the aroma of leather and smoke. Taking slow steps, he carried me inside before he sat me down on the sofa. He took off my dirty socks, covered with soil and grass. My jeans were also damp, so I took the liberty of slipping them off when he walked to the fireplace, tossing another log in. He took the blanket draped over the armrest and wrapped me in its warmth. His chest rose and fell with strenuous breathing while his hands grazed the sides of my arms, warming me. Desperate for his touch, I leaned in; his response—a pull back. A single tear slid down my face so slowly I could feel every inch of my skin it glided over. Wiping it with his thumb, he kissed my forehead gently and slowly. His jaw tightened, eyes flickering with something unspoken, before I was left alone.

The sound of his engine faded, but the ache in my chest begged me for it not to be over.

Chapter 18

Mateo

I wasn't a hateful person, nor was I unforgiving... Now, I've found myself to be both. The said hatred pointed at my cowardice; the unforgiving part set on the untruths spoken and shown by the woman who had captured my heart. In this moment, I felt a vulnerability I had never experienced before.

Why did she hide from me? What more is she still hiding?

Driving home with a mix of emotions swirling around me, I started to lose control, causing the front wheel to wobble. For safety reasons, I pulled up at the first clearing, stepped down, and kicked the air with my feet. Cars brushed by me, but I heard nothing; my ears were burning with an imaginary high-pitched noise.

Counting to ten with sharp breaths, I took off my helmet, commanding my body to settle down. Her eyes haunted me, the way they begged me to see her, to understand. And I wanted to, so badly. But I didn't know which version I'd be getting: the kindred, free-spirited one or the cover model. The internal conflict was tearing me apart.

I shuffled out a smoke when a flicker of fire appeared before me. I dropped it from my mouth when I saw Sabrina, barefoot, without any protective gear, in her freaking underwear. My fists clenched at her reckless stupidity, but my heart warmed with the risk she took to catch up to me. She was visibly shaking, her eyes bloodshot, and her hair messed up by the wind blowing on her unprotected head. She could've gotten hurt, or worse. The emotional turmoil within me was reaching its peak.

"Are you crazy?" I yelled out, but she didn't even flinch, only murmured, "It would explain a lot."

A smile was trying to form on her lips, but failed as more tears slid down her face.

"What the fuck is with these things?" She wiped her face and stared at her hands, as if it was her first time seeing them.

I spun, my boot grinding the dirt, fighting the urge to scream. That was when my eyes spotted her bike lying on the pavement. My chest tightened with anger or fear; I couldn't tell. She wanted to get to me so fast that she didn't put the kickstand down, letting it crash on the pavement. I snapped back to her, inspecting for any injuries that the action might have caused, and I closed in on a bloody cut on the side of her ankle.

How could she have been so reckless? She could've gotten hurt, or worse... I could've lost her. Something hard pressed on my chest at the thought. The sounds of screeching tires, shattering glass, and crunching metal came rushing in like someone had amplified them over a loudspeaker. My hand flew to my scar, the pain pulsing at the small dent.

I shook the memory away and focused on Sabrina, who was still shaking. My fists clenched, torn between shoving her away and pulling her close. Instincts took over when I took a step closer, her eyes locked on mine, chest heaving, shoulders tense. Her tears hit me harder than her deception, and I couldn't walk away—not yet. I opened my arms, the motion making her flinch, speeding up her breathing. Relaxing her shoulders, she crashed into me, and I locked her in.

She'd lied, but her trembling hands, her wrecked bike— that was real, and I couldn't let go.

Safe in my arms, her body relaxed with each breath, and her sobs quieted down. With a slight shaking voice, she said, "I ruined your shirt; it looks like it rained in New York."

A snort escaped me, making her pull back and meet my gaze. I grabbed her face between my hands and leaned in, only for her to evade.

"I'm sorry, but I can't. I wanted to clear the air and say goodbye."

"Goodbye? What the hell, Sabrina?" I snapped.

My rage took a back seat when I took the time to drink her in, the plea screaming out of her eyes, begging for understanding.

She'd hidden everything from me, but this—her, vulnerable, chasing me—was all the truth I needed.

"We're going to talk about this," I ordered, stepping closer. This time, she stayed put.

"Ok, let's go back, and we'll talk," she gave in, her voice wrenched, desperate. I removed my jacket and offered it to her. She shook her head, pretending there was something interesting on the ground.

"No, it's fine. If you have the spare helmet, I will take it."

I got behind her, slowly pushing her right arm through the sleeve, then repeated the same with her left, pulling the jacket up over her shoulders. With one quick step, I came to her front, zipped it up, grazing my fingers below her chin. I took out the spare helmet and placed it over her head, securing it with the lock. Then I picked up her bike to scan it for any significant damage, sighing in relief when all I saw was a minor scratch on the side. Holding it steady for her to climb on, I released it once she had a firm grip. The engine roared to life, and she waited while I backed up to my Royal.

Back at the cabin, it took one deep breath to hit me why she'd brought me here in the first place. The place smelled like her—books, coffee, freedom—this was her sanctuary.

She charged with her words, "Look, as much as you had every right to leave, I couldn't allow us to part ways like that. I need you to know that there is nothing I want more than not to be the girl on that cover, except maybe not being her with you."

She took my hands, pulling them between us. "I am not a good person, I am so far from it, and you don't deserve getting caught up in the messed-up web that I created."

Nothing was making sense. She might as well have talked gibberish.

"I didn't lie to you, not once, believe that. If only I had met you at a different time..." She trailed off, releasing my hands to wipe her face.

"I spent my life pretending, but with you—I wanted to be real." She closed her eyes, as if the words pained her. "When you first saw me, I meant it when I said I had a side hustle; it's not just a job, it's a fight I can't drag you into," she sighed. "I hope you understand, knowing you probably won't, but still I'm hoping."

She took out my pack of smokes from my front pocket, grabbed two, putting one in my mouth, the other in hers. Flipping the Zippo, she lit the fire, and we both brought the tobacco-filled tip to the flame. Three drags later, she continued, "Who knows... When I'm done, I'll seek you out and maybe..." she laughed away the rest of her thoughts.

Done with what?

I opened my mouth to ask, but she cut me off, "You were never supposed to happen! I tried so hard to stay away, not to think about you, to fucking erase you. But then you showed up under *my* tree, reading a *jebena* book. God!" She screamed the last word, bowing down and turning away. I could see the cloud of smoke forming around her as her head rapidly shook from left to right. I was frozen in the same spot she left me at the beginning of her speech.

"This was a mistake. I am sorry, but I need you to leave!"

The hell?

"No!" My loud shout snapped her eyes to mine.

I took a step closer, and she took two back. Backpedaling, she found the wall, and I caged her in, both my hands on each side of her head. I tossed our smokes into the

111

flaming fireplace before returning my attention to her. Her eyes switched focus from mine to my mouth, repeating the motion over and over until I broke it with a kiss. Her mouth took me in, but her hands tried to push me away.

Her body was at war with itself, not knowing which side to choose. Even if it would hurt, even if we were never meant to find something at the finish line, her eyes screamed at me to stay. I gripped the back of her neck, giving her an incentive, and another one when I pressed my hardened bulge to her. Her moan pulled me in, but her secrets still lingered, a shadow we couldn't outrun. I lost my fingers in her hair, and another moan escaped her. Her legs locked around my lower back when I picked her up, and I walked us backward to the sofa, settling her on my lap. She raised her arms, and I took off her shirt, taking mine off a second later in one easy swoop. Her eyes widened at my naked chest, fingers exploring every inch of it. Tracing my tattoo, she smirked, breathing out an "I knew it."

Chapter 19

Sabrina

Fuck me, he looked good naked.

My body had never felt such bliss as it did when he roamed all over my bare skin with his lips. The sight of his exposed body was a whole other story. I traced my hands over his hard pecs down to his happy trail, inspecting his tattoo more closely to take mental notes of the details. A stack of piled books and domino pieces tossed over the line of his first rib—burning, the flames rise to his neck. I tried reading some of the titles, but he was moving, and I couldn't catch any of the letters. I grabbed his chin, which was now at my belly button, pulling him to my eye level.

The twinkle in his eyes was all I needed. I kissed him so madly, so deeply, making it all count. He stood up with purpose, hand slipping into his pants pocket. This time, he came prepared. With a golden pack between his teeth, he shimmied out of his jeans and boxers, letting them fall to the floor. Watching him strip, I did the same, tossing my panties somewhere behind me. The rush of my heartbeat intensified when he took a step closer. I spread my thighs open, lifting my left leg over the back of the sofa, freeing the space for him. I watched him tear the foil with his teeth, take out the latex, and cover his hard-on before guiding it into me.

His eyes were hungry and something else I had no time to define. Never breaking eye contact, he slowly drove himself in. He kept a slow rhythm, allowing me to adjust to his girth. The burn was sensational, sensual, and intimate. We were saying goodbye, both of us needing to savor every moment. His breaths turned into panting, and I put my palm to his chest, detecting the vibration of his rapid heartbeat. I covered my chest with his warm hand, making him feel my heart, and he synchronized his thrusts with the beat.

My body began to build up tension, but something about it felt different. My back arched, my mouth fell open, and I released a loud moan. He penetrated me deeper and sped up to my frantic heartbeat, taking my control. To say I came would be putting it mildly. It was more intense than usual— fulfilling in a way; so much so, that it spread throughout my entire body. I felt the combustion from my head to my toes.

When there were no muscles left to spasm, I moved my hips for better access, more comfortable for his pleasure. He thrust once, twice, and groaned out his own release.

We spent the next hour on the floor facing the fireplace. Mateo's back leaned on the base of the couch, my back to his chest, and my head on his shoulder. With one hand dangling over his knee, the other went around me to fondle my arm.

"Can I ask you something?" I twisted my head enough to see his nod.

"Is 'The Book Thief' your favorite book? Is that what the tattoo is about?"

"Not really," he paused, and I could hear him swallow. His eyes flickered, like he was weighing whether he should let me in.

"It was my mother's favorite. She gave it to me to hold on to, and I lost it."

There was a moment, barely, but I felt it; that one shaky inhale. I didn't press for more, and the only reason was that he looked pained, and I wanted to wipe that notion away.

We sat in silence, neither of us wanting to start the discussion.

I want to keep you.

A part of me wanted to give up on the plan and stop the execution, but I knew better. It was too important, and I was already too far in to call it off.

His ache hung in the air, stirring my own buried wounds.

I hated my family to the core, my father especially. Their selfish decisions had set in motion a chain of actions that were now depriving me of my happiness.

Sranje!

God, how I wanted to stay, to choose him, but the truth I'd uncovered left me no choice. So I had to keep it locked in, knowing I would lose Mateo.

Becoming aware of the lack of movement, I shifted, my breath catching at his peaceful face. With his eyes closed, his thick lashes appeared longer—my personal kryptonite.

Carefully, without making any noise, I got dressed, grabbed my gear, and fought the urge to break. My heart fracturing, I left him to sleep, his warmth still on my skin when I stepped into the cold night. I pushed my bike far enough so the engine wouldn't wake him.

My getaway drive was dark and cold, with no other vehicle in sight. The empty road led me to the one place I could think of—Battle Road Trail. The irony of the name was not lost on me.

With my bike steadied up on the kickstand, I took out my phone, found the week's heartbreak playlist, and hit shuffle. How on earth I managed to stumble across Boyz II Men's 'End of the Road' was beyond me.

Jebi ga!

I turned it up, taking in the lyrics; my eyes, now accustomed to the moisture, began to well up.

Each step stirred memories I'd buried, my family's lies clawing their way out. I lost myself while walking along the path, thinking and making plans. There was a wooden bridge halfway along the trail, spanning the Concord River. Taking a seat on the bridge, I looked out over the water, my brain architecting my downfall. It was where I vowed to be free, but whatever I was feeling toward Mateo only showed what I had to lose.

A cataclysmic moment occurred as the sun rose, making the whole sky glow in various shades of red. The sight overwhelmed me with impossible beauty, the past year playing out in the back of my mind. Knowing I had lost a part of me, something I never thought to be possible, I mourned the loss and shifted to anger, my wrath now taking the lead. Ready for whatever was coming, I walked back to my bike, determined to end it once and for all. I'd face them tomorrow, armed with the truth I had uncovered, no matter the cost.

It's the right thing to do. I thought, not believing it for a second.

Chapter 20

Sabrina

Sleep deprivation was added to my schedule. I couldn't get his stupid, beautiful face out of my head, and I so wanted to; I honestly did. It was just that my mind somehow had all the control, and truth be told, I begrudged it a little bit. I'd barely slept through the night, a recurring state for the past couple of months, thanks to—well, you know who…

I shuffled downstairs, stomach growling, when my father's voice stopped me cold. "Sabrina, a word!"

Fuck! Fuck! Fuck!

I opened the door with a soft "Yes, sir?" making it into a question, a slightly shivering question. He stood up, beckoning with his finger for me to come closer.

My father was in his early fifties, looking better than ever. He had the whole George Clooney appeal going for him, and to top it off, he had a well-manicured beard. He was in the best shape of his life, hitting the gym every day, not to mention a tall motherfucker with dark gray hair and a muscled, steady build. His eyes were like mine, a perfect mirrored image, down to the beauty mark under the left one. Unfortunately, his allure was not solely due to his physical appearance; it was also due to his confidence. His demeanor had captured the attention of most of my friends during my teenage years. A roster of his admirers included my high school classmates and their mothers. There was an art in his prowl, making anyone weak for the hunt. Regrettably, my mother was also susceptible to his charms.

The moment I stepped up to the desk, he threw pictures in front of me with a slam. My breath sped up, panting at the sight of Mateo and me staring at each other under my tree.

"You had me followed? What the fuck?"

I want to scream at him so badly; more so, I want to shove a knife straight through his cold, dead heart.

"Language, Sabrina, we are not animals."

I scoffed, unable to restrain myself.

"What, you have something against my boy-toy?" I acted unbothered, not allowing any tension to show.

A new set of photos materialized.

Fuck!

Pictures of the five brothers and their mother sitting in their backyard.

"Ok, what do you want?" I crossed my arms over my chest and sat my ass down, keeping up the *'I don't give a fuck'* attitude.

With one almighty smirk, he took a seat, scanning me. Luckily, when it came to my family, I was impenetrable.

"So?" I raised an eyebrow. "Want me to stop seeing him? Done. It was just sex anyway, good sex, but still. If there is room for negotiation, I wouldn't mind fucking him further, with a bit more caution, of course."

One expected loud smack to the table, his palm spread over the middle, was not nearly loud enough to even make me blink. Always a game of chess with him, but I was the one three steps ahead, sometimes even more.

"So can I keep my fuck toy, or do I need to find a new one?" I stood up, head tilted, nonchalantly checking my nails.

There was nothing more I wanted to do but smile at his face. That stupid, surprised expression he made due to my indifference. He didn't expect it, just like I knew he wouldn't. It was truly sad how little the head of the family knew about his own daughter. No wonder I was so screwed up.

Still waiting for his rebuttal, I focused on my nails, trying to decide whether to cut them or maybe give them a new, fresh coat, but my father's words cut my decision-making process... "Be more discreet, and maybe pick up someone worthy of the headlines, not some punk from the ghetto."

"You do know that the ghetto doesn't exist anymore, right? I think it died with 2Pac." With that, I turned on my heel and stepped out of the most hated room in this house, my appetite lost.

As I drove my Porsche to the clinic, I turned on the radio. Last year, I'd stumbled on an old series thanks to one of my favorite Booktubers praising the famous 'One Tree Hill'. I was thankful for the awesomeness that was Brooke Davis. There was this thing she did with the radio, like a cooler version of the eight ball. She would ask the universe something and let the next song playing answer it.

And the universe gave me mine, in the form of ClockClock's 'Someone Else'. The lump in my throat grew two sizes too big, and the feeling of loss started to consume me.

Through the morning fog, my sight landed on an empty parking slot, and I glided my car between the lines. I paused before the entrance at the sound of a motorcycle. My body went into some sort of shock. It was unreasonable and unbelievable how much power Mateo had over me. His grin, that same crooked one he flashed before everything went to hell, hit me like a punch right to the chest. And now, with the threat of my father looming, it only made it worse.

My father turned out to be a monster, my own flesh and blood. Did that make me a monster as well? I certainly possessed some of his traits, not just the physical. But was I inclined to the same extremes that he had made other people endure? The selfish prick. Oh, the irony of his disappointment always pointed at me—his need for constant perfection, the importance of family, and the name.

Well, fuck the name; fuck the perfection.

My whole life was about it; I lived to show it, to flaunt it. There was nothing perfect about me, about *us*, but there was something perfect, yet tragic, about the two people who, against all odds, found each other.

With everything in me fuming, I took out a pack of smokes and lit up one cigarette. Two puffs in, I heard the car door slam before Simon's figure appeared in my periphery.

"Sabrina, what happened?"

I shook my head, taking another drag.

"I need you to do something for me."

"Anything."

I gave him a piece of paper with the location prewritten.

"What's this?"

"I place I need you to destroy."

"Sabrina, what's going on?"

"I slipped," I confessed, knowing damn well that it was a downright hard fall. "It doesn't matter anymore. It's a loose end, and I need you to send out a message."

"Who's the unlucky recipient?"

I gave him a pointed look, and he nodded, pocketing the note without another word.

As hard as it was, it needed to be done. I had to cut all ties with Mateo, delete that smirk of his, those eyes that had the power to see right through me. My heart ached, begging me to keep him. My head knew better.

"Where did you go?"

I must've zoned out, and who could blame me? I was being pulled in way too many directions.

"All over the place."

He let out a laugh. "You know, I always wanted a sister."

That kinda came out of nowhere, and the confession felt like a warm embrace.

I turned my head just enough to see his glasses fogging due to the moisture in the air. He took them off and started wiping using the hem of his shirt, giving me a soft smile.

"I always wanted a big brother," I admitted, turning slightly so that I could wrap my arms around his waist. I pressed my ear to his chest, feeling every beat pumping inside.

I had a brother, and he was the best sidekick a girl could ask for.

Chapter 21

Mateo

Days had passed since I woke up in the cabin all alone. I knew that the possibility of her leaving was high, but it didn't make it sting any less. I fought away any urge that tried to command me to seek her out. Closing myself down, I'd focused on school and my weekend job, thankful for any distraction. My brothers had been keeping their distance, understanding my need to be alone. My mama, on the other hand, didn't get the memo, so she kept pushing me to open up.

Halfway through my shift at the construction site, I took my break and searched the web for any news about her. The weird thing was that she had no social media presence. There were a couple of fake accounts, none verified, and it bothered me more than I would like to admit.

I had a reminder of her life plastered all over the building across the site—lying on a rock in nothing but a bikini, being worshiped by three heavily muscled men.

"Ouch, that's gotta hurt." Luka joined me on the bench, facing the billboard and handing me a sandwich.

"You have no idea," I confessed, annoyed by the circumstances.

"Wanna talk about it?" Despite Luka's hard exterior, he was a big old softy, not that he would ever, and I mean ever, avow it. He was always protective of us, acting as our guardian, but he never hesitated to share his wisdom.

"There's nothing to talk about, you were right. She's a hypocrite," I said, trying to sound indifferent.

I didn't know which version of her was the right one—the real one.

"Look, O, as much as I love being right, seeing you like this messes me up."

He placed a hand on my shoulder, giving it an empathetic squeeze. I must have looked like hell to get this kind of reaction out of him.

"I'll get over it," I spoke with my mouth full. After finishing lunch, we returned to work, the subject buried.

As soon as my shift was over, I ran away so fast I almost tripped getting to my bike. I was pathetic and gave zero fucks about it.

Driving just a mile over the speed limit, I got to her cabin only to find its remains.

Her message loud and clear.

I could smell the smoke as I stepped over the ashes, trying to see if anything survived the fire. How bad could it have been for her to go this far? This was her sanctuary, something she made for herself. And she shared it with me, only to burn it to the ground.

Why go to all this trouble?

The question played on a loop in my mind when I spotted something shiny right where the fireplace stood, still intact. I picked up a coin I had never seen before. The number one was on one side with a fox or a cougar behind it, and on the other side was a bird. Using Google Lens, I discovered it was the Croatian Kuna, the currency before it switched to the Euro. The bird was a nightingale, and the animal on the other side was a marten. After reading more about the coin and the country, I was ashamed to admit I had no previous knowledge of it.

It struck me that this coin must have a connection to her origins, or at least her family's. After scouring her Wikipedia page, I found no mention of such information. She was born and raised in Boston; her mother wasn't a native, and there wasn't much information available about her father, except for his political career. I had heard her say something in a language that sounded a lot like Russian, with her face indicating it was her cursing. This girl's evasiveness was driving me insane. I was desperate to piece it all together.

I'd spent my weekend sleeping and working, and on Monday, my tech professor gave me the good news that I made it into the second round of choices for the summer internship. I usually didn't get my hopes up, but at the sound of his praise, I couldn't help but feel a bit optimistic.

On my break between classes, I opened the Harvard school site, only to hit another brick wall. The administration still had her old schedule on file, and I had no insight into her whereabouts. Still high on my professor's exaltation, I decided to push my luck and typed Aria's name in the search bar. The fact that they were all famous came in handy. Aria was also a big-shot heiress, not as much in the spotlight as Sabrina, but with enough information online. She was a business student at Northeastern University, a 7-minute drive away from here. Using my incognito software, I bypassed the administration password and found everything I needed. Aria had another fourteen minutes of her Econ class in the auditorium. Gearing up, I set out for the Urban campus, my determination driving me forward.

I got there in five minutes, parked my bike across the brick-laid building, my heart racing with each step I took toward the massive double door. Taking my mark at the railing on the side, I patiently waited for the rush of students, focusing my mind to single out a tall blonde—hopefully an ally.

The moment she saw me, a grin appeared on her face as mine turned to full-on begging mode. Wearing a power suit, Aria strode toward me, arms crossed over her chest, all seriousness on her face and in her tone, "Nope!"

I never knew one word could have the power to shatter any flicker of hope, but I was nothing if not persuasive with a tablespoon of determination

"Please, Aria, this is important," I pleaded with a hint of desperation.

"Look, I can't tell you what is going on with her because she denied me any info, so don't bother asking."

Her words ruffled me, freezing my whole body.

"I love her to death, and she has a big heart, but when she sets out to do something, it will happen. So if she doesn't want you near her, it is something you should respect and trust to be right."

I couldn't accept that, not after everything that had happened.

"It's not that simple," I retorted.

"It is."

She took a step closer. "Listen, there is nothing more I would want for her than to let go of the act she puts out, to allow herself to be happy, but at the end of it, it's her choice and her choice alone."

Her arms fell to her sides, and there must have been something she saw that made her soften her expression.

"I can see you care for her, and I could see it in her, too, so here's what I can do..."

Hope fluttered, and I could feel my eyes double in size.

She took out a piece of paper, ripped it, and handed it over to me. "Write your number, but I can't make any promises."

I scribbled down what she asked, trying hard not to do one of those happy skips.

"Thank you. Thank you. Thank you."

What possessed me to hug the woman, I have no idea, but it was too late; she was locked in my arms, and by the looks of it, didn't mind it much.

"Don't thank me yet." With a hard push of her hand, I stumbled, but managed to stay on my feet.

"Just so we're clear, I am rooting for you, but if you hurt her, I know a whole platoon of men who can do some real damage," Aria threatened, and I narrowed my eyes.

A part of me wanted to dig into that, but I chose the smile-and-wave combo. As I watched Aria walk away like some boss woman, I couldn't help but smile, happy to know that Sabrina had a friend like her in her corner.

Chapter 22

Sabrina

"I got the last one," Simon's animated voice lit up the line.

"Fuck! I guess it's time. You know the drill," I gasped out and hung up.

This was it—the last step before implosion.

Between my classes, the clinic, avoiding my family, and executing my now two plans, I was downright exhausted. Pushing through my tiredness, I put on my big girl pants in the form of the little black dress, because it was time to finalize the '*Kill Mateo*' plan. Not to worry, I wasn't going to kill him—kill him, only his hopes about us. The first step was the burning of the cabin. Simon had done it for me, cuz I couldn't bear to do it myself, even knowing how essential it was to prove that point.

Sealing the deal with a red lipstick, I grabbed my lucky Cartier clutch and exited my house. A limo was waiting for me in the driveway with a vision in a tux leaning on the back door. I had to hand it to him; he looked good in Armani. A whistle escaped his full lips, and I gave him a little twirl, knowing damn well I looked good.

Dario was an up-and-coming actor who needed publicity to increase his public profile, and what better way to do so than by dating the *it* girl? We were on our way to a movie premiere, which was also our coming-out party. A night of fake smiles for the camera, making it believable with a lot of PDA, all fake but required for both parties. Mutually beneficial, with me showing Mateo I'd moved on and Dario getting his name plastered all over the news.

The drive was short and silent, but it didn't stop Dario from ogling me the entire time. I felt a little sorry for him, especially since I had no desire to even look at him.

When the limo finally pulled up, the flashing lights were all I could see. The red carpet calling, I waited for a hand to guide me out. The moment we were in each other's arms, the flashes hypnotized us; my name shouted from every direction, followed by screams, "Is this your new beau?" We smiled, looking at the cameras, then at each other. Dario was a couple of inches taller than moi in my 5-inch heels. He looked dapper, with his hair straight, thick, and pulled back with the shiny chemicals keeping it in place. His bluish-green eyes were locked on mine the entire time we both acted out sincere feelings. Leaning in for the money shot, he placed his lips onto mine, trying to invade them with his tongue, but I pinched his chest, letting him know that was not going to happen. On our way to our seats, I handed the security guard a USB drive. He was in my pocket; Simon made sure of it. The screening room went silent as the lights dimmed, plunging it into pitch blackness. The movie started, and I endured 103 minutes of something I could only describe as *'meh'*.

Before the credits began to roll, the place went back to pitch black, with people gasping in surprise. A robotic voice echoed from the speakers, marking the pinnacle of Phase 2.

"This is your country; these are the people who serve and protect you; these are the criminals you put into their high positions."

The screen lit up, and a slideshow appeared:

1. Congressman using his belt to punish a boy (his face was blurred out, but for your eyes only—it was his son)

2. The district attorney choking his escort, her eyes turning white

3. A video of the CEO of State Street Corporation forcing his assistant to give him head

4. Photos and photos of handshakes

5. Pictures of bank statements

6. Proof of embezzlement

7. A video of a gang rape

Panic filled the room, various ringtones echoing around me. I sat relaxed in my chair, smiling from ear to ear, finally seeing the fruit of my labor. Mr. Darcy's phone had the password that opened the secure server where all the information we needed was encrypted. With his password, we were able to access all the incriminating evidence that led us to the corrupt parties.

The last year had been spent gathering intel and collecting footage to accompany the paper trail I was sure would eventually emerge. It was now all out in the open. All the men on this list helped my father in one way or another.

The congressman secured his new identity, erasing the old one. It was back when he, ironically, served as chair of the Senate Committee on Ethics. My father repaid him by financially contributing to his congressional campaign.

The CEO of SSC helped him embezzle a large sum of money, which he used to start his empire by stealing from people's savings. The last video had nothing to do with my family, but I needed it to divert attention, and I also wanted the five men punished.

Men were the mere definition of pig-ignorant. Their idiotic insistence on keeping incriminating evidence was something I'd never understand. Why would someone doing something bad, not to mention illegal, keep visible trails of all actions? Don't get me wrong, it came in handy regarding my plan for destruction, but still…

Just bury your damn evidence! Am I right?

The rest was up to the people who had better means to dig deeper. I was merely serving the appetizer. The secrets were out, and now all I had to do was wait for tomorrow's headlines, hopefully filled with pictures of the mentioned party in handcuffs.

Oh, that would be an image to frame.

My heart was jumping, like a kid in a bouncy house, all the while my shoulders felt lighter. Half of the secrets were out; now it was time for phase three, one that had only one target in mind, one downfall to cause—the one and only Jacob Furst!

Proud of the montage, I triumphantly strode out. As the limo approached, someone's hand grabbed my wrist. I turned, ready to punch when Dario came into view.

Fuck.

His eyes were prowling, deliberately sliding over my body. I knew I looked good; the dress was tight, emphasizing my curves, and my long legs were on display. Honestly, who could blame him? His bubble had to be burst, and I felt a smidge of pity. There was no attraction on my end; he was merely a pawn in my game. I used him, and he damn well knew it; he used me, too. Biting his lips, he said in a husky voice, "Wanna go to my place?"

I freed my hand from his with spite, "Was the look of disinterest on my face confusing for you?"

"Sorry?"

"You should be, and don't play that CHS with me. I will 'huh' the hell out of you?"

"CHS?"

"Can't hear shit—" I winked with a soft—"Sorry."

Side-stepping him, I bit my tongue, with the lyrics *'It's just you and your hand tonight'* on my mind.

Chapter 23

Sabrina

I couldn't remember the last time I'd woken up with a smile. The anticipation for the Romano twins' annual lifestyle party filled me with excitement. It was the perfect distraction, *the* party of the year.

Aria and I manipulated Nala into joining us for the 24-hour yacht party. It took some hard convincing, but with the promise of half-naked men, great music, and an open bar, we managed to pique Nala's interest.

While it was still docked, we climbed on the mega yacht, and Aria and I couldn't contain our laughter at Nala's dropped jaw. "This thing is bigger than my entire block," she marveled. Saying hello to everyone, we spread fake hugs and kisses as we roamed the deck until we found a place on the sky lounge.

An hour later, we were soaking in the sun, sipping our cocktails, and talking bullshit.

"You won't believe what happened last night," Nala bellowed with excitement.

"What?" Aria and I sat up to face her.

"So I guess there was some big movie premiere and a lot of people ended up at The Brick afterward. I heard everyone talking about how it all blew up, like there was a hack on the screen and there were pictures of politicians and stuff..."

"Yeah, I read something in the paper this morning," Aria jumped in. She looked right at me while I stayed silent. She covered her eyes with shades, and so did I, yet I could easily interpret her stare—she knew, or at least suspected, who the culprit was. Remaining emotionless, I gave a vague "Hm" and turned to the sun, soaking in the vitamin D.

"Looks like Boston has its very own vigilante," Nala mused, her voice filled with awe and intrigue.

"I would hardly call it that; there was no fighting involved," I retorted, but Nala turned on the defense mode. "You don't have to be Batman to be a vigilante. Someone from the shadows uncovered crime; enough said." She flicked her hand for emphasis.

Her point put a new smile on my face, filled with pride... and it felt good.

"Yeah, I guess you're right... How should we call this vigilante?" Aria placed one leg over the other, and I knew she was side-eyeing me.

"Ooh, I like this game. Let me think..." Nala tapped her finger over her lips, and Aria chimed in, "How about The Boston Vamp?" making me choke on nothing. The two of them continued, while I lay back down, pretending none of it interested me, but my ears were burning.

"What makes you think it's a woman?" Nala wondered, her voice sparkling with curiosity.

"Just a feeling," Aria said nonchalantly.

"That would be amazing. Can you imagine?"

"Yeah, I can."

"Sab, you're oddly quiet." Nala turned to face me.

Necessarily so. My lips, generally quick to spill secrets,

were sealed this time, adding an air of mystery to the conversation.

"I was actually at that premiere," I confessed, sitting up to the shock of my friends.

"What? You saw it firsthand?" Nala practically screamed out, and I motioned with my hand to take it down a notch.

"Yeah, it was chaos. People were screaming, and some of the things were vile to watch."

"My God." Nala placed her hand on her chest, and Aria snapped her question at me, "What were you doing there?"

"I was on a date?" Somehow it ended up sounding like I was second-guessing myself, and I noticed Aria caught that instantly.

"What?" Nala yelled as Aria gushed, "Way to bury the lead. So you finally gave in to the bike guy?"

"No. I went with this actor, Dario."

"Is he cute?" Nala's interest piqued, I gave her a noncommittal shrug.

"I guess."

"You guess?" Aria's hand came to my forehead, and I snapped it away because no, I was not sick, just uninterested.

"Sure, he was your regular pretty boy, polished and whatever."

"Wow, you seem smitten." She played with the words, changing the intonation to emphasize the sarcastic tone. It felt like we were in a debate, with conversation just between us. Nala's head bounced back and forth, like she was watching a ping pong ball.

"It was more of a work thing. He needed a publicity boost.

My mother set it up," I admitted.

"Of course she did. God, I hate that woman."

"Join the club."

"Did you at least hook up?"

"He tried, but I wasn't interested."

"Hm… I wonder why?"

"Stop insinuating." My eyeroll was of the overdramatic variety.

"Don't play that *crazy* shit with me. I'm better at it than you are."

She sure was. Aria was the queen of avoiding her feelings. Sometimes I thought only I got to see that side of her, Nala too. Others weren't so lucky.

"Can we talk about the bike guy? Please?" Nala chimed in, fascination clear.

"No," I snapped, but with a more *'let it go'* kick to it.

"Come on," she whined, "I need something, guys, I am in a slum." She full-on begged, lashes flashing in hopes of us caving.

"How can you be in a slum? You have guys lining up at the bar every night?"

"You mean children?"

"Good point." Both Aria and I nodded.

"Come on, please." This time, the two joined forces, and I caved… If you could have just seen their faces, you would understand.

"We hooked up."

"The fuck?" Aria yelled, and Nala jolted. "What?"

"Twice." Two of my fingers went up.

"Sabrina Pearl Furst, you've been holding out on us." Aria

brought out the big guns, and my full name just cringed the hell out of me.

"It happened. Now it's over. Nothing to bring up. End of!"

"Yeah, right." Aria blew out, then took my hands, lifting them in front of me, nodding, her eyes wide with enthusiasm, her eyebrows wiggling in a teasing gesture. "Show us."

I spread my hands to the approximate width of his length, making their eyes widen and mouths fall open.

"What the hell is the matter with you?" Nala squeaked, pushing against my shoulder, causing me to fall back into the chair.

I don't know!

The sight of a half-naked, very familiar man railing against the fence came like an uninvited guest.

"Isn't that Cillian?" I nudged my chin in the direction behind Aria's blonde head. Her head snapped around so fast I was sure she would need a chiropractor.

"Fuck me," Aria gasped.

I lifted my shades to the top of my head, taking in the vision.

"Who's Cillian?" Nala asked, licking her lower lip.

"He's Ariaaa's..." I dragged it out, thinking of the right description, "Frenemy."

Cillian and Aria had grown up together. Their fathers were business partners and best friends. Once upon a time, so were Aria and Cillian. These days, they couldn't stand each other.

"Really?" Nala drawled, tilting her head to take in the man of the hour.

"They were childhood best friends; now they hate each

other."

"I love that trope."

"Who doesn't?" I winked, making sure both of them saw it.

"Guys, no book talk, please." Her hands were clasped over her chest, the tips pointing between Nala and me.

"Fuck Aria, he grew up good. Did you see the muscles on him?" I wiggled my brows. Every part of him was so well-defined, and his dark skin, my God, so lickable. When I was in my early teens, I had a crush on his older brother, but seeing Cillian now, all buffed up, I completely forgot about Mario. Earlier this year, Cillian's brother had gotten into a fight and ended up in prison. The story was shrouded in our circle, but I was aware of it. He received a five-year sentence, despite being only supposed to face civil liability for damages and medical expenses.

"I'm totally drooling." Nala stuck out her tongue, and we both laughed. Aria, however, tried hard to maintain her resting bitch face, one she had perfected for when Cillian was around.

"Whatever." She shrugged, still looking at the man she had obsessed over her whole life. It was something she denied on every occasion, but I knew better. She loved that man; he loved her. They were just too stupid, too stubborn, and self-involved to see it.

"Yeah, you go there; act indifferent, it will surely fool us," Nala mocked.

"What do you want me to say?"

"The truth," I stepped in.

"He's hot, always has been; doesn't make me hate him

138

any less," she admitted.

"When are you going to tell me what happened between the two of you?"

It was a thing she never shared. Growing up, those two had been practically inseparable; then out of the blue, they'd stopped talking. It happened overnight, a sudden and complete breakage of a longtime friendship. There was a time they couldn't even be in the same room, making every party blow up with the intensity of their fights.

"We both changed; he became condescending, egotistical…"

"And you?"

"I got powerful."

"Uh, I like that." Nala clapped, and Aria gave her a slight bow with a marveled "Thank you."

Cillian turned around, and their eyes met. I could see Aria's whole body react. The staring contest lasted about a minute before she broke it, turning back to face us. Oblivious woman, unaware of the way he was gazing, as if she were his last meal.

Chapter 24

Sabrina

By the time the real party started with the sunset, we were already buzzing to another level. Dancing, drinking, not giving a fuck about anything else, we marked the dance deck. It was everything I needed—a night to forget the mess I'd created, my family, my past, and the thoughts about the future.

The bass echoed the night air, and I suddenly wasn't at this party—I was back in his arms. I couldn't hear the music, too busy listening to his heartbeat drumming in my mind. And he was out there, somewhere, thinking that I had moved on.

It's for the best.

Aria pulled me back into the zone by sandwiching me between herself and Nala. Shaking my head, I allowed the cage and started moving in sync with their bodies. I knew what she was doing—three girls dancing in the middle of the floor was a sneaky way to tease the male population. My senses told me Aria's show was specifically aimed at one of them. My suspicion was confirmed when I spotted Cillian over Nala's shoulder, in the far corner, fist clenched, jaw locked.

You go, girl!

Just as I was about to dip between the two vixens, I felt I

was being watched. After a quick scan, I caught Dario's hungry gaze, his lower lip possessed by his teeth. A sight like that would make any woman drenched, and yet, my crotch could only be described as the Sahara Desert with only one mirage on its mind.

Pushing through the block, I sashayed to my partner in deceit, his hungry eyes doing a slow perusal of my figure. I took his hand and dragged him through the deck until I found an empty room. By the time I locked the door behind us, Dario was already on the bed, shirtless.

Nothing.

I waited for a flutter, some flapping of the wings in my stomach, even a skipped beat of my heart; however, it was all in vain.

My inner voice was screaming at my pussy to react to a sexy, half-naked man in front of me, but it got me nowhere. I paused, going through my wet roster in an attempt to spark something, but damn, was my pussy a crazy little spoiled ass bitch, fundamentally arid. My heart was worse, making me feel like some cheater. Stupid little fucker! The memory of Mateo turned into my biggest enemy, one I couldn't ignore.

Saved by the bell sounding from my phone, I shot Dario an apologetic smile and went outside. The screen showed an unknown number, which I wasn't a fan of, so I hit decline but pretended to answer. I needed time to think of a strategy. Thankfully, in the middle of my fake phone call, Dario stepped outside, whispered, "Mood killer," and left.

Thank fuck!

The knot in my chest tightened, and for the life of me, I couldn't understand why. Why the hell did it feel like I was about to cheat on Mateo? I was going crazy; that was the only explanation.

My hands on the rail, I took a deep breath, watching the hull form the foamy waves. It didn't take long for my best friends to appear by my side.

"Guy trouble?" Nala smirked, handing me a cigarette.

"We saw the actor come back on the deck with a sour pout," Aria added.

Shaking my head, I placed the brown tip between my lips, and Nala sparked her pink BIC, the flames hypnotizing me. All I could see was the Zippo, hear the sound of the flick, and smell the scent of leather.

What is this?

I asked no one since there was obviously something wrong with me.

Feeling Aria eyeing me, I took a long drag, the embers spreading at the bottom of my smoke.

"This is about O, isn't it?"

"Please don't call him that," I rebutted.

"Who or what is an O? Is that the bike guy?" Nala lifted one brow, leaning forward.

Aria muzzled me with her palm, gently pressing my mouth. "Yeah, his name is Mateo, but he goes by O!"

"Is it sexual, the nickname I mean?" Nala was no prude by any means, but still, her cheeks flushed while she asked the question.

"No!" I shouted at the same time Aria confirmed, "Damn straight."

I decided I hated them both, plotted their demise somewhere in between, with drowning sounding quite tempting.

They kept talking around me, but their conversation faded out.

I was being stupid. It was all the stress playing with my hormones.

Yes, that's it. Blame it on stress.

How did I end up arguing with myself again? Oh, right. Mateo. This was all his fault. I wished I'd never met him.

Lie.

Soon, we went on the bow, where we spent the night drinking and talking, ignoring the party happening on the three decks—no fucks given. It was mainly Nala and me talking about our latest reads, with Aria cursing at us and comparing our storyline to a similar movie plot. It was something we'd developed early on in our friendship. Unlike Aria, Nala and I were addicted to the words written on the pages... Aria was more of a screen girl, reading only the subtitles when necessary. I was lucky; I knew that. I was grateful to be part of this trio, triangle, or whatever you wanted to call it. They were my everything, the only light at the end of the tunnel, and I wanted nothing more than to stay here with them, far from the reality waiting on the mainland.

Chapter 25

Mateo

I woke up early and headed down to the kitchen, the freshly brewed coffee hitting as I took the last step. Luka came into view, sitting at the table, his fingers wrapped around his mug. Across from him stood another one, steam flying from it. Brows furrowed, tension filling my neck, I took my seat, all the while trying to figure out my brother's intention. He slid over his phone, and a knot tightened in my stomach, followed by muscles tensing as I glared at a happy Sabrina in a lip lock with some blond ass wannabe. Scrolling, I read a couple of keywords, such as 'official,' 'chemistry,' and 'love.' The last one hit hard, so, to add salt to the wound, I pressed play on the video linked to the article. On a loop, it showed Sabrina and Dario (even his name sounded pretentious) posing, gazes interlocked, culminating in a passionate kiss.

Well, her message was now louder and clearer.

Sliding the phone back, I raised my hand to stop the overdue lesson in its tracks. "Please don't." I was thankful for his nod that followed my plea.

Why go to the length of torching the cabin only to find a new toy?

It makes no sense.

If she hadn't already monopolized me, infatuated me, haunted me, I could've easily let it all go. But it was too late. Because now I was sure I haunted her. And I was going to prove it by any means necessary.

The auditorium filled up, and I opened my laptop, tabbing an empty doc file. I set my fingers in the starting position, waiting for the TA's monologue. Listening, I typed away, focused on the statistical data displayed on the white screen behind the tall, fresh-faced faculty member—every student's dream; young, dark, and handsome, with a nice set of glasses framing his face. The girl on my left was the only one not giving him her attention, like the rest of them. She was eyeing my fast-typing hands with frequent glances at my profile.

I'd be lying if I said I didn't get attention from women. It was clear I had plenty, especially when they saw me in my motorcycle gear or riding my bike, and I wasn't immune to it. Now, I was in a stand-alone, desperate for the attention of the one person who seemed determined not to give it to me.

The TA assigned us the task of creating graphs to summarize the given data. The seating arrangements paired us, so I got the blonde who couldn't get her eyes off me. She scooted closer, and I quickly drafted the setup while she gawked at the screen, not bothering to understand my intention.

"Wow, you're good at that," she gasped and left me to finish the assignment without any input.

The moment the class finished, a line formed behind the desk, all eager to invade the TA's personal space. I made my way through the crowd and stepped outside, breathing in the fresh air, trying to rid my lungs of the perfume mixtures I had endured for the last hour.

A hand touched my shoulder, and I snapped around, finding Tina, or was it Tracy?

"Hi." She had one of those sweet, innocent voices that would drive any man crazy. Any man, except this one. Apparently, my taste had changed, evolved; hungry for the daring, almost threatening, raspy tone.

"Thank you for doing the assignment for me." She played with a strand of her hair, twirling it around her finger. "Anyway, I wanted to repay you somehow. With coffee, maybe?"

"I don't drink coffee," I lied, desperate to get far away from this conversation.

This girl was pretty, with a clear interest in me, and yet I couldn't be more indifferent. All because I couldn't get Sabrina out of my head—the look she'd given me, that soul-searching, crushing stare we shared while I was inside her.

That was real, and she tried to deny it.

Both she and Aria mentioned something she was working on, a so-called 'side hustle'. One thing was for sure: I was going to unravel everything. My fingers might've been out of practice, but for her, I'd bring them out of retirement and get to the bottom of it.

Chapter 26

Mateo

The past few days have been chaotic due to the intense news coverage of numerous corruption incidents in Boston. I knew the whole system was flawed, but the broadcasters' statements, the pictures, not to mention the videos, were sickening.

"This is crazy." Mak pointed at the TV showing the twelve o'clock news. "Whoever got this uncovered will forever be my idol!"

"Right, my thought exactly. But why stay anonymous?" Luka puzzled, crossing his arms over his chest.

"Safety reasons, you know, vigilantes are not really in the scope of the law," I stepped in.

"True, but damn, whoever did that is ballsy." I couldn't help but agree with Mak on that one when Tristan stepped in. "With the books we are currently reading for the book club, it almost seems cataclysmic."

"There's a book series about that, like a modern Robin Hood. It focuses more on politics and society. It's called Ravenhood or something like that. Maybe we could do it next. What do you think, Mama?" I turned to face her, knitting in her spot on the couch, eyes focused on the news.

"You know I am always good with book recommendations. How did you hear about it?"

"Uhm..." I scratched the back of my head. "A friend mentioned it to me."

Luka coughed, and Mama's lips curved into a smile like they knew who I was talking about. Neither said a word, and I couldn't tell if it was a good thing or a bad one. Come to think of it, it was probably the latter. Everything, anything involving Sabrina was lined up with the word bad—in every direction—how badly I wanted her, how badly she behaved, how hard I fell.

She was consuming me to the point of self-destruction. The state of my mind, body, and soul was that of a zombie. I knew I was breathing, eating, and talking, but it was all just empty.

My brothers had been making fun of me; they had every right to, so I let them. Mama had been more worried than anything, but still tried to reassure me and keep my hopes high. If I had anything to show for my overthinking, it was that Sabrina had her walls bricked up, and I was the one who was going to smash them—a fucking wrecking ball on a mission.

Growing up with a strong interest in computers, I'd acquired a range of software-related skills, not just hardware. Over the years, I had picked up a few tricks but chose not to use my powers.

Until now!

So, with determination as my fuel, I kissed my mama, waved my brothers goodbye, and left for BU.

With little to no traffic, it took me fifteen minutes to get to the campus library. I parked in the shaded corner on the far end of the lot and took my steps into the building.

There were some heavy hackers on the ground, pricey SOBs... Sure, they were worth every penny, but for this task, my capable hands were more than enough. I knew one PC in the computer lab that was covered with the ultimate protection and equipped with all the right software, thanks to NOMAD66, and I was heading right for it.

Ten minutes of clicking later, I had her Social Security number, home address, and the place of her student employment. She had no number listed, probably due to her being in the public eye and all that messed-up shit. I couldn't show up at her house; that would be too weird, so door number two it was.

The drive was a short one, and when I finally reached the red mark on my map, my heart stopped, or skipped a beat, or maybe it even somersaulted; I couldn't tell for sure. There she was, dressed all in black just like the first time I saw her, a long braid falling over her shoulder, her bangs framing her forehead, and those greens hidden behind a cloud of smoke. With her back leaning on the building, she made circles with the vapor, not noticing me approaching. Our eyes locked when I closed in on the legal aid clinic, and she jumped. Without warning, her hand was on my chest, pushing me backward, her expression undecided—somewhere between the want to kill and fuck, maybe? Fiery for sure. Whatever it was, it made me shiver, not to mention fired up my body with the heat of her stare, making my dick hard. She pinned me to the tree next to my bike and whisper-yelled, "What the fuck do you think you're doing?"

She didn't pull away her hand when I leaned in, voice

sharp with conviction. "Why hello there, Blackbird. I see you forgot your manners, but no worries, I'm good. How about you?"

Her lips jerked; I could see it, the restraint, the need to let out a laugh, but she was too fucking stubborn to surrender, making me more determined to make her crack.

"How did you find me?"

"I have my ways." I lifted one shoulder.

"Whatever, I don't even care."

Oh, how she lied, poorly, by the way.

"What are you doing here?" she asked through gritted teeth.

"Isn't it obvious?"

Another twitch, this one a bit more noticeable. Her breathing also sped up, pumping up my own, her hand still firmly on my chest.

"Miss me?" I wiggled my brows, which got me an eye roll, but this time her lips curved fully.

"Ha!" I exclaimed, "You did."

"You wish."

"That was a weak comeback, baby; you can do better."

"I am not your baby," she sneered.

"Oh, I know, you're so much more," I confessed, noticing a slight hitch in her breath.

"That, that's not..." she stammered, as in actually stammered. Did I just make her mask slip? And why did it feel so good, fueling me to pull harder on it?

"That's not what?"

When she straightened her posture, her composed self came out to play, and I was all up for it.

"That's not what I meant. I am no one's possession. You need to go," she warned.

The door opened, and a blond guy stepped out, wearing all black, matching the Vamp. He eyes me curiously. I did the same.

"Simon, just give me a minute." He nodded, but remained at his spot.

Simon? Like the guy to whom the Jeep was registered?

No one's possession, ha?

Nothing made sense, and at this point, I couldn't even think over the anger consuming me. I felt stupid, played... again.

I got on my bike and drove away from her so fast, hearing her shouting behind me. Whatever she wanted to say didn't matter. Nothing mattered anymore. I got it all wrong; I twisted what happened and thought there was something real, but I was mistaken. She played me for a fool, and I was done.

Downshifting, I turned the corner and sped up when I got to the main road. It was only when I hit the interstate that the air got to my lungs.

Hell!

Despite my urge to scream, I maintained calm, something I had trained myself to do whenever I was in drive mode— total control.

I parked my bike next to Luka's pickup and found him sitting on the front porch. With my head down, I took a seat next to him and released a long breath.

I was more confused than ever.

Why did she lie?

Why did I let her?

And why can't I let her go?

She owned me, every part of me, and nothing could erase her possession of me, no matter how hard I tried.

Chapter 27

Sabrina

Mateo was here? He found me, God knows how, and he came here for me? What was I supposed to do with that? He came, gave me his little grin, and then, without any warning, drove off, leaving me utterly muddled.

"Is that him?" Simon came to my side while I was still looking in the direction Mateo had driven off into.

"Can we just not?"

"If you want to, sure, but maybe a new perspective would help."

I wouldn't. Analyzing it was the last thing needed. What would actually help was total annihilation.

"I don't want to get involved, but he can't seem to take no for an answer."

"Persistent, I like him already."

"Hey," I glared at him, "you're not allowed to take his side."

"Hey back. If he knows my sister's worth, I gotta give him props." He nudged my side with his elbow.

Sister.

That one would never get old.

My eyes were fixed on the spot where I had Mateo pressed against the tree, and I couldn't fathom why my heart felt so hollow. It was a feeling I wasn't used to.

"You like him." It was not a question, but I nodded anyway.

"You don't want him to be collateral damage?"

Another nod; no point in words.

I'd gotten so distracted that I didn't even realize my own father had me followed. That should be enough of a warning, but to have Mateo on my father's radar… I couldn't even think about it. I was aware of the risks, the lengths my father could go to. I prided myself on being strong, but now I found myself consumed by a feeling I couldn't control. The mere thought of it scared me more than I could admit. Because for the first time in my life, even if it was for a brief moment, I had something to lose.

"I am not gonna lecture you, or give you my two cents, but I'm here for you."

"I know," I whispered, because that was all I needed from him. From anyone.

We stood there in silence, both smiling for a beat before he finally broke it, "So what do we do now?"

"We need to take down that snake who ruined everything, starting with finding the dirty money."

"What about the cases?"

"Carl reached out to his FBI contact, who said that without the money trail, we had nothing."

Meaning we needed to figure out who my father had been conspiring with in all his cases to get this to the authorities.

"I tried; it's out of my scope of expertise," he faltered.

I hated that he felt helpless; I hated that I did too, that much more.

"I know, and don't do that. Don't blame yourself. When this whole thing started, neither of us knew how far it would go."

Understatement of the century.

"Yeah, we got into it to avenge my mother, only to uncover so many other people he harmed and ruined."

I dropped my head, thinking over all the screwed-up shit my father had caused, all the souls he'd crushed, and for what? For money? For power? But was the power real if it had been gained with lies and deceit?

"Hey, where did you go?"

"I still can't believe it all," I stammered, "even knowing what he had done, I still can't comprehend it."

"I understand that." Just as he uttered the words, his whole face turned to the expression I hated most—pity.

"Don't do that!" I took out a smoke and lit it. "Don't feel sorry for me."

"I know. I just wanted..." He took a breath. "I don't know," he finished with a shrug.

I flicked my cigarette with my finger, watching the ashes disappear in the breeze. "I get it, we're at a stupid standstill, and honestly, I don't know what my next move should be."

"You'll figure it out. I have no doubt."

When the last of the cigarette burned, I stomped it with my foot on the ground, and we both walked to my car. He opened the passenger door for me, and I slid inside, giving him an appreciative smile. With the roar of the engine, I went to the radio, begging for some help, some answers. And as I backed the car up, I got 'Run for the hills' as my answer. With Tate McRae singing away my feelings, I floored the gas, fighting off the tears.

I need to go numb. I need to stop feeling.

It was all too much.

I called Aria and put the call on speaker.

She picked up on the second ring, "Hi Sabby, what are you up to?"

"I need an escape, The Brick? One hour?"

"Meet you there."

Three quick sentences. That's how it worked with us. No need to get into any details; just whatever it took, we knew we were there for each other. I also called Nala to join. When she didn't pick up, I texted her.

ME: *The Brick, one hour? Aria's coming too.*

Nala: *Working, so see you there. You can crash at my place.*

ME: *Thx, see you... kisses*

Avoiding my house, I went to my hidden-in-plain-sight Jeep instead, took my killer red dress and my favorite leather heels. I quickly worked with what I had in my makeup bag and did a quick check in my Porsche mirror. The whole look was straight-up deadly, not to mention hella sexy, but the one on my face was plain white sad.

Chapter 28

Mateo

The chilly air did nothing to dim the flames culminating within me. Luka tried his best, but there was only one person who could remotely understand what I was going through— Tyler, and he was in a different time zone. We'd both lost our parents without warning, and even though we'd partially healed and found our place in this family, there'd always been this looming fear of losing it all in the blink of an eye. Maybe that was the reason I wanted to cling to Sabrina so much, why I refused to let her go. Outside my family, I never felt like I belonged anywhere, but with her, something was different, special, as if her arms were made to hold me and vice versa. I couldn't wrap my mind around it, the pull, even after everything, after she'd tried so damn hard to push me away— it only made the pull stronger.

Ready to call it a night, I stood up when I received a text from an unknown number with nothing but a location. Not entirely sure it was a mistake, I couldn't leave it to chance, so I texted back.

Me: *Who is this?*

After five minutes of no answer, I decided to dial the number, and the call went straight to voicemail. A familiar voice reverberated through the speaker: "This is Aria, don't bother leaving a message after the beep, I won't listen to it."

Filled with worry, I asked Luka if I could borrow his truck. He tossed me his keys without a word.

Fifteen or so minutes later, the red dot got me to a parking lot behind The Brick. I'd been here a couple of times during my junior year; it was a well-known club because of its prime location, near all the major universities and business buildings.

I arrived at the entrance only to see a line stretching around the corner; I cursed under my breath. The security guard waved at me, motioning to get closer. I did what I was told. The music blaring from the inside made him shout, "You Mateo?" I nodded, and the guy unfastened the chain so I could go through. Loud groans came from behind me, but I didn't care; I was on a mission.

With my spidey senses on high alert, I stepped inside, scanning the dark space, trying to lock on the blonde heiress, but it was not Aria that made my heart stop. No, only one person had that ability, and she was right there in the middle of the dance floor.

The siren was sirening.

With her curves swaying in every direction, I could count six sets of eyes glued to her seduction. I knew there were more, but I stopped my count there, not needing any more ammunition. Aria's eyes locked on mine across the floor, her smirk screaming, *'You owe me.'* And that might as well have been her approval and the push I needed. Then Sabrina's sway pulled me back, her red dress a magnet. As I closed in on the Vamp, she stiffened—sensing me.

Her familiar scent hit my nostrils, going straight to my semi, hardening it further before she pressed her perfect ass to it. Her moves turned torturous as she rubbed against my cock, moving like a cyclone, fully aware of the torment she was causing me. Reciting the roster of my brother's team in my head, I was determined not to come in my pants in the middle of a crowd, no matter how drunk the people around us were. Still, I was within reach of my personal temptation, ready to give in. I joined in on the swaying, slowly dragging my hand around her, stopping over her belly button just as 50 Cent started husking out 'Just a Lil Bit'. This club was loyal to the 90s and early 2000s hits, and right now, it was playing in her favor. She followed the beat down to the commands in the songs, crazing me out with a slow dip, her hands following, firmly sliding down my legs. As if whatever she was doing wasn't enough, she pulled her hair to the side, giving me access to her now-exposed neck and shoulder.

No holding back, I dragged my tongue on her flesh, giving her skin some needed sensation. Somehow, the act of my tongue swirling down her neck gave her the go-ahead to drag her hand inside my jeans. She hid her intent from the crowd with her body, pushing her arm behind her, stroking my cock with her firm grip. Wild! This girl was wild, untameable, and at the moment, all mine.

As if the DJ was set to accommodate her actions, 'Dirrty' by Christina Aguilera scratched over next, making her grip tighter and me seconds away from combustion.

"Bathroom now!" I gruffed, biting on her earlobe.

Her answer—a snap into action. Her hand flew out of my jeans and grabbed mine. As she dragged me through the crowd, I followed her like a lost puppy, doing my best to keep my tongue from hanging outside my mouth. When we reached the bar, she leaned over toward a cute bartender to whisper something in her ear while the girl eyed me with intrigue. They exchanged something over the counter before Sabrina retook my hand with a whole lot of pluckiness. She dragged me into a dark corner, in front of a black door with the sign 'Private' taped over, unlocked the door, then, with a firm grip on my shirt, pulled me inside.

The clicking sound of the door locking sent us both to work.

Despite the heat filling the room, I managed to pull away, my breath catching. Her eyes widened, and I fought the urge to kiss her before clearing the air.

"What's wrong?"

Honestly, I was surprised by the softness of her voice, her mask nowhere in sight, vulnerability taking over.

"The guy I saw you with at the clinic, who is he?"

Her throat bobbed, and then her mouth opened with a weird twitch in her eye. They narrowed like she couldn't see the apparent reason why I was asking the stupid question in the first place. Despite being in a household with four brothers, I was never prone to sharing, and when it came to Sabrina, I was as possessive as they come.

"Simon," she replied, seeming indifferent.

Annoyingly, I clipped, "I knew that already. What is he to you?"

She swallowed; her eyes dancing in surprise.

Yes, Vamp, I am fucking jealous.

As if reading my mind, she simpered, looking pleased with herself.

"Is that why you ran away?"

"I didn't run," I snapped back, my fist clenching. Not because she was wrong, but because she was right. Seeing him touch her had turned me into a coward, and I wasn't proud of it.

"Right," she drawled, bobbing her head in amusement.

"Well, you'd know, wouldn't you?" I regretted it the moment I said it, and her face fell.

"That's not fair."

"I am losing my patience, Sabrina. Who is he to you?"

If I'd blinked, I would've missed the flinch when I said her name. So, she preferred the nicknames. Duly noted.

"We work together. We're very close. I love him."

My blood boiled, but then she grinned.

"I also love Greg, his partner of ten years."

Satisfaction filled my lungs as I inhaled her gaze, growing warmer by the second. I closed in, her palm finding my chest while her other hand went right to the back of my head, fingers lost in my hair. Our mouths met, and then... then she kissed me like she had been counting the seconds since the last time our mouths collided.

Our clothes got discarded in record time before she jumped into my arms, locking her ankles around my waist. She claimed my mouth and gripped my hair like a hungry, starving little monster. I devoured her neck, played with her pink nipples, tucking, pulling, as her moans tingled my ears. She unlocked herself from my grip and dropped to her knees.

Oh, hell!

With a slow circular movement, she licked her lips, sending a strong pulse that made my cock jolt. Her hand covered my shaft, and when our stares locked, I could see it—the want, mirroring my own. With a sexy ass smirk, she stuck out her tongue, then she oh so slowly trailed my length, wetting it base to tip. She gave me one more look, a warning I thought, before she enveloped me entirely, right to the back of her throat. The sounds she made, those sexy little moans, made mine even more frantic. Her tongue danced around the tip, all the while she sucked and pulled and flicked, or whatever she was doing that made me crazy. Like dynamite, I exploded in her mouth, and she drank me dry, giving me one cocky look as she dragged her thumb over her fuckable lips. She knew exactly what she was doing to me, the power she had over me, and at this point, I didn't even care. Let her have the power, fuck, she's had it—me—from the start anyway.

Chapter 29

Sabrina

I am so screwed.

Mateo's hand slipped down, giving my clit some much-needed attention before his fingers dove inside me. I pulled on his hair, my voice sharp and focused in a direct order, "No. I need you."

I missed him. So freaking much that it pained me to think about it.

A foiled grunt escaped him, "I don't have a condom."

That line came out so cute that it managed to turn me into mush. I opened my mouth to tell him I was on birth control, but shut it, afraid of rejection. He read everything about me, so I was sure he was aware of my reputation. Would he believe me anyway?

You won't know unless you give it a try.

"I'm on the pill..." I hesitated, "and I haven't... not since..."

"I know," he cut me off, his words hitting somewhere deep.

"It was all for show, I never..." I didn't get a chance to finish before he interrupted, whispering, "I know," and settled his forehead on mine.

I blinked once, twice. Swallowed. Then trembled.

Something about the way his hand gripped the nape of my neck, his breath colliding with mine, made me... lighter.

I closed the small space between us, connecting our lips and pushing myself onto him. He pulled me up, and I wrapped my ankles around him, using the wall behind me for support. With a firm hold below my ass with one hand, he used his other to guide himself inside. The lack of latex, the warmth, the feel of the skin—it was all-consuming. I'd never done this bare; too intimate for my liking, yet with him, it was so much more. His eyes revealed everything I was feeling, and my default settings wanted to intervene.

"Fuck, Blackbird, you can't tell me that you don't feel it, feel this," he muttered, slowly filling me, giving me inch by excruciating inch. Shutting my eyes, I shook my head, and his hand went straight to the back of my neck.

"Look at me," he demanded, and I obeyed without hesitation.

"Say it!" he growled when he bottomed out, hitting one wall while breaking some parts of the metaphorical one. His hand on my neck held me firm in place, as if it were afraid I would run.

Everything in me was ready to bolt. Well, not everything. One part of me wanted to stay, and it was a vital one.

He started to pull out but stopped with his tip at the edge of my threshold, leaving us both suspended in the moment.

"Say it!"

I wanted to, but something wouldn't let me, like some higher force was pulling back the words. My heart pumped louder and louder, making a point about who was in charge, and then the thread broke.

"I feel it," I said in one breath, my lungs exploding.

His cock pushed deeper, his voice hoarse. "Feel what?"

"This…" I panted, "us."

"What about it?"

Sve!

God, I couldn't think when he gave me another inch.

"Say it!"

Those deep browns of his got eager, and when he hit the jackpot again, I cried out, "It's real."

"Good, now repeat it for me," he whimpered, and pulled out halfway through, the suspense driving me crazy. The bastard was glaring at me; this all-knowing smart-ass was gonna make me break right here in the middle of a freaking bathroom.

O Bože!

"It's real. Fuck, it's real!"

With that, he pistoned inside, his movements unforgiving, deliciously possessive—as if to mark me, claim me, have me.

"Finally." It was a whisper, soft and close to my ear—declaring his victory. He knew from the start and felt it all along. He was just waiting for me to catch up. And I was in deep now, drowning in the sensation of our bodies working in tandem. The skin-to-skin contact, the friction, the mere sound of his breath drove me over the edge. He never stopped, not allowing me to inhale fully.

My heart was a mess, beating, stopping, pumping to the beat of his thrusts. His tongue moved over every part of my body it could reach, all the while my nails were marking every muscle on his body, from his biceps, over his abs, to his glutes.

This was not just another level; it was a completely different game. There was no mistaking it, this earth-shattering ache that consumed me whole, down to my core. Unprepared, totally lost in the moment, the feel, *him*—I disintegrated, shattering around him just as he filled me up, warming my insides in every sense of the word.

"Let me in," he grumbled, both of us frozen in time and space, riding the high. "Come on, be the Harpy Eagle, and just let me the fuck in!"

I could feel the imaginary walls crumbling from the earthquake his words caused.

Tears, those damned tears, welled up and ran down my face of their own accord.

"Let me figure you out, just... Fuck!" he shrilled, slowly pulling out. His essence slid down my thighs, causing my body to shake. I couldn't move, though; completely exposed, defeated with a side of voiceless. All I managed was to watch him grab the back of his head and hear him release mumbled curses. I tried, I honestly tried to speak, to say anything, but my brain couldn't find the words. What was there to say? I couldn't give him what he wanted, not really. Not without putting him in danger.

Jebote!

It hit me.

How the fuck did I allow myself to forget? I just put him in danger—again.

Oh fuck! Fuck! Fuck!

My palms started to get all sweaty, my knees weak, and I was one step away from acting out the entire opening lyrics of 'Lose Yourself'. Except I wasn't so lucky as to have mom's spaghetti to vomit.

This was no time for more hand-wringing; it was time to bolt.

Turning into The Flash, I quickly hunched down to pick up my discarded underwear, but before my fingers could reach the lace, my wrist got caught. Mateo's strong arm pulled me up, so we ended up face-to-face. Feeble in looking at him, I averted my gaze.

"Don't do this," he begged. I knew, because I could hear the crack in his voice. He framed my face between his palms, the act itself compelling me to regard him.

"Ali moram."

His eyes narrowed. Fuck, I said that aloud.

The Croatian in me was strong whenever I felt overwhelmed, and being trapped between fight-or-flight would undoubtedly be considered overwhelming.

How do I get out of this?

His stare turned scrutinizing, and I dreaded every second of it. And when he opened his mouth to speak, I opened my heart to listen.

"You've got it in you, I know you do. All you have to do is trust me and let me in. You owe it to us to at least try."

Us.

One word, two letters. The power of it? Endless.

I nodded.

Chapter 30

Mateo

Progress report: although the walls were crumbling, we still had a long way to go. I was all in for it, knowing the strength of her barricades. This would have to be more of a one-step-at-a-time approach. She was worth it. The way we fit together, the way her body reacted to mine, the quivers her breath sent down every inch of my skin, the soul-searching eye lock. It was all too much and not enough.

Ruined!

That word could, from now on, be used to describe me. Completely and irreparably ruined, and I couldn't be happier about it.

Taming the caveman within me, the giddy teenage boy took over, using a paper towel to clean her thighs of my mark. I gathered our clothes and helped her slide into her red seduction dress. I carefully pulled the delicate straps over her shoulder. They brushed against her skin, making her shiver and break out in goosebumps. Her lips were swollen, makeup smudged, hair ruffled from my touch, and in all honesty, she had never looked more perfect.

"Perfection," I gasped.

The words made her blush, revealing a shy side of the

temptress, the sight of it making my dick twitch.

"Let's get out of here," I demanded. No question mark at the end, leaving no room for excuses or misinterpretation. Now that I had her, I was never letting her go. On that note, I cleaned her face, took her hand, and got her out of the club, but not before giving back the key to the bartender who gave us an approving wink.

Outside, we were welcomed by clean and fresh air, so we just walked around the streets of Boston, hand in hand, fingers intertwined. I couldn't help it, honestly; it was all my fingers doing. The impulse to drag over the inked mark, to remove the meaning behind it.

"You hungry?" I asked when we closed in on a concession stand near the boardwalk.

"Always!"

"Two, please," I said to the guy, but Sabrina gave me a look that could kill.

"Four, please?" I drawled, waiting for approval.

That quantity earned me a nod from her and a smile from the guy wearing a red hat with the sign 'Love Dog' plastered in yellow.

"Ketchup or mustard?" the guy asked, handling four hot dogs at once.

"Both," we said in unison, making the guy release another chuckle.

With our hands full, we took a seat on a bench overlooking the harbor. The crescent moon shimmered over the water, its reflection making the current more pronounced.

Before I finished off my first hot dog, both of hers were devoured without a single drop escaping the buns. She gave me a *'don't judge'* look, though it turned out more endearing than she'd intended, and I couldn't help but laugh at her perfect combination of deadly and adorable. The idiot in me forgot to get us something to drink, but before I could show my chivalrous side, she was already on her feet, walking to the cart. She grabbed two bears, and I watched those long legs saunter toward me, making my mouth go dry. She twisted the lids and grabbed a pack of smokes out of her purse, handing one to me before taking the other to her flushed lips. With one quick click, I opened my Zippo and fired up both of our cigarettes together.

"Where does that leave us? Thirty-four years?"

"Don't ask me; you're the smart one."

"Was that an actual compliment?"

"Only stating the facts. You're all kinds of smart, mister," she said through a chuckle, and I gulped.

"Are there different kinds of smart?"

"Yeah," she scoffed. "There's book smart, hand smart, and smart-ass. And you, my pretty friend, got the trifecta right there." She circled her palm in front of my face, making me snort out a laugh.

I ignored the 'friend' remark and went for the confusing part. "What the hell is hand smart?"

"When a person knows how to use their hands, and yes, it's a double entendre," she finished with a *duh*, then added, "as I said, you're all kinds of smart."

"What does that make you, miss Econ to Law?"

"I'm not that smart, I have a photographic memory."

"No shit?"

"No shit."

"What's that like?"

"Depends on the situation," she said with a shrug.

"I'm gonna need some more concept there," I gaped at her.

"When it comes to studying, it comes in handy, but when it comes to personal stuff, it's a killer."

I said nothing, but I knew she could read my face, the one demanding her to continue.

"For example, the whole summer I couldn't get your face out of my head. Our meet-cute is forever mapped out right here." She tapped two fingers to her temple.

Knowing she was haunted by me as much as I was by her gave me some much-needed confidence. Unlike her, I was an open book, but hers was sealed shut, so this one admission was a grand opening of sorts. Now, all I had to do was show her I was the right guy to read out the rest.

"I've gotta ask, did you let your hair grow because of me?"

"What do you think?"

She raked her fingers through it, revealing a knowing smirk.

"No one got to pull on it except for you," I spilled, causing her cheeks to blush.

"How did you know where to find me?"

Points for changing the subject.

"Your friend Aria sent me the location." I had a feeling her friend wouldn't mind me throwing her under the bus, considering she was rooting for me.

"I ambushed her after class, but she wouldn't budge, so we settled on me giving her my number." I shrugged, and she gave me a soft smile.

"Do you live on campus?"

"No, I live outside of the city, Port Norfolk, with my mom and my brothers."

She didn't laugh, didn't even bat an eye at the fact I still lived at home, like most before her had. There she was, this rich Vamp, not a single shred of spoiled on her, and somehow it didn't surprise me. Here, with me, she was down-to-earth, raw.

"Tell me about them?"

Talking about my family was one of my favorite sports, so with a beaming smile, I cleared my throat. "Mak's in med school, the oldest and the smartest, but don't ever tell him I said that. His ego is already big enough."

She let out a chuckle, and I felt it in my core. "Luka's next; he works in construction. He's the closest to a father figure we have, though we never needed one. Our Mama made sure of that. I'm the middle child, which leaves Tyler and Tristan, both athletes of the family. Tyler plays basketball in a Tennessee college, and Tristan is the high school quarterback."

"Which one is the tall tank one?"

"That would be Luka, and don't let the exterior fool you; he's a softy."

She murmured something in Croatian, and hell, I had to get myself a dictionary.

"Is Tyler your biological brother?"

The fact that she didn't use the word 'real,' like any other person would, cemented all the feelings I held for her. Most people in the system didn't like that type of label, including us.

We were a family—blood meant shit.

"Yeah, we're two years apart."

"How old were you when you got adopted?"

"We never got adopted. Tristan was the only one eligible, but he refused out of solidarity. We all legally changed our last names, taking Mama's when we turned 18."

She took a breath, and I could see the wheels spinning, trying to form the next question. And I loved her for trying to find the best way, so to save her the trouble, I intervened. "Our parents were in a car accident; they died when Tyler was 3. We were both in the car but survived. Afterward, we went straight into foster care, and our first stop turned out to be our last. We were lucky."

"I am so sorry; you were just kids." Her eyes turned soft.

"Tyler doesn't remember much," I revealed, "he feels guilty about it."

"Bet you didn't forget."

"I got a sexy ass scar to prove it." I tried to get all playful, but her expression wouldn't allow it. Her hand flew up, fingers hovering for a beat, waiting for approval. I closed my eyes, and she slowly grazed the vertical cut, sending shivers all around.

"It was a drunken driver. He got a year of probation."

"What?" she cried out.

Wrapping me in a hug, she whispered, "I am so fucking sorry."

Her hand grazed my upper back in comfort, and I felt each stroke go straight to my chest. When she pulled away, she gasped, "Wait, is that how you lost the book?"

She remembered that?

"Yeah, I was holding it for mom on our drive home from our road trip. Somewhere between the hospital and the group home, I misplaced it," I rued, the endless sleepless nights spent crying over it came like a rush of wind, down with the nightmares that followed. Every detail of it, the smell of the fire, the screams, the blood... All of it was permanently engraved inside every brain cell.

I refocused my attention on Sabrina, the way her fingers played with the label of the beer bottle, trying to scratch it off.

We both sighed, hers a bit louder than mine, and I could feel her observing my hand movements, my shaking knee, and the rise and fall of my chest.

"We tried to find it... Mama made a lot of calls, and she went back a couple of times, but no one saw it." My eyes went glossy, obstructing my view.

"Do you remember what it looked like?"

"Yeah, it was one of the earlier editions with the domino pieces on the cover, but this one had a stamp. My mother had this personalized wax seal stamp she used to mark all her books. It was a jasmine, the flower, which was also her name."

"Pretty," she said through a shy smile.

The moon's reflection played with the shadows covering her face, as if the current's movement wanted to highlight her features, one by one. First, it was the apple of her cheek, then one side of her full lips, next her nose, then her eye, and it stayed there until I opened my mouth, making her turn. "What about you?"

"What about me?"

"Your family?"

"I have a mother and a father, on paper at least. We cohabit under the same roof, and that's pretty much it," she said, a bit detached.

"So, you live with your parents?"

"Only for a couple more months, then I'll get my full trust and move out."

Her face lit up at the possibility, and my heart skipped a beat.

Chapter 31

Sabrina

My eyes were closed, yet my mind was fully awake and aware that the thing under my back was not my mattress. The smell of coffee, mixed with the most amazing scent to be woken up to—fried bacon, gave me the courage to slowly, carefully crack open my lids. Sunbeams tried to pierce through the window, but the wooden shutters served to protect my eyes. I was in a state of confusion, not knowing where I was or how I got here, and it added to the mystery of the situation.

I sat up, taking in my surroundings. So by the looks of it, I was on a massive couch, big enough to sit four people, in the middle of a large, colorful living room. Head spinning, I looked around, but all I could focus on was how cozy it was. It had that homey feeling filled with warmth and love. Across from me were two armchairs next to a rocking chair with a glass coffee table in the middle. Most of the hardwood floor was covered with a colorful, round carpet that spread under all the furniture. Walls filled with framed photos and knick-knacks on the shelves let you know that an actual family lived there. A glass clattering noise cut through the air, and I jumped to my feet.

"Sorry, honey, didn't mean to scare you." The 'Mandy

Moore' from the restaurant looked right at me with welcoming eyes and a genuine smile, framing the picture of hospitality. Her words were like a warm blanket, comforting me in this unfamiliar situation.

"I'm sorry, Ms. Hart, I..." My mind went blank; there was no way I could finish the sentence. Truth be told, I had no idea what I was doing here, nor how I got there in the first place. The last thing I remembered was slow dancing with Mateo under the moonlight. Ok, it had been more like us swaying a bit, our feet firmly glued to the same spot, though there was some heavy groping involved. I could still feel his firm grip on the small of my back.

"Just breathe," she said softly. "Do you want some coffee?"

I got a bit too excited when I said, "Yes, please!"

"Oh, good, another one," she singsonged. "Don't worry, this house is coffee friendly."

I chuckled because, frankly, I wasn't expecting the woman to be so... chill, especially with a complete stranger.

"Come here, I don't bite," she said through a laugh, getting another chuckle out of me, and by the look on her face, she was proud of it. With a skip in my step, I got to the kitchen area with my hand held out. "I am Sabrina. It's nice to finally meet you." I accompanied it with my most sincere smile.

She snapped my hand away and enveloped me in a tight hug, depriving me of air.

"We're all huggers here; you'll see."

My whole body went from stiff to relaxed, and my hands moved around her upper back at their own accord.

"I'm Eva, and it's nice to meet *you*."

Despite it being a quick hug, I felt the weight of it in my fluttering stomach.

Wow! The woman was gorgeous, and I took my time soaking it in. Every wrinkle of her face was as beautiful as the rest of her.

"I'm sorry to impose," I faltered. "I'm embarrassed to say that I have no idea how I got here," I confessed, head still weary.

That came out wrong, and panic took over. I sounded like someone who drank her way into oblivion.

"I had only two drinks; I was not—" I was cut off by her raised hand. Since I had no idea how to get myself out of the gutter, I was somewhat thankful for her stopping me.

She motioned me to sit, and like the obedient girl I was, I obliged, wrapping my fingers around the black mug waiting for me.

"Don't worry, honey." Why that word hit a nerve was beyond me, but I wanted to hear it again. "Mateo called me, saying you fell asleep before giving him your address, so I told him to bring you here."

"Oh." A mix of embarrassment and humility washed over me, but amidst it all, I couldn't help but feel a surge of gratitude toward them both.

"He carried you inside, and you didn't even budge. You must have been so tired," she said softly.

I hadn't slept since I got back from Croatia. I mean, I slept, but there was a lack of that deep sleep, the one that regenerated a human.

"I am sorry I got him in that position, and... I..." again with the stuttering… Have I lost the ability to hold up a conversation like the grown-up I was supposed to be?

"Oh, honey, please stop apologizing. I'm sorry to put you on the couch, but I figured it would be better than waking up in a boy's room. I hope that's ok?"

It wouldn't have been my first time waking up in a stranger's room, but I wasn't gonna tell her that. No way, Jose.

"I think your couch is more comfortable than my bed," I blurted out.

"You don't have to do that." She tilted her head to the side and took a seat across from me. That's when her words reached my brain.

"Oh no, I mean it. I can't remember the last time I slept like that."

"Well, if you don't mind me being straightforward here, I don't think that has anything to do with the couch." She winked, and not a quick pass-by wink, but a knowing one, saying it had everything to do with the boy who got me on said couch.

"So we're feeding the strays now, are we?" I turned around to find a grinning Shrek, whom I now knew to be Luka.

"Be nice." Eva gave him a look.

"Can't make any promises."

My hand lifted into a wave with what I believed to be a nice smile, with a side of a soft spoken "Hi."

The way he looked at me, it was clear I was on Luka's shit list, and my new life's mission was to remove myself from it.

"I'm Sabrina," I said, standing up and extending my hand. The moment stretched, leaving me hanging. He eventually accepted my hand and shook it with a grunt. "I'm Luka."

"Nice to meet you," I wheezed as I took back my seat with trembling legs, while pretending that his not saying it back didn't sting. With his tallness, he took two steps, opened a cabinet, grabbed a mug, and filled it with warm brew from the pot. He repeated the action three more times and placed two cups across the table from me, one left in his hand. Leaning against the wall, he took the mug to his mouth, never blinking, his stare fixated on me. His big arms grew two sizes when he crossed them over his chest. The Shrek was scary. This guy could play The Hulk better than any of them so far, with a square face, short brown hair, and a large, muscular body frame that made him look impenetrable. The youngest brother stormed in with curious eyes pointed right at me.

"Well, well, well, it isn't Sabrina Furst." His smile was genuine with a hint of cockyness. "I knew you looked familiar, but I couldn't place it. Let me say, I'm a huge fan!"

How was this the conversation I was having right now? How was this my life?

"Tristan, manners," Eva yelled at him, one firm finger in the air.

"I'm being nice here. Anyway, I'm Tristan, future NFL star." He opened his arms in invitation. Practically jumping to my feet, I flew into his embrace, curious to find out how each of their hugs felt. I was barefoot, not as tall without my heels, so he towered over me, causing my face to collide with his upper chest. The Harts gave out some good hugs; I had to give them that... OK, OK, great hugs!

Chapter 32

Mateo

When I got downstairs, I found everybody cozied up around the dining table, except for Tyler, who was many miles away, but in his place was Sabrina, looking surprisingly at ease. Her presence gave my heart that all-familiar fuzzy feeling. When the floor creaked under my foot, all eyes snapped to me. I pretended not to notice the blush spreading across the cheeks of the Vamp that stole my—well—everything. Luka nudged his chin toward the empty stool and my fuming mug.

"Morning, family," I stated, a bit of a skip in my voice, just as it was in my step.

"Morning," they all said in unison, but somehow I managed to isolate one voice on top of all the others, the one voice that had some exceptional hold on me. It wasn't hard to imagine more mornings like this one, welcomed by all the people that meant the most to me, down to the newest edition staring shyly back at me, making me all giddy like a freakin' schoolgirl.

I took my seat between Mama and Tristan, right across from the beauty that captivated my sight. The light from the kitchen window illuminated all her features, highlighting her perfection.

"Sleep well?" I asked her as I wrapped my fingers around my mug.

"Yeah, sorry you had to drive me here."

"No problem."

No problem at all.

When she'd fallen fast asleep in the passenger seat, the moment the truck started moving, I couldn't bring myself to wake her up. So I kept driving around until I got tired myself. Frankly, I could've easily driven to her house, but it didn't seem right, so I called my Mama for advice. Luckily, she'd said to bring her home, even demanded it. Without a second thought, that was precisely what I'd done. The whole drive, she'd never moved, and when I transported her to the couch, she still hadn't even flinched. That's how strong a sleeper she was, so damn cute doing it, by the way.

One of the greatest gifts of my upbringing was the unwavering support of my family. I knew that no matter the hour, my mother would always be there to offer her wisdom. Thanks to her, Sabrina was now a part of my world, a world I was finally ready to share.

"Mama, remember we have to call Ty; he has a game later today." Mak stood up and placed his empty cup in the sink. One pointed look from Mama made him turn back and rinse the mug before he went to the family room. We all followed the same actions and direction, all but Sabrina, whose mug I took to clean. She stayed glued to her seat, waiting for a command, maybe, only to be pulled up by our youngest brother. He dragged her to sit next to Mama on the couch before he opened up the laptop. I came up behind them just as the ringing tone sounded from the coffee table. Two beeps later, Tyler appeared on the screen. We were all huddled up with big smiles, and Ty's eyes got wide when he noticed the 'imposter' among us.

"Well, who do we have here?"

I could see, and not to mention feel, her cheeks flush; she quickly regained her composure. "I'm Sabrina, nice to meet you, Tyler."

"So you got dragged to the book club? Welcome."

She turned to face me, forehead wrinkled and eyes somewhat narrowed. When my pretend indifference didn't completely satisfy her, she turned to the screen without saying a word.

"Ok, let's get this over with. I have a big game today." Ty clapped his hands loudly. He grew up playing basketball, and it was his first love. He'd received many offers to play college ball, but Tennessee was his number one choice. He was missed, but we tried hard not to let it show as much, solely to make it easier for him. He was the first of us to live alone, though he didn't want to. None of us did, which was a weird thing for most people to comprehend. We were all grown-ups (save Tristan); Luka and Mak both had financial stability, so they technically had no reason to stay, and I could have easily moved to campus—we just didn't feel like it. We loved living here, had all the freedom, and we genuinely loved each other. There was a great deal of mutual respect and understanding, allowing us to function in unity.

"Are you a reader, honey?" our mother asked Sabrina the question we've all been dying to know, so we leaned in, curious.

"I am. However, I've converted to audiobooks. It's a whole new experience. I do use my Kindle when there is no narration available," Sabrina answered animatedly. I quickly glanced at my brothers, all bobbing their heads in approval.

"Have you read 1984?"

"Only recently, it was mentioned in one of the series I was reading, so I was compelled to read it to get the full picture."

"What series?" Tyler asked through the screen.

"The Ravenhood."

Shit!

Yup, my family shared a knowing look because my woman had unknowingly ratted me out. She noticed the looks spread across the traitors, and once again graced me with her blushing cheeks.

"So this is your book club?" She sounded surprised, even though I had shared the story, but it dawned on me that she might not have believed me.

I nodded with a bit of a smirk.

"Wow, and to think I thought it was some girl club you infiltrated to get into a variety of panties." Her eyes widened, as if now realizing there were other ears around. "I'm so sorry, Miss Hart, I didn't mean it like that," she said apologetically.

"It's Eva, and of course you did, understandably so." My mother patted her knee, causing Sabrina to cough up a storm, choking on air.

"Mama," I whined, getting on the defensive.

"Oh, come on, she had a point there; it would be my thought if any guy told me he was in a book club."

"Fair enough." I shrugged.

"What got you to do it?" Sabrina turned to face my mother.

"It was a way to get them to read, maybe have something to share, and look forward to. But mostly, it was a way for them to cope."

In the beginning, Mama had picked self-help books to get us through our losses and traumas. Later, she'd turned us to fictional stories, all infused with love and growth.

"Wow, that's very admirable of you. You introduced them to so many new worlds. Do you only read classics or?"

"We do everything. We usually do an author's marathon. Last year, we did R. L. Stine, and over the summer, we did Ana Huang," Mak chimed in with that one.

Sabrina froze, opened her mouth only to close it about five times until finally uttering through a shaky voice, "Ana Huang? Like the Twisted series?"

"Yeah," Tyler chimed in from his screen, "precisely."

Another blush to her cheeks, with a lot more redness on them this time, a deep, peppery red.

"So, you..." She took a breath, then another, some humming, followed by another inhale, all the while her hand gripped the back of her neck.

"Read smut?" Tristan came to her rescue, making her whole body fidget with a dry cough.

"Yeah, we know all about the peppers. Don't worry about it, we don't exactly discuss *that* stuff." That was Tristan for you, always straightforward.

"Right," she drawled, her eyes dropping to the floor. Her inner cheeks were caught between her teeth, the sight making my knees weak. I wanted to read her mind, get inside, and see the wheels turning. A part of me hoped she had a dirty mind like mine, thinking over all the spicy scenes for us to bring to life. Hopefully, sooner rather than later. And yup, that thought built up a tent in my shorts, right there, in front of my entire family. Thank God for the back of the couch hiding it.

Chapter 33

Sabrina

Sluggish—that was today's mindset.

Every muscle in my body was working overtime, overloading to the point of risking some serious injury. What exactly were they doing, you ask? Keeping me from spiraling. I tried to wrap my head around all the facts that were brought to light, showing no emotion.

It was just a book club.

I told myself.

It was a totally normal thing, cool even, to the point of making me jealous for not having such a family. All that aside, the red peppers dancing around my head, like stars would in the cartoons when a character got knocked out, made my whole body freeze. I was in the middle of a family huddle, fully aware of the fact that they all read some nasty, hot scenes, filled with steam and spice.

How crazy was that?

How was I to keep a straight face in front of them with that information? And let's not mention Mateo, a person I could never look at the same way again. The worst part was that all the spicy stuff occupied my mind, like a Pandora's box opened with kinky content escaping it and going straight to my thoughts.

So I was blushing, embarrassed that I was turned on in the middle of the living room with all the members of the Hart clan. If the Earth were to open a large hole for me to be swallowed, it would be much appreciated.

As the Harts rambled on about totalitarianism and the genius portrayal of it in 1984, I excused myself and snuck to the kitchen in the pretense of getting more coffee.

There was something special about this family, something I envied. There was no blood, no DNA shared, but there was so much love. Unlike with my family, despite blood ties and all, we couldn't be or feel more apart. I couldn't help but notice the particular stares they shared, the way they communicated without a single word.

And, as on cue, my eyes chose to betray me once again, with all their now well-known leakage. A hand squeezed my shoulder, stopping the shaking that was about to happen, a side effect of the tears.

"Come, honey, why don't you and I go for a walk?" Even though Eva posed it as a question, her voice was calmly authoritative, making it more of a statement, one I was bid to follow.

When we stepped outside into a warm day, I finally noticed my new attire. I spent the past hour or two wearing a t-shirt that was way too big for me, covering the shorts that fell just below my knees. When the hell had they changed me out of my dress?

No, scratch that—my dress was still on me, underneath the baggy ensemble. At this point, it was unimaginable that I hadn't noticed a simple wardrobe change, something that had practically been forced into my psyche.

"I am sorry," were the only words I could utter since my brain decided to stop functioning altogether.

"Honey, please stop that. You don't owe me any of your apologies." She linked her arm with mine, and we started our stroll around the neighborhood. The street was quiet, except for the chirping of birds and the occasional passing of a car. We crossed the road, and Eva waved at the neighbor watering his plants.

"You got yourself a new one?" the man shouted with a smile. He was older, with gray hair and a plaid shirt, and from a distance, he seemed tall, really tall. Eva squeezed her grip and shouted back, "Mateo brought in a stray, but I think I'll keep her." The way she'd said that, all sincere, even through a laugh, made me want to hug her again and never let go.

When we turned a corner, she cleared her throat. "Now, tell me about yourself."

"Everything you need to know about me, you can find online," I answered sheepishly.

"Well, that is not true," she deadpanned. "Whatever is written on the Internet is how the world sees you. I want to know the real you, the you that captured my son's attention," she put forth.

I wanted to tell her that my looks probably caught Mateo's attention, but it would be a lie. He'd proven it over and over, with all the pursuit he led. I couldn't understand it, though. All I had to offer was my looks and the money. At least, that's what got brainwashed into my core—that I held no actual worth, personality-wise. Many people had told me I was funny and clever, but it was hard to tell whether they genuinely meant it or were being polite. And let's not mention all those who put me in the pretty but dumb box.

"I'm not sure he has the right idea. If he knew the real me, he would be running in the opposite direction."

And that was putting it mildly.

"I doubt that, Mateo has a good head on his shoulders and good instincts when it comes to people," she asserted as we took an earthen path between two houses.

"Everybody makes mistakes. I happen to be one of them." Well, that came out of nowhere.

I didn't do heart-to-hearts. I dealt with commands and orders, following them to perfection. Feelings were not a part of it. I was molded into this perfect version of a doll, forced into obedience, and deprived of the chance to develop any character of my own. I played different parts, all with plastered fake smiles, and somewhere along the way, I got wrapped in it all. I lost any sense of self, as if I had any to begin with.

As if she could read my inner turmoil, Eva's hand took mine, clasping over with the other, covering my fingers with warmth.

I'd spent the last year finding myself outside of my family, fully immersing in a fight I knew would be the end, but I was prepared to go down swinging. I was ready to lose everything, including myself in the process, determined to take them down. I had nothing to lose, no one to shield, nothing to be considered leverage over me. Except now I had crossed paths with this amazing woman and the man she had taken under her wing, waiting inside their home. A major mistake I should never have allowed to happen. How could I live with myself knowing that I'd put them all in danger? A clean slate, a way out... that was what I needed now, a way out of this without leaving any trace. After giving myself a mental pep talk, I finally gathered whatever was left of me and, with renewed resolve, I put on another mask, hiding all my emotions.

"I come from a fucked-up family, excuse my French... so seeing yours got me a bit emotional, that's all."

"Come here." Eva opened her arms, and I crashed into her, allowing the warm embrace to take over everything I had left in me. This version of me was no longer allowed; it was time to suppress it, making this moment of weakness my last.

Chapter 34

Sabrina

Extra! Extra! Read all about it: Sabrina Furst was officially addicted to hugs.

Yeah, yeah, I was deprived of physical touch by my parents, boo freaking hoo. No need to be sorry for little ol' me. I was a tough ass bitch, and I proudly carried the label.

When Eva and I got back inside, a weird feeling tingled my senses, reminding me of my last night's conversation with Mateo. I grabbed my phone, excused myself, and went straight to the bathroom, where I called Simon. He answered with a yawn.

"Can you look up a case for me? A Mateo and Tyler Hart, but I don't know their last name before they changed it. It was sometime in 2006, a drunken driver hit a car. The parents died. Mother's name was Jasmine."

"Shit," he mumbled, and I could hear him typing.

Does he sleep with his laptop?

"What do you need to know?"

"Who was the judge on the case?"

Silence.

And yet, it spoke volumes.

"Give me a minute."

More typing, a pause, some clicking.

Please be wrong, please.

I tapped my foot, nerves taking over.

Simon cleared his throat, "Jacob fucking Furst."

It shouldn't have come as a surprise, and yet, my chest tightened, the unmistakable feeling of drowning taking over. The walls closed in. I lifted my clenched fist, ready to swing at my reflection staring back at me from the mirror, but Simon's voice stopped me. "Sab? You ok?"

I shook my head, tears on the verge of spilling.

Serendipity indeed.

"I'll be fine," I told him, and after he hummed disbelievingly, I hung up. When I exited the bathroom, I was met with curious stares. Desperate for an escape, I looked at Eva. "I need to go. Is there a train or a bus I can take?" I queried.

The disappointment on Mateo's face was more than obvious, as was the relief on Luka's. "I can take you; I have to go to the city anyway," he offered, stunning me with the gesture.

"You don't have to; I can grab whatever ride there is."

"Don't be silly, Luka is headed there anyway, so you just go on with him." Eva closed in on me, placing both her hands on my shoulders. "Don't be a stranger, ok?"

Since it was a promise I couldn't keep, all I could give her was a barely noticeable nod and a smile. Both Tristan and Mak gave me goodbye hugs, and never in my life had it been harder for me to fight back the tears. Mateo walked me outside to Luka's truck, framing my face between his ruffled palms. Luka got behind the wheel and waited.

"I know what you are doing, and I won't let you," he said

hoarsely, eyes piercing all the way to my soul, making every part of my body aware of the intensity. This was wild; he knew nothing about me, and yet he read my intention, my thoughts. I could feel him peeling back the mask I had hidden behind. I was sure that this man could shatter my entire world. Worst of all, if I stayed, I'd give him the sledgehammer. Instead, I did what I do best: I pulled back and pressed down all the emotions clouding my judgment.

The urge to drown my sorrows took over, fully aware that they had learned how to swim.

Unable to look at him any longer, I backed into the passenger seat. Mateo shut the door in silence, then Luka backed out of their driveway.

As we drove away from the only place I could ever, possibly, consider home, Mateo's face ripped through me. That knowing look, filled with sadness and disappointment, was the only thing I could see, and it tore me apart.

The stopping of the vibration snapped me out of whatever that was, only to knock me down into another state of nervousness. Luka opened the door for me, but I sat there frozen, unable to step out.

"Come on, it's just coffee," he voiced, calm, his expression somewhere between kind and commanding. With a large lump in my throat, one I tried to swallow, I got out of the only protection I had and followed Luka through the bar out to the small back patio. Spotting one empty table in the corner, we walked to it. I blindly dropped into the chair he pulled out for me, glancing around as he lowered into the seat across from me. I chose not to look at him, knowing what was coming. From our first interaction, I was sure Luka was the family protector, the father figure, the rock of the bunch. I was used to being scolded, as well as being a disappointment, and let's not forget the *'you're not good enough'* spiel. It was all imprinted in me, deep and permanent, and yet, knowing all those things were going to come out of his mouth scared the hell out of me.

Deciding to stand my ground, I took a firm stance, though in a sitting position, and cracked. "Look, I know all you are going to say, so save your breath. I know I'm not good enough for your brother, don't deserve him, and he's better off. You don't have anything to worry about. I will stay away. He was the one who sought me out last night, and it wasn't my intention to fall asleep or to come to your house. So whatever you want to say, please spare me," I articulated.

"For someone who goes to Harvard, you sure seem to be," he trailed off, then quipped, "How to say dumb without sounding mean?"

"If I may be blunt, anything coming out of you sounds mean," I pointed out.

"Don't judge a book by its cover," he placated.

"Like you did?" I raised a brow, and he pulled back, grinning.

"Touche." He took a deep breath. "I was wrong!"

Well, that was unexpected.

"Sorry?"

"I. Was. Wrong." Each word got louder, clearer.

Too bad. I couldn't even gloat.

"No, you weren't," I rebutted.

There was something in this little back-and-forth we were having... it almost resembled the vibe I shared with Simon.

196

Wow, that was an odd thought to have.

"Yes, I was; it took me a couple of minutes to see you to realize it."

"What's that supposed to mean?"

There was a glint in his spiky glare, one that scared the shit out of me.

"I am an observant person; it comes with being compared to the Hulk or a tank."

"I was going more for Shrek," I said playfully, but regretted it instantly, not sure if I'd offended the guy. He surprised me with a chuckle, and I took the chance to make it right.

"Sorry about that, but you're intimidating."

"Only to the people who don't know me."

"Fair enough, sorry about that too."

"Don't apologize. I, too, made judgments and jumped to conclusions. I see now that you are far from the cover girl plastered all over the city. And you are not your father's daughter."

From our first interaction at the Apollo, I've had a feeling he knew exactly who I was, and he has now confirmed it. But before I could say anything, he cleared his throat. "You care about him." It was a statement, but somehow I still wanted to answer it, elaborate, maybe…

"I do, that's why I am going to stay away."

"I don't think that's a good idea."

A way-too-young-to-be-a-working-waitress came to take our order. Luka was the one doing all the talking since I was too busy phasing out.

"You don't know me, and frankly, I don't want you to, so

let's cut the bullshit and get it over with," I snarled, turning hostile at that point, wanting this charade to end.

"It was you, right?"

"What?"

"District Attorney, the CEO of that bank, and all the others?"

"How?" I gasped, and there was a slight chance that my jaw might have hit the floor. I didn't even try to deny it; I couldn't really, with that serious, scary face staring at me.

"I had my doubts when the news broke out, especially the coincidence that it was revealed during the movie premiere you attended in an attempt to fool my brother." His huge neck twitched, revealing a pulsing vein.

"You got it all wrong." I waved my hand just as two cups were placed on the table between us. Luka slid mine over, cocking a brow.

"Don't patronize me; I may not have a college degree, but it doesn't make me any less aware or intuitive."

"That was not my intention. Besides, I didn't know—" He put up his hand, stopping whatever I was trying to say next.

"Let me interrupt you right there. I am sure you dug up information about us, so don't play dumb with me."

Well, Fuck.

"Now," he exasperated. "I brought you here with one question, and I want you to give me an honest answer."

There was a minute-long staring contest happening, and due to the intensity in his ambers, I blinked, giving in to it. This man had a gorgeous set of eyes.

"What is your plan?"

"I can't tell you that."

"Why?"

Dropping my head, my eyes went to my fingers, pulling on the skin around my nails. When I didn't answer him, he murmured, "You don't want to get anyone involved?"

Now, how does he do it?

"If you know that, why ask?"

"Because I need to know if you're worth it."

"I can tell you right here and now that I am *not*," I asserted.

"That's a lie, but I'll give in to it. Do you care about my brother?"

"You said one question!"

"Let's not play any more games, just answer me," he demanded, his tone harsh and firm, matching his whole vibe.

"I do, and that is the problem. He was never supposed to happen, not when I..."

Stop it, Sabrina, don't share!

"When what?"

"I get that you love him. I can tell you care about me too, even if I don't know why. But if this gets back to me, I want no collateral damage," I confessed. "You knowing any of it puts you in danger."

"I can take care of myself." He pulled closer, placing his elbows on the table. It made him look even more intimidating.

"Not when it comes to this." To add to the point, I crossed my arms over my chest.

"And what exactly is this?"

You know what, fuck it!

My mind just yelled at me; that inner voice took over, deciding to lay it all on the table, consequences be damned.

"My father was never a good person, at least not when it came to the people closest to him. To the outside world, he is the epitome of rags to riches. The public has no idea how he got to the top, and initially, we wanted to uncover it. Then we found some disruptions in his judicial career; cases we are sure he took bribes for each ruling, some to bury, others to put innocent people away. I have all the information, all except the money trail, and twenty minutes ago, I found out he also wronged your brothers."

I watched for his reaction to the last thing I said, but he remained still, a poster man for calm and collected.

"You knew?"

He nodded.

"Does..." before I could finish, he snapped a quick "No!"

Fuck, it would be easier if Mateo knew about it. Or maybe it was for the best.

"What do the men you outed have to do with it?"

"Some of them helped my father bury his past, while others built his present. I want to tear it all down, including his future."

"Is that why you switched to law?"

Why was everyone hung up on that? Was it so hard to believe I would turn to law?

"Not the main reason, but yes."

"Ok, thank you for sharing." His shoulders relaxed; technically, it was an impossible task, given how naturally tense they were framed.

"Don't thank me. When this comes back to me, play possum."

"I told you already, I can take care of myself. Now, onto

the other matter…" His eyes looked straight at me, cutting in deep. "If you care about my brother, as I am certain you do, you need to share it with him. He could help you out; he has a way with computers."

"No," I whisper-yelled, "that is off the table. He stays as far away from this as possible."

A shadow appeared from behind me, darkening the table, and my heart stopped beating altogether.

"Too late for that."

Chapter 35

Mateo

I took a seat next to my brother, who'd texted me their location, knowing I would be following.

"How much of it did you hear?" Her soft voice called out, but her eyes wouldn't look at me.

"All of it," I said point-blank.

She turned to face Luka, giving him a somewhat angry stare. "You set me up?"

"Yes." My brother shrugged, the biggest smirk on his face.

"Why?"

"Because you infiltrated the inner circle," Luka stated it so matter-of-factly, and Sabrina glared at him like she wanted to slap him.

"What does that mean?"

"You got the stamp of approval." He gave her that 'duh' look only I could read.

With her perfectly arched brows, she gawked, "Not following."

"Mama likes you," Luka professed.

The moment he uttered the words, she turned to face me, her features slightly softened, giving Luka a chance to continue. "Our mother read you the night at the restaurant. I was the one blind to see it, but she knew straight away. From the start, Mama appealed to your character. And after she met you, it was clear to all of us."

"I'm sorry, I still don't follow." Sabrina switched her focus between the two of us before landing on Luka.

"Mama has a way of reading people, it's a gift, she says—claims is more appropriate. She saw your 'soul'—" he air-quoted "—that night and only confirmed it this morning."

"Damn it, I am going to start leaking again." Sabrina fanned her eyes with her hands. "No, I'm not leaking; it's nothing but some eye hydration."

My brother and I both laughed, and the look on her face was one of instant regret, letting me know those words weren't meant to escape her mouth.

I gave Luka a look, and with a nod, he stood up and left, giving us a moment.

"Let me in. Please, let me the fuck in."

"I can't." Her voice cracked.

"Why?"

"I'm scared, all right. I am so fucking scared of this." She motioned her finger between us.

"That makes two of us. This is far from normal for me, but I'm here, ready and willing."

"You shouldn't be; I don't deserve it." A tear glided down her face, and I swept it away with my thumb.

"Now that's a load of crap, and you know it."

"My father…"

I stopped her before she could finish. "I don't care. You didn't do anything, except keep it from me, but I will look past it."

A soft chuckle finally got her lips to twitch, fighting a smile. I scooted my chair to hers, grabbed both her hands, and placed them between our beating hearts.

"It doesn't undermine how strongly I feel about you or you about me."

"You don't even know me."

"That's another load of crap, but fine; let's go with that. Let's go with the fact that I don't know you hate your life. Let's say I don't know how good a friend you are, how much you care, or how big your heart is. Let's say that you are not a strong-willed woman, and, God forbid, you care about anyone except yourself. And to add a bit of icing, let's not acknowledge how much happier you get inside a small wooden cabin despite living in a mansion, or how you tore down your favorite place to keep me safe." Her hand in mine twitched. "And yeah, I read right through that, so you burned it for nothing. But don't worry, my brother has a knack for building things."

She averted her gaze, not allowing me to see what she was thinking, but her recoil spoke volumes. I could feel her whole body tremble as the words sank in.

"I know you, I know your heart, so don't you dare deny me."

There was a beat of silence, but I was on a roll here, so I kept going, "At the beginning, I honestly thought it was lust at first sight or some shit; but the more you gave away, the more it turned into something else."

"I hate you for this." She wiped her soaked cheeks, a sight I never thought would be so meaningful. "Showing any emotion is not allowed in our house, and I always felt like a robot, and now..."

Pride shot through me. "I infiltrated your walls," I verified.

"Well, stop it," she yelled, pushing at my chest.

"No way, it's too late; all you have to do is let me in all the way."

"That's not going to happen." She shook her head, and I grabbed her face, pulling all her attention toward me.

"I love a good challenge."

"Stop it!" Another crack in her voice.

"Stop what?"

"Saying things like that," she gasped, her greens at full display.

"Why?"

"Cuz it's making me uneasy." She bit her inner cheek, and I saved it with my thumb.

"That's how it's supposed to be," I stated, grazing my thumb over her jawline.

"How what's supposed to be?"

"Catching feelings."

Her eyes widened.

"That's not what this is." She tried to pull away, but I wouldn't allow it.

"You couldn't be more wrong." My words once again got her eyes averting to the floor.

"You've got it all mixed up."

"You can't hide anymore. I see right through it. I see you."

I drank her in, the way her leg jumped, nails grating her cuticles, and the biting of her lip. She was at a breaking point, right there on the edge of falling, and I was ready for it, with my parachute all in hand.

"You felt it under that tree, in the cabin, yesterday—you felt it."

"It's called sexual tension."

"Vamp," I roared.

"Don't call me that," she snapped, making me grin.

"You want me to call you Sabrina?"

She cringed at that, saying "No" under her breath.

"Blackbird?"

Her leg stopped bouncing, so I chose to stop her heart.

"How 'bout mine?"

Her eyes snapped up, and I could see it all in those beautiful greens—the fear, the apprehension.

"Stop it," she whined.

"Stop what?"

"Looking at me like that." She blinked.

"Like what? Like I want you? Like I care? Like you're mine?"

"I'm nobody's property," she snarled.

God, she was stubborn.

"Wow, the lengths you will go to shut me out are impressive." I clicked my tongue with a tut.

"The secret is out, and I am fully aware of your endgame. You have one choice: we do it together or separately. But mark my words, I'll be doing it, with or without you," I claimed.

"Please," she begged, her tone shaky.

"Please, what?"

"Don't do this."

"Do what? Make you face your demons? Tough luck; now look me in my eyes!"

Nothing, not even a flinch.

"Look at me, dammit!" I wailed.

She slowly opened her lids, taking my breath away.

"There you are." I smiled.

I cupped her cheeks tighter, grazing the side of her lip with my thumb, and she leaned into my touch, making my entire body react on impulse alone.

"Let go, and trust that I've got you."

Her eyes, teary and wet, played ping pong, focusing on both of mine, undecided on which one to lock onto fully. All I could see in that moment was her, the real her, the love she was desperate to hide.

"Don't fight it," I cracked, desperation taking over.

I saw the moment she made the decision. Right then and there, she let go of all her defenses, broke down the armor and all the bricks surrounding her, answering my plea. The kiss she initiated, the one giving in to me, us, felt like a promise. With it, she gave me her trust, her fears, and her hopes. With that one kiss, she answered all my questions and ignited the fire she tried so hard to put out. Eager for the connection, I pulled her onto me, not a single fuck given about our surroundings. One single gasp made me feral, and I lost all control when she opened her mouth, inviting my tongue. This drive between us, the thing she described as sexual tension, was so much more, almost cataclysmic. The pull she had on me, my heart, was so strong that it felt like physical pain, and right there with her, I welcomed the hurt.

Whatever she wanted from me, I would give her, down to my heart, ready to be broken, stomped on, and pierced right through. Everything was on the line; for her, I could and would do that because being with her was the best feeling in the world. No matter what was to come, no matter the consequences, as of this moment, I was all in, and finally, so was she!

Chapter 36

Sabrina

Who was Mateo Hart?

To put it simply, he was the person who broke me. Technically, he broke down all my defenses, but in doing so, he broke me. He infected my DNA, changed the way my heart was beating, and made me serve all my weaknesses on a silver platter. Never in my life have I shown one smidge of fear, not a slip of insecurity, until *him*. Before, I was a walking definition of poise and power, and somehow that woman got lost in the pull of his brown eyes. He held me captive, yet somehow I was the one who tossed away the key.

And I never wanted to go back.

Stopping the full-on PDA in front of a packed patio, we pulled away, at least physically. Mateo took out his wallet and tossed a couple of bills on the table for the two barely touched coffees, then took my hand, guiding me through the crowd, ignoring the nasty looks. We got to his bike, his helmet waiting for him on the mirror. He unlocked the top box and took out the spare. Sparkly eyes stared at me as he handed it over. With shaky hands, I took it and slid it over my head, all the while looking at him as he did the same, covering up that beautiful face of his.

"Where to?"

"The legal aid clinic. I'll guide the way."

"You wanna drive?" he asked, holding the bike for me.

"No, I like it when you do it."

He cleared his throat, his Adam's apple bobbing, and I smirked.

"Then how will you guide the way?"

"You trust me?"

He nodded, taking my safety buckles and clicking them together.

Both saddled up, my arms wrapped tightly around him, locking firmly in place. The vibration started to build under me when he shifted into gear, and then we were flying. At the first intersection, I tapped his left shoulder, and he understood the assignment, taking the turn. I navigated our way through the city, repeating the same actions until we reached our destination. He found a spot under a tree, and we stepped down, placing the helmets on the mirrors.

The place was closed, but I had my key, so I unlocked it and swung the door open. He followed me inside, taking a look around with curious eyes. The place smelled like a library, and I could never understand how that was possible.

Getting into this clinic to get my hands on my father's cases, I never would have imagined that I would end up loving it.

The place was messy, six cubicles forming a rectangle in the middle, each stacked with files and papers. It had only one private office, one that Carl shared with Lisa, our other lawyer, next to a small conference room.

I walked to the far-right desk and placed my palm on the surface. "This is me."

"It's nice," he said, scanning the personalized items in the corner.

"What do I have to do to get a spot next to that one?" He pointed at the framed photo of Nala, Aria, and me hugging on the floor of Nala's apartment.

That was cheesy, yet extremely cute.

"Are you jealous?" I taunted, my voice raspy.

"I prefer territorial. I mean, you are wearing my clothes. I should probably mention, you in my shorts and t-shirt is your best look by far."

God, I've forgotten all about it. I didn't even dare to imagine how I must be looking. I bet my hairstyle is sporting a bunch of flyaway antennae.

"Possessive much?"

"Want me to go full caveman on you? 'Cause I will."

"You're unbelievable." I rolled my eyes, and he wrapped one arm around my lower back, pulling me to him.

"Right back at ya." He grazed his nose over mine before his lips found my ear. "So, do you want me to bend you over your desk before or after we come up with a plan together?"

Together.

I shook my head with a laugh and took him in, that fearless smirk that always seemed to hit deep.

"You know your way around a computer?"

"I dabble."

That came out way too cocky, and damn, it only made him sexier.

"How's your money tracing dabble?"

"Pretty good."

While still wrapped in him, I twisted to unlock my drawer.

Sliding it open, I took out my laptop and placed it on my desk.

"It's encrypted and everything; paid a guy a small fortune to twerk it up."

"What do you need?" He took a seat, opened the laptop, and fired it up.

"To find a connection between the money and the other party, we need to figure out who he was conspiring with."

Over his shoulder, I punched in my password, and my background appeared. It was another picture of my best friends and yours truly. I navigated to my latest file using the touchpad and double-clicked. When it filled the screen, I pointed with my finger.

"Those are the dates of all the cases he worked on. If I could..." I cleared my throat, correcting myself, "If *we* could just find matching invoices..." I trailed off, swallowing hard. I didn't even know how to finish. We had no idea who my sperm donor was working with, let alone if there was even money involved. It was all speculation on my part, since it was the only thing that made sense. All my father ever wanted was power. Dollar signs equaled power. Hence, my entire hypothesis.

"Ok. I'll dig, but there's something I need to tell you..." He paused for dramatic purposes, and my lungs froze. "I'm hungry."

I released a breath, shaking my head.

"What are you in for?" I snickered, pulling up my Uber Eats app.

"Pizza? Best food for hacking and scheming." He sealed it with a wink, and it honestly didn't have to be so damn sexy.

"Pepperoni?"

He gave me a nod and quipped, "Extra cheese."

My kind of man.

Shit. As if I needed any more reasons to like him.

"Done," I said, and sat on his lap, leaning to the side so he had a better view. With one hand on each side of me, he typed away at an impressive speed, windows on the screen popping up by the second.

Something about this setup got me feeling confident and assertive. I could picture it, the future—the two of us working together, with me sitting in my new favorite seat, watching him do his thing. I liked the concept, the possibility.

"Did you check your mother's accounts, or the company's?"

"Yeah, we went through them all."

It was far too easy, with my mother's accountant being an idiot and using his name as a password.

Mateo hummed and turned his focus back to the screen.

Pizza came soon after, and I fed it to him while he continued typing. I took a seat at the desk, marveling at his concentration, the way he puckered his lower lip and narrowed his eyes.

"Sab?" My name on his lips was my newest drug.

"Yeah?"

"How big is your trust fund?"

"10 million," I answered, as if the sum meant nothing.

"There are 35 million currently on your trust balance."

"What?" I cried out, sliding off with a hop. I blinked at the numbers right there, staring back at me—35 million of dirty money under my name.

"It says here that one Jacob Furst is in control of your

trust until you turn 21."

Of course he is.

The bastard had been using me this entire time.

Well played, Daddy, well played.

"So that means he can withdraw and also deposit it?"

"Yeah," he mumbled, "by the looks of it."

Guess I was wrong. I haven't been three steps ahead. While I'd been busy daydreaming about his downfall, my own father had been playing me dirty, and now it was my name attached to his crimes.

"When was the last transaction?" I asked, letting it all sink in.

"Back in August?"

"Show me," I said, my eyes zooming in on the screen. He pointed his finger right over the number. After thorough cross-checking, we identified a significant number of conflicting dates, which made the heavyweight a little lighter.

"Now we have to figure out who the money traces back to," I concluded.

He was going down, and not only that, people were finally going to get some well-deserved justice, one that he had taken away from them.

Chapter 37

Sabrina

A hand tried hard to wave me out of my hypnotic state. It was a mixture of confusion and excitement, followed by a severe overload. A minute ago, I'd felt my eyes widen, as if I had found some long-lost treasure; then everything went blank. Poof.

"Talk to me," the soft voice that owned me tingled my ears.

I blinked once, twice, and took a breath. "It's a long story."

"I have time."

I dragged my desk buddy's chair and took a seat next to Mateo. He eagerly waited while I gathered myself, and after taking a deep breath, I monologued my life story. With too much detail, I recollected the very first memory I had of my mother yelling at me for mispronouncing our brand name. At three years old, I had problems with the letter R, so the 'Furst' part of 'Furst Design' had been a nightmare for me. My mother hadn't cared, though; she'd yelled the obedience out of me until I'd gotten it right. I laughed at the memory of me peeing my pants at her scrutiny, in front of an entire team of people working on the commercial for the children's fall line I was the face of.

I skimmed through my PG-13 teen years, focusing more

on my life in that house, in the semi-spotlight, revealing the dynamics of my relationship with the people who gave me life. I told him about Simon, our connection, and about the people we've taken down so far. And I apologized again for the injustice my father had committed against his parents.

Mateo hugged me then, wrapping me in his warmth, not letting go until I was ready to. I chose that moment to let out a frantic laugh that kept on going, turning hysterical. I couldn't stop it; honestly, I haven't even tried to. Mateo didn't say a word, just waited until I let it all out. My laughs turned into sobs, and without warning, I broke down. He caught me, held me, calmed me—the rhythm of his breathing like a life raft keeping me afloat.

When I finally composed myself, I pulled back to wipe the tears, but he took charge and did it for me. I leaned into his touch, feeling the shivers spreading out.

"At first, Simon and I wanted to expose Jacob's fake identity, and in our search, we stumbled on a case that made no sense. That's why I started volunteering at the clinic." I took another breath, but it was a failed attempt to calm down. "Carl, my boss, gave me access to all legal files. He went to the FBI with all the cases we red-flagged, but unfortunately, it wasn't enough."

Unease settled, remembering the tightness in my chest while I read over all the files.

"I decided to take matters into my own hands to reveal to the world all the bastards that helped my father along the way. But I couldn't bring myself to let it bury all the people he had wronged, so we started to build a case for a class action."

I could see the tick of his jaw. I didn't know much of the trial he remembered, but the way his fist clenched, I could only assume he remembered it all.

"Mateo, I am so sorry."

"It's not your fault."

"Doesn't mean I can't feel it."

He placed his chin on my knee, and my fingers went straight for his hair.

"I will make it right," I reassured him, then cleared my throat. "After Simon saught me out, and told me how my father left his mother pregnant, only to fake his death and start anew, we looked into Jacob's entire history, the life he created. Everything. I had my doubts about the authenticity of his law degree. Jacob was good, his picture is on the academic board, there are photos of him working for the paper, the report cards, everything was there, official and all."

I turned on the laptop and typed in the official website of his alma mater. I had honestly thought his diploma was fake, but now I wasn't so sure.

"He's on the alumni committee, and there's a picture of him at graduation."

Mateo's head left my knee to take a look.

"I don't know how he did all of that, considering he was not in the state during his fake education."

Water started building up in my eyes as I released a breath I had been holding for God knows how long.

"My father is the reason why there are a lot of innocent people behind bars, and now I have proof." My chest started heaving, and I wanted to burst out crying. It was a different kind of sensation; it felt like a reverse panic attack or something. We were still waiting for the program to trace the money when Mateo muttered, "Do you think maybe he was working with the prisons?"

Fuck, why didn't I think of that? It made sense. They would receive more funding as the inmate population increased.

"It never crossed my mind. Can you work your magic?"

"Anything for you."

That turned me into a puddle.

Frankly, I had no idea what he was doing; all I knew was that he looked hot as hell doing it. My guess was that he was filtering the search.

"Will this get back to you?"

He looked so worried, scared even, and a part of me broke at the sight. Aside from Aria and Nala, I've never had anyone care for me, especially not to this extent.

"Hey, this is bigger than me. I am not important."

"You are to me." His palm found my cheek, and I melted.

"Look who's being all sweet."

"I'm serious."

I could tell by the intensity in his eyes.

Trust issues were a problem. Who could blame me with my family history? But there was another word, the four-letter one, that was incomprehensible. I lacked in that department, deprived of the one thing that made the world go round. I wouldn't be able to see it if it were staring me right in the face, right? Except I saw it, or at least I thought I did… and it was right there in those brown eyes, the same eyes that fired up my entire nervous system. The thing was, the look came with some side effects, primarily guilt. It was a look I couldn't reciprocate, down to the feeling it represented, and he deserved the look. He deserved the world, and I couldn't give it to him, although I wanted to badly. It was not something I had in me.

I had a choice to make, and it was as simple as they got—be selfish or selfless. Given that, the latter was the correct answer.

"I don't care about anything other than everyone getting what they deserve."

Including you!

With that, I closed the laptop, straddled his lap, and kissed him with purpose. The way his hand instantly went to my waist and under the fabric of the oversized shirt sent out a moan, making me whimper at his touch. His fingers found my breasts and did wonders around the hardened nipples. His neck was the next victim of my attack, with my teeth grating every inch of his skin, followed by my tongue tracing back the path, remedying.

He grabbed my ass and, in a quick swoop, I was airborne for a split second before he set me on the table. He played quickly, discarding our clothes, everything except his shirt, which was covering me. There was a moment when he took a step back, his chest motioning the depth of his breaths while his eyes traced over me.

"Fuck Blackbird, you look so sexy in my shirt," he admired, his voice hoarse.

His possessive expression only made him hotter. I was burning up in another way, though, a hazard furnace second away from overload. Then he was inside me, filling up my body and my darkened soul. He was the only light I knew, the only one not blinding me, opening all my horizons to see them more clearly. His torture was slow, savoring, making every slightest move articulate my heightened senses.

We looked into each other's eyes, and he took my hand, intertwining our fingers. His gaze grew deeper as he deliberately grazed his thumb over the tattoo on my ring finger, as if erasing its meaning.

And when the built-up curled from my toes, every fiber absorbing the spreading power rising, I came apart for him. I knew he saw it; the moment realization struck, hitting the deepest parts that had long been lost and forgotten. And as if the sight of it fumed him, he shattered, infusing me.

I didn't know what love felt like, but whatever this was, I was in it.

Chapter 38

Sabrina

After I took an Uber to the house, I got a strange feeling in my gut. There was no security at the gate, and Javier didn't meet me at the car. When I got inside, the house was too quiet, every creak screaming trouble. Then my mother's voice hit me like a whip. "Sabrina, a moment." My heart raced, my palms grew sweaty, and a knot formed in my stomach. I knew this was going to be another one of those confrontations, and I was not ready for it.

I honestly thought I'd been chipped as a child because I wondered how on earth they knew to expect me. My body protesting, knowing damn well I wasn't getting any sleep, I dragged my feet to the study, preparing myself for the worst. I popped my head through the door, surprised to find my father in his chair, Erica, my mother, hovering over his right shoulder, and our family lawyer seated in a chair across from them. The lawyer, a regular fixture in our family disputes, ensured the legality of their decisions without providing any form of justice or fairness. Daddy dearest only brought him in when shit was about to go down.

"Oh great, the Unholy Trinity's all here," I tweeted.

"Take a seat, Sabrina." My father issued his command, leaving no room for argument. I scanned their posture, focusing on the way my mother kept her shoulders straight. Dark-haired, brown-eyed, tall, my mother was the epitome of sophistication in her burgundy Prada power suit; shame that her soul was as dark as her hair.

"I think I'd rather stand." I crossed my arms in defiance, but my father wouldn't allow it. He barked, "Sit!" And, like a good dog, I did just that, my boldness simmering beneath the surface.

"Your dad tells me you have been fornicating with a slum dweller."

I squinted at what she came up with. My mother liked using big words to appear intelligent and give the illusion that she was superior to others. The thing here was that I knew better.

"So?" I cocked a brow.

"You are to stop seeing him this instant," my mother snapped back at me.

"You do know that I am an adult, and that you have no right over who I see?" I said it more rhetorically sarcastic, and I sensed the steam coming from my mother's ears.

"Considering you are living under our roof, I have to disagree with you." Daddy dearest stepped in.

"That's an easy fix. Give me an hour to get my things, and I will be out of your hair."

Frankly, it would take me less than half an hour, but it was beside the point.

"You are not moving out!"

"You're sending mixed signals here." I rolled my eyes at my mother.

A loud slap, I honestly didn't see coming, struck my left

cheek. Sure, my face was familiar with my mother's palm, though it had been long since they last collided, but the sting still stung. The shame in her eyes was evident, but I kept my head held high, feeling the burn without acknowledging it.

"How dare you speak to us like that?"

"Like what, mother? Like a human?"

That remark made my father let out an exasperated breath, making my pride tingle.

"You have a choice," he told me, and I gawked at him.

"I do? That's a new development."

"Stop it!" he yelled, except it was not directed at me; it was directed at my mother, who was already in her striking stance, her hand frozen mid-air. She turned to face him, only to submit, hand falling to her side. It was a new dynamic altogether. By the looks of it, it was new to my mother as well.

Sick and tired of the charade, I stood up. "You mentioned a choice," I reminded them.

Sperm donor cleared his throat, standing up to show off his dominance.

"It's either us or him." My mother laid it out for me.

The true colors of my parents, ladies and gentlemen. You could see the selfishness just by the fact that she put them as the first option.

"Oh, mother. Do you honestly think that I would ever choose you?"

The only problem here was the timetable not playing in my favor. My endgame was to leave this prison right before the big reveal, but now was as good a time as any.

My mother gasped, as if she hadn't seen it coming, but there was no surprise on the male side of the family, which made me a bit uneasy.

"Fine. If that's what you want." Her cold tone was an Oscar-worthy act.

"Just to clarify, you will no longer be a part of this family." The father took his signature serious pose, elbows on the table, closing the triangle with his intertwined fingers, his voice cold and final.

"Never really was, was I?"

I swear, there was a bit of red covering his features. Like my words somehow hurt him.

Not likely, I thought.

"Are you going to leave it all? Your cars, your inheritance?"

I might, possibly, maybe miss my cars… the leather seats… the AC…

"If that's the price I have to pay, so be it." I shrugged, not a care in the world.

"Sabrina, this is no joking matter," my mother pointed out. And for a fraction of a second, I thought she actually cared.

"Good thing I'm not rolling on the floor laughing."

"You're a disgrace." With clear disgust, she pointed her polished finger at me. I could lie and say it hurt, but, unsurprisingly, I felt nothing.

"Right back at you."

"How dare you?"

I had to hand it to her; she looked wounded.

"How dare I? Are you for real? All you ever did was treat me like I was a puppet. Well, I'm cutting the strings, mother!" I growled, playing my fingers like scissors.

"Go to hell!" Her loud shriek hurt my ears, but, much to

her dismay, nothing else.

"Can't do that…" I dragged a breath through my clenched teeth, hissing, "You see, I've sent too many people there already, so it would be kinda awkward, don't you think?" I finished off with a wink, and I swear, both their jaws dropped in shock at my audacity.

"Get out of my sight."

"Gladly," I added with spite.

I stormed out of there, as if it meant nothing, given that it was true. On my way to the garage, I glanced back at the house that was never my home. I took a minute to think about whether there was anything I wanted to take with me, but came up blank. God, that was pathetic somehow. I had nothing of worth to me in there, not one thing. And still I smiled.

Stadling my Honda, still wearing my heels and Mateo's shirt, I took it all in for one last time before my grand exit. As the prison reflected in my side mirror, getting smaller with each passing meter, I felt the tightness around my heart loosen.

If I thought jumping off a cliff into the water felt liberating, I had a new thing coming. For the first time, I felt unshackled, free, and like myself.

Chapter 39

Sabrina

The moment I turned onto his street, I saw him and Luka relaxing on the front porch. My insides instantly lit up, warmth spreading through me. I parked in their driveway, behind Luka's pickup, and kicked out the kickstand.

"I didn't know where else to go," I revealed when their gazes shot to me. Mateo stood up, beckoning me with his finger. "Come here."

I took the necessary steps until I was right in front of his open arms.

"What happened?" He wrapped me in his embrace, and I leaned into it.

"I've been disowned," I said through a chuckle.

The silver lining in all this was that it all felt right. I was exactly where I was meant to be. This right here was my true endgame.

"What?"

"Don't worry, it was by choice."

He pulled away, and I took my time looking at him, a cigarette poised between his fingers. I turned my attention to his brother, bobbing my chin. "Shrek."

"Princess," he retorted, and I let out a laugh. "Coffee?"

"Please," I answered with a smile, and Luka went inside,

leaving Mateo and me alone. With my hand tucked in his, he walked me to the wooden bench, took a seat, and pulled me onto his lap.

"Are you ok?"

"I'm perfect," I reassured him before my lips fell onto his. He wrapped his fingers around the back of my neck and pulled me closer, taking away every breath.

A couple of months ago, I might've even cared that I lost everything, but here, in his arms, nothing else seemed important, except this man who somehow spread his poison through my veins, infecting me with a disease... and in all honesty, I hoped it was fatal.

"Well, well, well," Tristan teased, his head peeping through the cracked door. "If I didn't know any better, I would think you like us," he said, stepping outside, grinning.

"Nah," I kidded, "I came for the coffee."

"Sure, sure."

"Where are the others?"

"Mak took Mama to pick up Tyler at the airport," Tristan answered, and I smiled with a nod. Luka came outside with a full tray, and I stood up. "Is it ok if I use the bathroom?"

All three brothers chirped a "Yup," but Luka added, "You know where it is."

"Thanks." I smiled and went inside. The house was quiet, as if it were missing its heart. I sure could've used one of Eva's hugs right about now. In the bathroom, I washed my face and stared at my reflection. It was an indescribable look I had on my face, calm and at ease, despite the hobo-chic look I was somehow pulling off. Heavy grunting noises came from outside, and I tore to the front yard, wishing I hadn't.

I didn't even know where to look: at the two men who betrayed me or at the family members hurt because of me.

My eyes locked on a beat-up Mateo lying on the ground, and I slid down on my knees to his side. Grabbing his face to see the damage, I cried out, "Shit." My heart broke at the sight of him.

I stood up, the traitors getting my full attention. I stared at their heaving chests, fists clenched at their sides, boots ruining the work of the freshly mowed lawn.

"Wow, I must say, I am disappointed." I let out a sigh, turning my attention from my former valet to the security guard, snarling, "My father chose poorly."

Derek's nostrils flared at the insult, but Javier didn't even bat an eye.

"Who did this to him?" I asked, my eyes flying to Mateo.

You, Sabrina, you did this to him!

His breath was painful, almost as if he couldn't inhale fully.

I turned to his brother. "Luka, which one of them did this to him?" I yelled out, and he lifted his chin, pointing with it at Javier. I took one step in his direction, checking my nails with my head tilted.

"Of all the staff, you were the last one I'd expect, but I guess money talks."

I tsked, spotting a chipped nail, my heel digging into the soil. I slowly dragged my eyes to meet his.

"You could've come to me; I would've paid you more."

He hissed in an attempt to brush it off, and I smirked. "You know he doesn't even know your name, right?"

His breathing shallowed, and I knew I had him. I took

another step, bringing me right in front of him. With my heels, we were at eye level, so he had the front seat to my fury. He'd witnessed me shooting from a rifle when my father entertained guests... was the one who'd taken me to every practice when I was little, had seen every belt I'd gotten, including the black one. God, I could see his pulse working in the vein on his throat. So I gave him one last pointed look before I barked, "Run, Javier."

Built like an Olympic weightlifter, he bolted, wobbling a bit, and I cackled dramatically, like a true villain. My long legs strode in his direction, almost gliding. He turned over his shoulder and stumbled over his feet. I let out another laugh and picked up the pace. When I closed in on him, I jumped on his back, locking his neck into a chokehold. I pressed my knee into the middle of his spine, making his back arch as I pulled his head back, gripping tight. I got to his ear and hissed, "You have exactly 10 seconds to answer. How many?" He tried to free himself, but it only made it worse for him, so he caved, "Three."

Shit, now I had to find the missing traitor.

Easing the pressure on my knee, I asked the last question, "Tell me, Javier, are you left or right handed?"

"Wha-at?" He stuttered, and I grinned, "Which hand did you use to punch him?" I could feel his forehead forming the wrinkles before he gasped out, "The right."

"Good," I whispered and squeezed tighter, "Nighty night."

He fell on the ground before me, and I landed on my knees. I stood up, dusted myself off, feeling lucky that the guy was an idiot and didn't make any sudden moves while I was airborne on his back. Glancing at the thick, long, pointy tip of my heel, an idea formed. I nicely straightened his palm on the pavement before I smashed the tip into it, making his whole body jolt, followed by a scream. I squatted down next to him, pulling on his hair. "Tell Jakov not to be such a pička (pussy) and come right at me!" I gave his head a nudge, introducing it to the cement.

Taking off my heels, I ran back to Mateo, who looked like he had been hit by a train. His face was swollen, his left eye shut, and blood was coming from his lower lip. The sight of him broke me. "I am sorry." Tears poured down my cheeks. "I am so fucking sorry."

I turned to Luka. "Did you call the ambulance?"

He nodded. "Yes, they should be here any minute."

"The bastard got away," Tristan panted, bringing his hands to his knees to catch his breath, sporting a split lip.

Three men to handle three brothers. My father knew exactly how many of them were here.

Sranje.

The sound of the sirens closed in. I gently placed my hands on Mateo's ears, trying to avoid the swollen pressure points. "I am so sorry. I should have..."

"Ma'am," a soft voice interrupted me, then a hand moved me to the side. The EMTs placed Mateo on a gurney and carried him to the ambulance. I cried as they took him away. "I am so sorry," I sobbed, pulling my hair. "I should've stayed away."

I wanted to go with him, but couldn't. I didn't deserve to.

"You go with him, I'll call Mak," Luka commanded, and Tristan listened, tagging along in the ambulance.

My knees buckled, and I fell to the ground as I watched

them take my heart away.

"Why the fuck couldn't I just stay away?" I faltered.

I felt a firm hand on my bicep, and then I was pulled up to my feet. I stared at Luka, choking on my words, "I am so sorry; it's all my fault. Please tell your mother I am terribly sorry."

His expression was soft, and so was his voice, "C'mere." He embraced me into his arms, and I sank in, gasping for air. He pulled out his phone, and I heard the dial tone, followed by Luka's firm voice. "Go to Mass General, O was taken there. I'll be there soon."

I pulled away from him, knowing he had to go and be with his brother. There was nothing I could say, so I just beelined to my bike. A hand on my wrist stopped me. "You're shaking."

Was I? All I felt was numb.

"You're in no condition to drive. Let's go inside so you can catch your breath."

What Luka didn't know was that there was no breathing without Mateo.

He guided me inside, straight to the kitchen. I stood there, frozen, while he poured what I could only assume to be coffee, since I couldn't see shit thanks to the moisture disturbing my vision. I felt his hand on my shoulder before he gently sat me down.

"Look, I have to go, but please stay here. At least until you're calm enough to drive."

I nodded, or at least I thought I did until he shook me. "Tell me you'll stay."

"I'll stay," I said, and then he was gone.

Chapter 40

Sabrina

A beeping sound was what got me to blink. It kept on going—annoyingly, so I followed the direction of the noise that brought me to a laundry room under the stairs.

I took the clothes from the dryer and folded them neatly. There was a load of laundry in a hamper next to the washing machine. The whole fight club scene must have interrupted someone's chore. I gave the house a thorough sweep for any lingering clothes, and when I couldn't find any, I put everything from the hamper in the washing machine. Selecting 'Quick wash' lit up the digital clock to 30. I returned to the kitchen and decided to wash the dishes to fill the remaining 29 minutes.

"What the hell am I doing?"

I asked myself in wonder. What was I doing here? I wasn't sure why I stayed, but I knew one thing: I didn't want to leave. I couldn't go to the hospital to face Mateo either, but I wanted to make sure he was ok.

Stopping myself from spiraling out of control, I focused on the dishes. When I was done, I checked the timer that showed 23 minutes. I gave myself another unauthorized walk-through of the upstairs. Was it wrong? Sure. Was it a necessity? Probably not. Did it stop me? Absofuckinglutely not.

Mateo and Tyler's room was small, just right to fit a bunk bed on one wall and two study desks on the parallel one. A large window was spaced right between the two sides. The lower bed was made up, looking as if it had not been slept in, which only indicated that the upper bed belonged to Mateo. The table by the window had a stack of books and a poster of the newest BMW M 1000 RR above it. Next to it was a poster of a naked blonde riding a Ducati. For a brief moment, jealousy started boiling up, something I'd never experienced before. An idea popped into my head of a private photoshoot just for Mateo, with me naked on his bike, but I quickly brushed it away.

Taking two steps forward to the desk, I took a closer look at the books. They were all about engineering, technology, and innovation. The rest of the wall was covered with basketball posters, one featuring Jordan playing against Iverson and the other of LeBron, surrounded by a couple of photos of kids in basketball jerseys and a framed article praising little Tyler.

My chest tightened, and I took out my phone, pulling up Simon's contact and hitting dial. He answered right away, "Is everything ok?"

"No," I faltered, trying hard to keep my voice sharp and not break down. "Do you have a way to check hospital records of a patient who was brought in about half an hour ago?"

"No, but I know someone who can give me the information."

"Do it! It's Mateo; he was taken to Mass Gen."

"What happened?"

"You have one guess."

"He didn't!?" The fact that it came as a surprise to him made me happy in a way; he was lucky that he never got the chance to meet the monster that was our father.

"Yeah, he sent a couple of guys as a warning. Mateo got beaten up pretty badly, and I want to know if he's ok."

"Give me five minutes, and I'll get back to you."

"Thank you."

"Do you need me to come?"

I melted at his concern, and a part of me wanted his comfort, but a bigger part wouldn't allow it. I wasn't used to it.

"It's fine, I'll crash at Aria's."

"Ok." He sounded disappointed, and I couldn't blame him. I was so accustomed to doing everything on my own that it was difficult for me to accept help or comfort from others. Aria was different; she knew me, knew that I liked my distance, to drown my sorrows in dancing and alcohol, much easier and familiar. I hung up with a quiet 'thank you' and returned downstairs.

Not knowing what to do next, I went to the kitchen and opened the fridge, scanning the contents of the produce. I decided to cook dinner, hoping no one had any deadly allergies. Aunt Mara was the one who'd taught me how to cook over the years. She also taught me how to make the most of my resources when I had limited supplies. My lessons came in handy tonight, considering it was a six-person household and the fridge was fully stocked.

My phone chimed, and I opened Simon's text.

S: *He's ok, no broken ribs, no concussion, just some bruises. He'll be released within the hour.*

I sighed in relief, only to be washed out with guilt. I should have been there with him, holding his hand. But how could I? I was the reason he was there in the first place. I was the reason he got hurt. Me.

I typed in a quick 'thanks' and got back to slicing the onions. While the meat sizzled in the pan, I prepared the rest. When all the layering was done, I slid the dish into the preheated oven.

While I waited for it to bake, I turned to the living room and skimmed through the bookshelf. The books were worn out, and they gave off the distinctive smell of a library. I smiled at the entire shelf filled with Dumas's classics, including my favorite.

Hearing the beeping chime, I went to the laundry room, emptied the washing machine, and filled the dryer. The soft chirp sounded when I hit start. I set the table and cleaned my mess, somewhat proud of the setting. When dinner came to the perfect crisp, I turned off the oven, stepped outside, and rolled my bike to the corner of the street. Hiding behind the tree diagonally across from their house, I set up shop and waited.

Half an hour later, Luka's pickup pulled up, followed by an SUV. Doing a head count, I released a breath when I reached number six. Using my tunnel vision, I focused on Shrek lurching down, crutch-carrying Mateo, who seemed a bit woozy, probably due to the effects of the painkillers. Seeing this family taking care of each other, something inside of me flicked, and I took out my phone, pressing the dial button on the last contact.

"I could use a hug," I said the moment Simon picked up.

"You know where to find me. I'll have my arms at the ready."

I nodded, knowing damn well he couldn't see me.

Taking one final look at Mateo, I waited until it was safe for me to once again disappear from his life, my heart left behind right there on the pavement.

When I arrived at Simon's house, he was on his porch, pacing. I demounted my bike and set it on the kickstand. When I took off my helmet, Simon ran down the steps right to me with open arms. I collided with his chest, allowing him to comfort me.

"It's ok, he'll be ok," he whispered, grazing my hair in a soothing motion. I didn't know why, but I trusted his words like I'd never trusted anyone else's. We got inside, and a coffee mug was already waiting for me. I have been in his house many times before, but something was different. It felt warmer. I sat on the couch, and Simon followed suit. With curious eyes, he quipped, "Tell me everything."

And so I did; I told him about our weird little meet-cute, about the connection that went from lust to need or whatever it was I tried my best not to define. I told him how I wanted to keep the distance, only for Mateo to refuse it, the determined bastard.

"So now you ran away because you feel responsible for what happened?"

I nodded.

"You know that it's not your fault, right?"

I remained still, letting my silence speak for me.

"Sab," he sighed and took my hand, pleading, "look at me."

I lifted my gaze, meeting his soft eyes. "This is not on you, and he knew the risks."

"Not really, I wasn't even aware that it would get this far. I knew Jakov would retaliate, but I thought I would be his target."

"Well, you kind of were. He found your weakness."

Shit, he had a point, which only made my guilt more potent.

"Don't run away from this. From what I gathered, they all care about you. Don't let Jakov ruin that. Don't let him take another piece of you. He already took so much."

I let those words sink in, and I knew that I should've come here. I didn't need these thoughts. I needed to drown my sorrows in something much more substantial than my brother's peace of mind.

Chapter 41

Mateo

Luka swung the door open, holding one side of me, and we were instantly hit. "Why does our house smell like lasagna?" Tristan pointed his nose in each direction, sniffing, while Luka slowly planted me on the couch.

"That's not Mama's lasagna, though?!" Mak halted.

Walking to the dining table, Luka's hands found the back of his head, giving it a scratch.

"Your girl fucking made us dinner," he gawked, shaking his head. I stood up, overpowering the pain, and dragged myself to him. My eyes went to the note sticking out of the flower-filled vase in the middle of a six-place setting. Words scribbled in delicate handwriting stared at me:

I am so sorry Hart Family!
Dinner is in the oven.

My mother, who was an all-around emotional wreck, patted my back on her way to the kitchen. "Eat first, rest, then go get her."

I nodded, not even surprised she read my mind. We took

our seats as Mama removed the dish from the oven and placed it on the table. All noses went into some heavy inhaling, the steam slowly evaporating. Our mother was a fantastic cook, and she passed her knowledge down to us. However, I must admit that, by the looks of it, Sabrina had put us all to shame.

Fighting to take the first piece, Mama coughed gently at our behavior, making all eyes turn to me. Mak broke the tension, placing the first piece on the plate before me. No one talked as we ate; only moans drifted around us as we all but licked the glass pan clean, leaving it spotless.

"Now, that was some of the best damned lasagna this belly has ever stuffed," Tristan smacked his stomach, giving Mama an apologetic look.

Mama just shook it off with a scoff.

"I say you put a ring on that brother," Mak taunted, "and fast."

I laughed, and instantly regretted it, causing the sharp pain in the rib area to flare up. Nothing was broken, but the pain was hard to take. I couldn't help but think about Sabrina and how she must be feeling right now.

After dinner, Luka took me to the couch, gave me my painkillers, and I dozed off into a blissful sleep, dreaming of green eyes.

In the morning, we all huddled in the kitchen, taking in the vitamin caffeine.

"She kept apologizing," Luka spoke from across the table. "She said something like she should have stayed away and that it was all her fault." His voice was calm, but his eyes showed deep empathy. He turned to Mama. "She explicitly told me to apologize to you."

When I'd woken up in the hospital surrounded by my family, I couldn't deny the sting of not seeing Sabrina there. Now, the picture was clearer.

Mama placed a hand on her chest, sighing, "That poor girl, she must be terrified."

"Didn't look terrified when she beat the crap out of that guy," Tristan jumped in.

"She what?" Mama shrieked, and we all flinched a bit.

"Yeah, I didn't see the whole thing, but I did witness her digging a heel into the guy's hand after she asked him which one he used to beat the shit out of O."

"What?" I bellowed.

I had been pretty out of it after getting ambushed by three large bulk men. By the time Luka had returned from fetching another chair for Sabrina, I was already knocked to the ground. Tritan had rushed out, jumping right at the blond dude who'd chickened out pretty fast. Everything was a blur after that. I did remember her sobbing and feeling her hand on my face.

"Yeah, your girl was fire," he added, then Luka stepped in, "She jumped on his back and choked him. I hate to admit it, but it was impressive as fuck."

I looked around the table; everyone shared the same expression—stupefaction.

For someone who kept running away, she sure as hell kept giving me reasons to chase her. And chase her I would, but first, I needed the *'go away pain'* pills. Physically, I was hurt, but mentally, I was bruised beyond repair, because now it all made sense—her refusal to let me in, all the evasive behavior.

Let's analyze together, shall we? She'd let out her plan—wanted me out—I forced in, and after I'd helped her, I got attacked... No coincidence there.

Honestly, I was surprised her father went to such lengths, even after she told me everything the fucker had done. But to go after his daughter like that, how low could the guy go?

Frustration and anger boiled inside me as I thought about her life, how hard it must have been growing up with parents like hers. No wonder she was so hard to breach. With insight into her story, I was even more determined to help her.

Admiration took over next because, for her to remain such a pure heart and spirit despite it all, was damn right impressive. It dawned on me how strong she truly was, the balls it took for her to go against them at the risk of losing it all. And yup, right on cue—guilt shot up. Hell, she walked away from her whole life, the money, inheritance, everything, and for what?

For you, you idiot!

Because she cared, even though she refused to admit it, she cared, and I loved her for it.

I love her?

That sounded about right—no other explanation for all the feelings shared for one person. Warmth spread through me, and I could only hope she felt the same way.

Let's get our girl - my head told my heart, and I stood up, feeling nothing but determination.

"Luka, will you drive me?"

"Already one foot out the door, little brother," he said with a grin, and I glanced over the rest of my brothers, all smiling widely. Our united front was a testament to the strength of our family bond. My eyes landed on Mama last, hers all glossy as she gave me her nod of approval.

Chapter 42

Sabrina

"I knew it was you. I just knew it," Aria marveled, eyes filled with pride before they turned to empathy.

Last night, after I'd invaded her place, we'd chosen the drinking-no talking route. That didn't stop my best friend from demanding answers the moment the sun started to rise. So now, we were sitting on her couch with me pouring it all out. But hey, there was coffee, so we were good.

"Why would Jacob do that?"

"Because I chose Mateo over him," I stated.

Her blue eyes narrowed. "What do you mean?"

"He pulled out the 'it's either him or us' bullshit." I gave a slight shrug, my palms turned upward, hands loosely spread and raised to the sides, signaling the 'meh' attitude.

"Seriously?"

"Yup, no money, no inheritance, no Porsche, no nothing." I gave it another shrug, relaxing my posture.

I'm gonna miss that Porsche.

"Shit." Aria couldn't hide her shock.

"You said it." I snapped my fingers with a frown.

"What now?"

I finish the job and make sure no one else gets hurt—

emphasis on the last part.

"Now," I hesitated, "I bring him down."

"What can I do?"

"No, Aria," I shouted, not in a mean way, more like caring, "look what happened to Mateo because of me."

The place where my heart used to be was hollow, cold. I missed him so freaking much, and all I could do was wallow.

"You know it was not your fault!" It was not a question, but a full-on declaration.

"Of course it was," I argued, taking a sip of my now cold coffee.

"You love him, don't you?"

"If you mean how I can't breathe when we're apart, only for it to get worse when we're together, then it might be possible."

I could see the hearts in her eyes staring at me.

"I don't know what to do with it," I mumbled, and she smiled at me.

"You leap into it."

The buzzer sounded, going straight to my headache, and I wiped my eyes, still far too heavy to keep them fully open. Aria stood up and walked to her door while I stayed put. I had no view of her entryway, but I could easily identify the muffled voices. Trepidation washed over me as I got up, compelling my legs to move. When I reached the entrance, I was met with Luka's wide frame. When the figure behind him came into view, my heart broke into a million pieces.

Mateo took a step toward me, and on instinct, I pulled back. Him being here… I couldn't take it. Merely thinking about it all hurt, but seeing him was so much worse. The bruises on his body, the split lip, all because I couldn't protect him. And yet, he was looking at me as if I were the one in need of medical attention. His eyes filled with concern, and all I wanted was to leap into his arms.

This was the part where feelings had to get hurt.

"What are you doing here?"

"We're here to take you home!"

I couldn't have heard that right. There was no way they were going to take me back to that hellhole. I didn't even have a home, for crying out loud.

"Come on," Luka said, gesturing the invitation with his hand.

"No!" I shook my head, panic rising.

Why are they doing this to me?

"It's ok." Mateo's soft voice went straight to my core, almost as if reminding my heart it was still beating.

"It's not," I sobbed, slowly backtracking. Mateo's hand wrapped around my wrist, stopping me in my tracks.

"I'm ok."

"Stop it," I faltered, "I, I just, I can't..."

This time, Luka firmly stated, "Of course you can!"

"Please, just leave." I was hanging by a thread, begging for it all to stop. I couldn't even recognize my own voice; it sounded defeated. My head was twisted, my heart divided, and my body too weak to fight it.

"Well, that's not going to happen," Mateo huffed.

"We're not leaving without you," Luka added, his voice filled with determination.

"Come on, Blackbird," Mateo begged, knowing the effect his nickname had on me, though any name he had for me would bring me to my knees.

It felt like a standstill, or better yet, like a scene straight out of those Western movies when they did the noon showdown with the tumbleweed rolling past to highlight the tension. Both our hands were on the buscadero holsters, but I was the one who shot first. And by shot, I meant bolted to the bathroom, locking myself inside.

Ever since I met Mateo, everything I had done had been out of character, including my now-very-cowardly behavior. I was not the one who ran away from a fight. Hell, I was the one who instigated them. So what was I doing hiding in the middle of a cold bathroom floor?

Beats me...

The knocks were banging straight into my headache, and I tried my best to cover up the yelling with my hands. It was pointless. Their voices penetrated my stupid palms.

"Don't make me break down this door," was Aria's threat, one that made us all laugh.

"Fine, don't make me make Hulk break down the door."

Knowing Luka for as little as I had, one thing was for sure—he would happily do so.

God, I was tired of all of it, so fucking exhausted. I swung the door open, unexpectedly being pulled into Mateo's arms. I relaxed instantly, giving in.

"I'm sorry." I focused on his lip, the clotted blood staring at me.

"I know," he said within a breath, taking my hand, then whispered, "Come on, let's go home."

With a heavy heart, I said goodbye to Aria and went with the two brothers. When we arrived at Luka's pickup, I noticed

Tyler in the back seat. We'd never met in person, so I gave him a wave, and he returned one. I slid to the middle of the three-seater, sandwiched between Mateo and Luka, who pushed the key in the ignition and roared the truck to life. While Luka backed up from the parking place in front of Aria's building, I felt that itch in my finger.

"Mind if I dabble with the radio?"

"Be my guest."

One long glance at Mateo, I asked the music gods my question: to tell me what to do, how to feel about the man looking at me with so much affection that it was unbearable. The chorus of Zara Larsson's 'Ruin My Life' played after I pressed the seek button, and I burst out laughing. The look on Mateo's face turned annoyed, and his eyebrows furrowed at me, posing the question of my sanity.

"I do this thing with the radio; it's like an eight ball, kind of."

Luka snorted, but I ignored him, focused only on my favorite pair of brown eyes. "I ask a question and let the radio answer for me with the next song that comes on."

"And this one made you react like that because?"

"I asked about us," I whispered the last part, but he heard it; his scarred brow cocked.

Another laugh escaped me, uncontrollably, and he only smirked.

"Why is it funny?"

"Because I verbatim ruined your life."

"That's not how the song goes," he puffed.

"It does the way I interpret it."

"Well, you're doing it wrong. So, stop overthinking, shut

247

the fuck up, and ruin my life, will ya?" He snapped at me, but the flair in his eyes didn't match the tone. The moment stretched, our eyes locked, focused on each other as I kept replaying his words.

It was like flipping a switch with him, one that turned the entire world around us—off.

Chapter 43

Mateo

My mouth was on hers the second that light in her eyes registered. The fake coughs coming from my brothers were waved away by my middle finger with zero fucks. The need to seal this was imminent and crucial. When it came to Sabrina and me, actions spoke louder than words, goes without saying. The importance of this kiss was significant and heavy. The pumping of my heart drummed in my ears as her tongue played circles around mine. It was only when the truck stopped vibrating that she pulled away, eyes narrowed at the sight in front of us.

"What are we doing here?" she asked, looking ahead where my mother stood on the porch, Tristan at her side in the rocking chair.

"I told you…" I took her hand in mine, her fingers coiled, locking mine. "We're taking you home." Her hand twitched in mine, and I soaked it all in, down to the tears forming in her eyes.

"I don't understand." She squinted, tilting her head.

When realization hit, she gasped and sank her head, letting go of my hand to play with her fingers in her lap.

Luka opened the door and got out, leaving it open for

Sabrina to follow. When her feet touched the ground, he sniggered at her, "You know, you'll have to learn how to open the door for yourself from now on, Princess."

I couldn't see her face, but her head tilted with a dragged-out "How rude!"

He was playing with her, maybe testing her limits to see if she could handle the family.

"I'm not rude. I simply have the balls to say what everybody else is thinking!"

I got out, circling the car, expecting her to be angry or worse, only to find her amused.

"What? You want a high five for that? Maybe in the face—with a chair?"

I bit down on my lip at her bravado.

"Don't turn all drama queen on me!"

"Don't worry, I avoid drama. But not because I'm scared of you." She crossed her arms over her chest. "I just have anger issues, and this need to avoid jail time."

Luka snickered and pulled her in a hug, surprising both Sabrina and me. His hold was tight, patiently waiting for her to reciprocate. When her hands lifted around him, I saw a full-blown smile forming on his face, something I didn't get a chance to see often. Only when satisfied with the sincerity of the hug did he let go, allowing us to go inside. My mother warmed her some more with her signature tight hold, followed by Tristan doing the same. He noticed my cocked warning brow and quickly retreated. My sixteen-year-old brother was crushing on my woman.

Once inside, we all took a seat at the kitchen table while Mama put on a fresh pot of coffee. Mak came downstairs and joined us, his leering smile in place.

After what seemed like hours of silence, Tristan clapped his hands. "Ok, so how is this going to work because I'm not giving up my bed?"

"Neither am I." Mak lifted his hand high.

"I'll be gone tomorrow; she can have my bed," Tyler settled it.

"What's happening right now?" Sabrina asked, her expression strained as she glanced at us. It was as though she understood the topic but refused to believe it. She then turned to face me with furrowed brows, fiery eyes, and a whole lot of something else. Something she still hadn't wrapped her head around.

Patience. It will come.

"Let it play out," I simply stated, and it seemed to do the trick, seeing her shoulders finally relax.

"So couch tonight and tomorrow, Tyler's bed," Mama concluded, and we all nodded, all except Sabrina.

I counted six times her mouth opened and closed before she finally spoke.

"You want me to stay here?"

"Of course, honey." Mama took a seat next to her and placed a hand on her knee. Sabrina's eyes snapped to the spot where Mama's hand lingered and stayed locked that way.

"You belong with us now," Mama declared, plastering a broad smile on that beautiful face of mine; I meant Sabrina's.

"Yeah, we kind of claimed you," I whispered, but loud enough for everyone to hear.

"Just so that you know, we are not discussing the float

scene," Tristan cajoled, making the room burst into laughter, save one staggered Sabrina.

"You lost me," she murmured, and Tristan lifted his brow, looking at her point-blank, letting it come to her. When it didn't, he handed her a bone. "Our current read, we're discussing it over the weekend." And then it hit her, evident by how her cheeks turned crimson.

"You're reading 'Flock'?" she gasped, excitement screaming out when she turned to face me, and I knew why. I understood why it was her favorite series, and reading about the men in the book turned me full-on jealous, fictional or not. I made it my life's mission to delete any trace of book boyfriends from her memory, all the while using them as inspiration.

"Uhm, Eva, if you could please tune out, maybe cover your ears for this one." She looked at our mother, all serious, which only made Mama laugh.

"Oh, honey, no need to censor me. Trust me. None of these boys know how to be subtle, all using the laundry room, thinking that the machine could hide what they were doing."

We all choked on air, turning dead silent while Sabrina held her belly in order not to burst into a full-on guffaw.

"You're now officially my idol," Sabrina told her. "I can't believe how open you are around each other. It amazes me!"

"There is no point in hiding; we are who we are. And if you want to know, Mak is the house slut."

"Mama," Mak sputtered; we all nodded. It was true. His on-call room reputation preceded him.

"Wow, just wow," Sabrina gushed, her hands flying in a wave, like she couldn't handle it.

"We have a bet going on." Mama kept on going, and I loved it.

"Oh?"

"Yeah, we all agree that Mak will be the last one to settle."

"That's never going to happen," he pointed out, but we wouldn't have it.

Mak had a firm stance against monogamy, something we were all sure the right girl would stomp right over.

"Who will be the first?"

"Luka!" We all cheered in unison. No matter how closed off he was, Luka's one goal in life was to have a family of his own. He wanted a house full of kids and someone to love fully. Truth be told, no one deserved it more than him. He had a tough childhood, with terrible parents who left physical and mental scars to linger over him. I had high hopes for my big brother.

Our family was one of a kind, special in every sense of the word. And now Sabrina was a part of it, no matter how much she tried to fight it.

Chapter 44

Sabrina

Wow—this family.

There were no words to describe it better… just 'wow'.

How comfortable and open they were, not to mention that sense of safety that was always present. Love was the all-encompassing notion, and all I wanted was in.

Surrounded by the Hart clan, all I felt was blessed. My future was unknown, especially now that I had nothing left; still, it all seemed insignificant. Being here with them gave me a sense of comfort, and I became more assertive about what I had to do. For the first time in my life, I had something to lose, something I was determined to keep safe. My bed was already made, but they didn't have to sleep in it.

"What is it?" Mateo dragged his chair closer to mine; I shook my head.

"You just made a decision, and I want in on it."

God, how was it that this man knew me so well? He made it look so easy.

I turned to face him, and I knew it the moment our eyes met—he read it, he read my every single thought. Putting my hands in his, he thundered at me with one sharp, "No!"

Every head snapped to us, and Mateo turned to Luka. "She wants to give it up."

"What?" Luka blurted, stunned.

I hated the confusion on everyone's faces, so I cleared my throat to take the stage.

"There is something I need to tell you all..."

Everyone's attention shifted towards me, so I let it all out in the open, sharing every discovery, every piece, and every move made so far. The more I spoke, the easier it got for me to continue, without even realizing how much I needed this type of support. It was clear in their demeanor, in their eyes— I had it fully. It felt good, like I could do anything. I gave myself my wings, but they were the wind beneath them.

"You are officially *my* idol." Eva gave me back my words, sending them right to my pumped-up heart. The guys stood up, taking turns giving me high-fives like I was some hero. Little did they know, I was far from it.

"What can we do?" Tyler spoke first.

"You don't understand. I am not going through with it."

"What?" "Why?" "What are you talking about?" came out in one major pile, with me unable to distinguish which question belonged to whom.

"I already put Mateo in danger. I can't risk any of you."

I've become attached. But I kept that one to myself.

"Oh, honey, you don't have a choice. You have to do it for the sake of all those people," Eva asserted.

That notion made my heart sink because I knew she had a point. All those people deserved justice. We had proof, fifteen of them, but I was certain more would emerge eventually.

"Mama is right, you can't back down now," Luka spoke, the voice of reason right there. They all nudged, reassuring me to continue. With Mateo's arm tightening around mine, keeping it all in became impossible.

Friday came quickly, and I was deep in discussions with Lisa, our litigator, as we reviewed all the cases at the Clinic. We decided on Carlos as the face of the class action; the youngest of all the plaintiffs, who'd gotten caught shoplifting and was prosecuted for assaulting an officer during a brutal arrest. Back then, his lawyer had argued self-defense, citing that it was his first offense. Despite the evidence and an impressive closing argument, the kid had gotten a three-year sentence.

My work frenemy waltzed in, Tony, or was it Tom? I wasn't sure. I was terrible with names, and he had an awful attitude.

He handed Lisa a file and turned to me. "I have a feeling I need to apologize."

"A feeling, you say?"

"Yeah," he cleared his throat, "I misjudged you. I thought you were some stuck-up, dumb model trying to be the next Elle Woods."

His tone seemed sincere, but his eyes contradicted the words. He was not very convincing.

"That was your first mistake; there's only one Elle Woods."

He rolled his eyes, and that confirmed it. He was sucking

up, meaning none of what he'd said was true.

"Full disclosure, I knew you were a major suck-up dick."

He started coughing, as if I had somehow offended him. I didn't know jerks could get offended, though... That was riveting.

"Sometimes, I wish that people came with trailers, you know? So that I can see what I'm getting into. Would make shit a lot easier." I gave him a pout, with a pat on the back. "No worries, *dude*. At least now we both know I'm better than you!" And with that, I made my dramatic exit with my stuck-up nose high.

Chapter 45

Mateo

"Knock, knock," I announced, cracking the door open. All eyes snapped to me, and as soon as everyone noticed the coffee tray, smiles lit up their faces.

I was a frequent visitor to the legal clinic and was commissioned to do some investigative work for them. Though I said I'd do it for free, Sabrina's boss wouldn't allow it.

"Hi, O," Carl hollered from his office, and I waved at him, lifting the tray. He immediately stood up and grabbed his cup with a thankful nod, then added, "She's in the conference room." I left the tray on her desk and beelined to the separate room.

Leaning on the door, I took my time staring at her, back turned, leaning over a stack of papers, marker in hand. Unaware of her surroundings, she bobbed her head to whatever song was coming out of her earbuds. Her hair was up in a messy bun, exposing her neck. Then I saw it—the goosebumps, because like always, she sensed me. She snapped around and plastered a beaming smile before standing up and rushing into my arms. I did a quick twirl, holding her with one hand while the other removed one earbud and placed it in my ear. The last verse of 'The Takedown' by Marc Ferrari played out as I claimed her lips.

"Pumping yourself up?"

"I have a themed playlist!" she exclaimed.

"I bet you do." I grinned, letting her down. "How's it going?"

"Pretty good," she answered, grabbing my hand and guiding me to the desk. I took a seat, and she did the same, taking her favorite spot, which was, in fact, my lap.

"We managed to collect twenty-two cases," she piped with pride.

I looked over the board in the corner, where pictures of 22 young, multiracial men were pinned. Something tightened around my throat, and Sabrina took my hand, noticing my line of sight.

It amazed me how well she knew me; more so, how she knew what to do to calm me or ease the tension. I was born and raised in Boston, and even as a child, my skin tone made people judge me. It only got worse when I added my bike to the mix. With that said, Sabrina squeezed my hand tighter and continued, "We decided on Carlos for the face of the lawsuit, so I'm going over the appeal Carl drafted for the class action."

"So you'll review all the cases?"

She nodded, hope evident in her gaze. "Anyway, give me a minute, and we can leave," she said, starting to gather all the papers. I stepped in to help, but she smacked my hand away.

"Auch, what the hell?" I scowled, and she shushed me. "Oh, don't be such a baby. You know better than to touch my stuff."

Yeah, you'd think that after so many smacks to the head I would've learned, but nope—I haven't learned shit. It was pure instinct, really, to put the need to help into action. And I knew she refused it only when it came to the confidential files. So with that notion, I pulled out my best apologetic ass puppy eyes. "Sorry."

"Good boy, now shoo," she waved her hand, "wait for me out front."

Like the good boy she just called me to be, I did exactly that. Yeah, I was a total wuss for this girl, and I fucking owned it. I strode through a sea of cubicles, saying my goodbyes, and went outside to meet the sun. I took out a smoke, lit one up, and dragged in the poison. I glanced at my bike parked right next to Sabrina's and laughed under my breath. It had been two weeks since she moved in with us, and she had already taken control of the place. She'd created a ridiculous bathroom schedule so that she could spend extra time doing her makeup. Mak was the only one putting up a fight since his hair was a spoiled little bitch. It was pointless, really—all Sabrina had to do was raise a brow, and the wimp waved the white flag. Fuck, even Luka was afraid of her.

Living under the same roof came with benefits, and not all were of a perverted nature. I got to know her, her ticks, her ways, her little routines. Also, I'd managed to uncover that my badass had an irrational fear of spiders, so much so that she never set foot in the attic or the basement.

I stubbed the cigarette with my boot, and the door swung open. "You ready?" Sabrina's voice was heard before she stepped into view.

No.

That was what I wanted to say, but ended up with, "Tell me again why I'm doing this?"

"They specifically noted you need to be vetted," she said matter-of-factly.

That's what they'd called it, like I was some applicant for a job. Her friend Nala, whom I hadn't met yet, and Aria put this plan in place. I acted as if the whole thing bothered me, but truthfully, I was prepared to take the hot seat and answer all of their questions. They were a huge part of Sabrina's life, so obtaining their stamp of approval was practically mandatory.

"Yours or mine?" I asked when we got to our bikes.

"I was thinking about selling mine," she said, uncertainty in her voice.

"No," I snapped.

"It's brand new, minus two barely noticeable scratches." She gave the side of my mouth a little peck. "We could get a lot for it," she asserted. That little *'we'* made my heart skip a beat. Then she placed her hands on each side of my waist, pressing her boobs to my chest, her usual tactic to get what she wanted out of me. I sighed, and she grinned, knowing she had me. "Fine, I get to drive you around more often," I smirked, wiggling my brows.

She frowned, "I didn't think this through."

I pinched her ass cheek, and she squealed before it turned into a giggle. "Stop that! I don't need a freshly fucked face when you meet my friends."

"I kind of think that it will give me some extra points," I snarled.

Shaking her head, she pulled me into a wet lock, her tongue digging deep to meet mine. Her hand went from my waist down to my throbbing cock, and I whimpered—I fucking whimpered. If she didn't stop, I was gonna take her right here on this parking lot, in broad daylight, for everyone to see. I bit her lower lip in warning, making her release a moan.

"How late can we be for them to tolerate it?" I asked, my breath uneven.

The elevator door dinged open, and we walked to Aria's apartment. We stopped in front of 3B, and my foot started tapping, my nerves deciding to manifest. Sabrina knocked, and I eyed the doormat, snorting.

"She's a big Potterhead, don't ask," Sabrina chuckled, looking at the bolded-out words, stating: '*Doorbell broken, shout Alohomora!*'

The door flew open, and Sabrina immediately went on the offensive: "Sorry, we're late."

"You've got to be kidding me," Aria snarled, and a brown-haired woman stepped to her side. "What?"

I remembered her from the club, working behind the bar when Sabrina and I had hooked up in the bathroom.

Her hazel eyes traced Sabrina's face when she grinned and laughed out an "Oh," followed by, "Did you at least get an orgasm out of it?"

I choked on air. This was going to be a long night.

Aria narrowed her eyes. "Okay, you gained a point after losing one for being late. Better be a damn good orgasm," she finished on a high note and moved for us to enter. Speechless, I followed Sabrina inside while she hugged her friends. The brown-haired one extended her hand. "I'm Nala, nice to meet you, bike guy."

Hate to say it, but the nickname was growing on me.

"Hi Nala, I'm Mateo, nice to meet you too." I shook her hand and gave her my best smile. Aria pushed Nala away and took a menacing stance in front of me, her arms crossed over her chest. One of her eyes narrowed further, while the other was wide open. How the hell she pulled that off was beyond me.

"You ready?"

"Ready as I'll ever be," I wavered, "Lead the way."

I followed Aria until she stopped in front of a single chair and motioned for me to sit. I plastered my ass down, and the three women took their seats across from me on the couch.

"First, do you need some liquid courage?"

Well, shit. This was a trick question, I was sure. But I wasn't planning on lying, so I outed, "Yes, please."

"Good answer," Nala winked at me.

"What's your poison?" Aria asked, going to her kitchen.

"The strongest one you have."

Chapter 46

Sabrina

I was wrong... Tipsy Mateo was my favorite because the bastard had won them over. If I didn't have seniority, I'd be seriously worried about him taking my place.

We went from the couch to the floor, drinking and playing 20 questions, though it looked more like an infinity of questions, all pointed at Mateo.

"Sabrina told us you got an internship at ENOVA?" Aria tapped her fingers on the half-empty glass. We decided on margaritas tonight, and we were on our third pitcher. Nala did the pouring, but her attention never left Mateo.

"Yeah, I got the call yesterday. I never pictured myself in the medical field, but with Mak's help, I think I can do some real good there," he answered, puffing out his chest.

I bit my inner cheek thinking about the call. I was so proud of him that I'd dropped to my knees and sucked him dry. My panties dampened at the image, the sounds he'd made while I pumped him and twirled my tongue around his shaft. I had to suffocate my groan. It amazed me how much I've come to know his body and mind in such a short period. I expected the hunger to die down, but it never did. Mateo had mapped me out so well that it took merely a glance for me to get halfway there. He must've thought the same because I saw a bit of flush running through his cheeks. My eyes immediately went south just as he shifted to hide the erection.

Aria, ever the clairvoyant, gave me a knowing stare, and I shook the thoughts of taking Mateo into her bathroom to jump his bones away.

"That's the doctor, right? Is he single?" Nala wiggled her brows, and Mateo choked on a laugh. "Trust me, you don't want to go there."

She frowned, and I stepped in, "I don't know; I could see her taming him."

He kept on laughing, then stopped abruptly, mulling it over. "She would eat him alive, and I hate to say I like that fact way too much," he concluded.

"I bet he is good with women's anatomy," Nala said gleefully, pursing her lips. The fact that she was this comfortable in front of Mateo spoke volumes. Although she was surrounded by men daily, she struggled to open up, so seeing her like this made me feel a mix of emotions, all of the happy variety.

Aria made the 'time out' signal with her hands. "How about we deal with this Hart first, before going through the roster?" she sneered, her boss woman showing.

"More margaritas?" I offered, noticing she was on edge for some reason. I needed her to be relaxed, not for Mateo's sake, but for hers.

"What the hell," she shrugged, then handed me her glass with an empty expression on her face.

"What's wrong?" I asked, and she shook it off. "We are here to get to know your..." she hesitated, "Wait, what is he exactly?"

Point Aria - perfect attempt at a sidetrack and another ten for sticking the landing.

I turned to face Mateo, unsure of how to respond. We've never labeled it, so I wasn't sure what we were—roommates, fuckbuddies?

"Her future husband," Mateo chimed in, that stupid smirk on his face beaming. I smacked him over the back of his head. "I thought I made myself clear."

"Hey, a guy can dream..." He took my hand and planted a kiss on my knuckles. On instinct, I scooted closer over the floor, dragging my feet under me while my free hand held my weight. I took a good look at him, thinking it over. This man had done so much for me, becoming my safe space; in fact, he was my lifeline at this point. Something in me shifted.

"How 'bout, babe? He's my babe," I repeated the word, like I was taking it for a spin. "I like it," I committed, and both Nala and Aria nodded in approval. I turned to Mateo. He hummed, his gaze piercing through me. "As long as you're mine, I don't care what label you use."

The fainting 'Aaaaaa' came from the two women, and I giggled like a star-struck teenage girl.

"Babe, it is." I clapped, my friends joining me while Mateo rolled his eyes. But I could see it, the little twitch on the curve of his mouth, trying way too hard not to pull into a smile.

Intertwining my fingers with his, warmth spread from my palms all the way to my toes, but it came to a boil when his thumb grazed over the tattoo on my finger—something I've caught him doing on more than one occasion.

"Stop doing that," I whispered, and he leaned forward, his mouth reaching my ear. "Doing what?" he whispered back, voice deep, and I jerked my hand away.

"Whatever it is you do or think or manifest or spellcast..." I trailed off, at a loss for more verbs.

"Spellcast? Seriously?"

I released a loud grunt and groaned, "Whatever mojo you conjure when you drag your stupid finger over the tattoo," hiding the ink in question between my thighs.

"Don't go insulting my finger," he snapped, but more playful than mean.

"Oh my god, are you two serious right now?" Aria glared at us, annoyance obvious.

"Oh, come on, leave them alone, they're cute." Nala shoved her, and Aria stumbled to the side, bursting into a laugh. Sharing my thoughts, Nala gave me a nod, and we both jumped on Aria, sandwiching her in a hug mixed with tickles.

"Stop it! I hate you!"

Lies, all lies.

"You love us, admit it!" Nala teased while Aria tried to escape our hold. My fingers dug into her sides, making her squirm. "Stop it!"

The sound of her laughter felt like a victory, and I knew that for a moment, whatever was eating at her took the back seat

Mateo cleared his throat, letting us know he was still there, but no one batted an eye.

Then my phone rang, and I let out an exasperated sigh, knowing whose ringtone it was. All eyes went to me, and I shook my head. "Ignore it."

I sure did. My mother had been calling every day, adding

a couple of threatening texts to the mix. No matter how mad I was, I couldn't get myself to block her number. Some narcissistic part of me needed to know the lengths she would go to get me back.

Thankfully, I had plenty of distractions. I've been cramped up in the legal clinic every single day, making my eyes burn with all the reading. There's a possibility I've consumed my weight in coffee beans. Carl had said that if we made it to court, I could tag along. He'd already petitioned that I participate under supervision. It did mean more work and less time with the Harts, but they'd been supportive every step of the way, making this whole thing easier.

Having Mateo helped immensely. Every night, I'd slump on the couch, too tired to breathe, and he'd rub my feet while I went on and on about the cases. He'd listened like every word coming out of my mouth was important, which made me feel all the more so. He made me feel valued and loved. It took me a while to realize what it was, but now I knew, with every fiber of my body, that this man loved me.

Can you keep a secret? I loved him right back.

Chapter 47

Sabrina

Before Mateo left, I told him I'd sleep over at Aria's. He nodded in understanding and drove Nala to her place. He sent me two separate texts, one when he safely dropped her off and another when he arrived home. His reassuring presence was a comfort amid the storm.

"You didn't have to stay," Aria whispered, getting the sofa ready for me to sleep on.

"I know, but whatever is eating you up, I'm here for you."

"I don't want to talk about it, not yet at least." She started cleaning up, but I stepped in and took the reins.

"We don't have to talk," I muttered. I knew my best friend. Much like me, she too liked to keep it all bottled up. Her comfort was a screen, preferably with a gut-wrenching theme showing.

"How about we binge something?" I offered, which piqued her interest.

"We can do 'How to Get Away With Murder' for inspiration?" She wiggled her brows. After I'd finally come clean about everything, both Aria and Nala were supportive. Aria had even given me some contacts and offered to ask Cillian to help with protection. He was a high-ranking Marine and had a large number of armed men at his disposal.

Though the image of muscled men following me around sounded appealing, I'd kindly declined, relying on my fists. A thought occurred to me, and I grabbed Aria's hand. "Does this have anything to do with Cillian?"

Her eyes widened, giving it all away.

"Tell me!"

"He was in an accident," she said under her breath, and that's when I noticed her shaking hands. Tears flooded her eyes, and her knees wobbled, so I grabbed her shoulders and guided her to sit down. How long had she been holding this inside? Her vulnerability was palpable, and I couldn't help but feel a surge of empathy for her.

"What happened?"

"Some gun misfired, and he jumped to save his friend, but the bullet hit him." She sobbed, barely getting the words out, "He was in a coma for three days."

"What? Why didn't you say anything?"

My suspicion crept up. How is it possible that I hadn't heard anything about it? The thought lasted a second, because knowing Aria, she must've worked her magic and kept it out of the press. It was something she had been doing for Cillian ever since he'd started filling tabloids with his conquests.

"He's ok now, they said he was lucky the bullet didn't do much damage."

"Oh, Ari, come here," I said, opening my arms for her, and she dropped into them so fast it took me off balance. I wrapped her in my embrace and held her as tightly as I could, knowing how much she cared for him, no matter how skilled she was at denying it. In that moment, I felt a sense of pride in how far we had come in our relationship.

"You could've called. I would've been there for you."

"He looked so helpless," she shuddered, and I caressed her hair, trying to calm her down.

"You were with him?" I asked even though the notion didn't surprise me. The two had been inseparable for most of their lives, practically family.

"He doesn't know, so don't let it slip."

"Don't worry, but you know I will be using it as a bargaining chip." I tried to lighten the mood, and it worked, as evidenced by the soft chuckle.

"Wouldn't expect anything else." Her lips twitched, trying to produce a full-on smile, but I saw the lack of strength.

After she calmed down, we turned on the TV, jumping into the lives of law students following a badass lawyer. We swapped our margaritas for popcorn and Coke. It took her two episodes to start snoring, and my heart melted at the sight. She had been through a lot. I really hoped she and Cillian would work things out. Honestly, those two were endgame, even if they hadn't realized it yet.

I pulled out my phone and fired off a text to Simon.

Me: *Meet me at the clinic in the morning, I have an idea.*

S: *I'll bring the coffee*

Turning off the TV, I snuggled next to my best friend and dozed off.

When I arrived at the clinic, Simon was waiting for me in the conference room with the rest of the team working on the class action.

"We hear you have a plan?" Carl spoke as soon as I entered, intrigue covering his face.

"Boss man, cover your ears a bit so you can play ignorant, because what I am about to lay out is out of a badass playbook," I started, voice firm, stance dominant.

Carl gave me his signature grin and handed me the podium with his full attention. I disclosed the new plan, finally finding a way to get the big guys involved. We'd tried before, going to the FBI to review the case, but were brushed off in a pleasant, professional manner. Somehow, all the dirt we'd had wasn't enough for them to open a federal investigation, but after Aria dropped a couple of names, a lightbulb lit up. It turned out Mario, Cillian's brother, was serving a sentence in one of the prisons we suspected was in cahoots with my father.

His sentence: five years.

Judge's ruling: involuntary manslaughter

The story: A drunken fight where Mario had sucker-punched an asshole who then headbutted a brick wall at a right angle and ended up in a coma. So instead of getting charged under the principles of negligence and self-defense, he'd gotten far more than the norm.

Conclusion: another state judge was on the wrong track of the law.

With Mario's deep pockets, I figured he could persuade the warden in the right direction. So, just like that, a door cracked open, waiting for the full swing.

"So what do you think? If it works, it can have grounds to open up a federal investigation now, right?" I inhaled, my lungs protesting as if I'd said it all in one breath. My big brother beamed at me from the corner, and I swear I could see a tear going down his cheek. Carl lifted his hands. "I was never here. Great job putting those smarts out of you."

Well, shucks. What was a girl to do with all that praise coming at me? So naturally, I puffed out my chest and swung my hair in a quick flick. And, like the girl I was, I jumped with a squeak, which got everyone laughing. I pulled out my phone and called the one person whose voice I was desperate to hear. He answered on the first ring, and I went straight to it. "So, wanna hear about a new idea in the works?"

"Always." And there was that sexy-ass smirk that I could hear through the line. And then he hung up.

The hell?

I was about to hit redial when the door swung open, and my heart stopped. There he was, all dark and handsome, in his leather jacket, smirk pointed right at me. I ran to him so fast, but he was prepared, catching me mid-jump, and those strong arms got to work, pulling me up.

"How did you know I'd be here?"

He licked the seam of his lips, his brows lifting as he gave me a pointed look, as if it were the most obvious thing. I couldn't help but smile.

I kissed him with so much fire that it felt like I was gonna self-combust.

"Easy on the PDA, please, big brother coming through." Simon covered his eyes, and I grinned, hiding my face in the crook of Mateo's neck.

"Sorry, man." Mateo managed to sound apologetic, and I knew it was for my benefit. Those two'd clicked right from the start, and something about it screamed family, and I was part of it.

"Yeah, yeah… Come on, lovebirds, let's grab breakfast," Simon said as he walked past us, but not without giving Mateo a threatening stare. I warmed at the sight of his protective role. I'd never had that before; no one had greeted my dates at the door, no one had given me the talk. Having someone who cared, even if it was mostly playing around, made my heart melt. I grabbed Simon's wrist, and he pulled to a stop. He wrapped his arms around me, allowing me to snuggle into him.

"Thank you," I mumbled into his chest.

"For what?"

"Everything. For believing me, believing in me, for blindly following…" I trailed off, and his grip tightened around me. I felt his kiss on top of my head, then heard his words in a hushed whisper, "Thank you."

I pulled away, lifting my head slightly to meet his gaze. "For what?"

"For giving me closure, for trusting me, and giving me a family."

I turned to look at Mateo, who stepped away, giving us the privacy; then I lifted my head to face Simon. "Thank you for giving me mine."

Chapter 48

Mateo

Four months later

The TV in our living room was on full blast while we all waited for the exclusive, tension around us palpable.

"Breaking news—Rebecka Young here in front of the Supreme Court. After a grueling three-month trial, Judge Furst was convicted of bribery and misconduct."

The text scrolled at the bottom of the screen, stating _'Furst was initially charged in a class-action suit back in October 2023, followed by his indictment in November of the same year.'_

The frame went from the reporter to photos of the courtroom with Jacob Furst front and center. Tristan yelled, "There's the badass," pointing at Sabrina, who was standing behind Carl. We all stood up to get a better look before the screen turned back to the reporter.

"All the plaintiffs are cleared of previous charges by the ruling of the miscarriage of justice. Their release date is set for tomorrow, along with full restitution."

Tristan pumped his fists, Luka wiped his eyes discreetly, and Tyler spun in a giddy circle. Mak's hand found my shoulder; I nodded, still dazed.

She did it. She fucking did it.

"With new evidence brought to light during the trial, a new investigation has been opened regarding all the parties, with a case building against three incriminated prison wardens, two more state judges, one state congressman, and the attorney general."

Luka turned off the TV, cutting the woman off while we all let it sink in. My phone rang, and I answered immediately, putting it on speaker.

"Babe?" Her voice reverberated, sending shivers up my spine. God, I missed her.

"We're here," I said while the rest of my family yelled over each other with congratulations and praise.

"You did it!" I shouted, wanting to do so from the rooftops.

"For all the families like ours." Her voice cracked, the *'ours'* cutting deep. Mama gasped, her hand flying to cover her mouth.

"They're all free, babe." I could hear her sob. We were all so damn proud of her. The work she put into this case, her whole body and soul went into it.

"He got 10 years, no chance of parole."

There was a brief moment when all I could hear was her deep breathing.

"I..." she stuttered, "I love you."

The room fell silent, and my tears found their way to my cheeks, slowly gliding over them. I knew the importance of those words, how hard they were for her to say. I saw them in her eyes, in her actions; I knew she'd felt it before she was ready to share it with me. Even over the phone, their power went straight to my heart. I knew I'd loved her from the very start, so I waited patiently, not wanting the pressure of it to consume her.

"I love you," I bellowed.

"God, I hate that I am not with you right now, Mateo, because I love you so freakin' much," she declared, and I could hear the shake in her voice.

"I know, baby, I know." I kept bobbing my head, fully aware she couldn't see it.

"We love you too, you know?" Tyler hollered, and the others joined in, shouting their love into the phone.

"I love all of you right back, but I love him the mostest," she said, and I could feel her smile with every fiber of my body.

"When's your flight?"

"First thing in the morning, I'll be home around 10."

Home.

When it came to Sabrina, those words carried a great deal of weight. She had never had a real home before; had never known love. And it took time to learn, to accept their meaning. And now, with her using them so freely, I felt like I was on a high. Over the last couple of months, she'd been flying back and forth between Washington and Boston. We'd spent more time on the phone than we did together, with regular FaceTime calls (phone sex per her request), but we'd made it work.

And she was finally coming home.

I took the phone from the speaker and whispered, "I can't wait to see you."

I heard 'oohs' and 'aaahs' behind me, and I waved my hand at my brothers.

"Watch it, babe. Someone will think you actually miss me," she teased, her voice getting raspy just the way I liked it.

"You have no idea," I admitted, and she chuckled.

"I miss you, too. I have to go, but I'll see you tomorrow." She made the kissing noise and hung up, saving me from doing the same in front of my brothers.

I looked over at Ty, his fingers playing with the pendant around his neck, one he had gotten for Christmas. We'd surprised Sabrina with a leather briefcase featuring a harpy eagle embroidered on it, and her name stitched on the inside. None of us expected any gifts, since she had walked away from all her money, but she managed to surprise us all. Tristan had gotten a signed jersey from Travis Kelce, Mak a pink stethoscope with lips printed all over it, and Luka an apron with Shrek's belly covering the front.

I choked at the memory of opening my gift.

"How did you find it?"

My fingers brushed over a jasmine impression in the copper-golden wax. Mama gasped over my shoulder and then knelt in front of Sabrina.

"Oh, honey… I…" she shuddered, and I was at the brink myself.

"I'm sorry, I thought…" Sabrina went on the defensive, and I chuckled through my sob. This woman… this fucking woman knew nothing about emotions, the good kind… she couldn't register the happy tears, the appreciation coming from any of us, and as much as it pained me, I was selfishly glad that we were the ones to show her.

"Oh, honey, no… this…" My mama took the book from me

and lifted it in front of Sabrina. "You don't know how much this means to me, to him." She pointed the paperback at me.

"He cried for over a month every night, screaming how it was the only thing he had from his mother, how it was all his fault!"

This time, it was Sabrina losing it, chest heaving with pain, her eyes releasing tear after tear.

"I felt hopeless when I couldn't get it back for him, and I have tried," Mama wheezed.

"How did you find it?" Tyler asked from across the room before he got closer.

"I had Simon dig up the name of the group home. They moved into a bigger place a couple of years ago. The social worker told me that everything from the old place was stacked up in the attic, so I just full-box-dived."

I eyed her, stunned, my fingers going over each crack in the spine, the cover, the title.

"I had to fight a family of spiders for it," she snorted.

The beating of my heart seized at her words, because in true Sabrina fashion, she just told me how much I meant to her, that she loved me, and I was a goner.

Her closed fist came between us, followed by a nudge at Tyler to come closer; he obliged.

"I also found this." Her palm opened, revealing a golden necklace with a round pendant engraved with jasmine. She flipped it over, showing us the letters T and M surrounded by a heart.

"I went to the police station first, the one they took you to after the accident. I requested the case file using my legal ID. In the box, there was an evidence bag with house keys, *sunglasses, and this."*

I froze; all I could do was stare at her palm, my mother's necklace right there... I saw glimpses of it skimming through my head, of it dangling around her neck while she read us bedtime stories.

"I figured the other stuff wasn't as important, but I couldn't leave the necklace, so I stole it."

"You stole it?" Tristan marveled, impressed.

Sabrina shrugged. "Worth it though, just for that." She pointed at Tyler, who was smiling through his tears.

"I remember this," he said, then took it from her hand, stretching out the chain and taking the pendant to his fingertips. "Sometimes I dream of this. I used to play with it while she read to us?" It was a question, pointed at me, and I nodded. His smile widened, and I looked at Sabrina, mouthing a 'thank you'. She wasn't even aware of what she had done for him, us. Growing up, Ty used to get angry for not remembering anything, so this—this one thing, the memory coming back to him... was everything.

It took us a while to calm down after some heavy hugs, mostly between Tyler and me. Sabrina received her fair share of thank-yous. And just as we thought the sob fest was over, my little Blackbird took out another present and handed it to our mother. "I have a friend who's a miracle worker with a pencil, so I had her make you this."

When Mama opened it, tears welled up in her eyes. She turned the framed drawing to us, and we all forgot how to breathe. We were all a ball of mush. It was a drawing of a woman's hand surrounded by five smaller ones, and the text said:

NOT STEP
NOT HALF
NOT FOSTER
NOT ADOPTED
JUST FAMILY

"Honey, this is perfect. Thank you!" Mama said, pulling Sabrina into a hug. We all went in, wrapping her in a big group embrace.

She fits in perfectly with us.

Family!

Chapter 49

Sabrina

Although it was overrated, somehow I missed sleep. I did have a nap during my flight, at least. Coming down the escalator at Boston Logan Airport, I had to blink more than once. Six Harts, one Simon, one Greg, one Aria, and one Nala holding up a huge sign saying "Welcome Home Badass" with huge smiles on their faces. The way those people melted my heart had been a recurring sensation. The time spent away from them had been unbearable, despite the numerous intense phone calls and video chats.

I was a full member of the book club, joining Tyler from different parts of the country over Zoom. They'd all kept tabs on me, never making me feel alone, so we naturally grew closer. They knew me, my core, and vice versa. I could proudly say that I was successful in conversations happening without words, making me a true insider. Everything with them was easy; I never had to censor myself, never had to bite my tongue, or hide my opinion. They embraced the worst parts of me, the curse words, the attitude, the heart... Everything... They loved me! *Me*! Not the model, not the heiress, not the cover girl... Just me. And I loved them right back.

They've even accepted Simon and Greg, welcoming

them with open arms, just as I knew they would. It was their signature move, after all.

Simon's true identity was kept secret from my father. He was not ready to reveal himself, and I wasn't sure if he ever would be. I would respect any choice he made, just like he had been respecting every single one of mine.

During this process, my life got turned around—I'd lost everything, but gained so much more. A support system and the love of a man I didn't deserve...

Still, I embraced it all.

My eyes started leaking as I drew closer to them, feeling a sense of completion.

"What are you doing here?" I choked, taking it all in. Without words, they surrounded me in a massive huddle. Naturally, I had to fall apart, full-on sob fest right there in the middle of the airport. I didn't care, though. And who could blame me? I was in the middle of everything that mattered, a part of something bigger.

My family.

Back home, champagne was served, with toasts that played a bit on my ego. I wasn't someone who needed praise or reassurances, but it felt nice to hear them. It was a hard period for me, but they made it easier.

Everyone was focused on me while I talked their ears off

about the case. During the preliminary hearing, Carlos's mother had told me, between heavy cries, that he was on the verge of a breakdown. She was afraid he would hurt himself inside if he didn't get out. When that gavel had smacked, I felt so much relief. I knew he had a long road ahead of him, but I had faith.

As to the Furst family... Every case Jacob had ruled over would be investigated and reopened. My mother had run away the moment our name started to get dragged through the mud. So after she'd taken all her jewelry, she fled the country. The mansion was put up for auction, and a megastar won it. Leaving me, the last one standing.

"What are you thinking about?" Mateo's voice whispered in my ear, sending electricity right through me.

"I want to change my last name legally," I voiced. His eyes flared at that, and I felt a slight ping.

"Don't look at me like that." I shook my head, smiling.

I'd mentioned my stance on marriage to him a while back. What I didn't tell him was that I was slowly, maybe, warming up to the idea—with him. A life together, sharing a future... I could picture it so clearly: the white picket fence, a tire swing just like the one in the front yard here, children running around. One was not an option. We could maybe even adopt...

The possibilities were endless.

He was it for me, the one who never gave up, sledgehammering my defenses, turning my averted gaze to him, to everything we could be. The sculptor of my clay who built me up from the ground up, making me whole.

"Sorry to disappoint, but you read me wrong."

Regret washed over me. Was he getting tired of me? Was I too much to handle? I hated how this man brought out all my insecurities, especially since I'd never had them before I met him.

"Make no mistake, I still have high hopes about you changing your mind about that," he asserted, and I gawked at him.

I mentally wiped my forehead.

"How so?"

"I know your stance on marriage, but it doesn't mean you can't take our last name." He was so sure of himself, shoulders straight, eyes focused, not a shred of doubt, confident about that idea.

"And why would I do that?"

While I was still in the chair, he turned it so I would face him fully.

"You want me?"

"Yes," I said with a nod.

"Forever?"

I smiled at that, seeing as nothing sounded so good, except maybe when he called me his right before climax.

"That's the plan," I breathed out.

"You want kids?"

I flinched at his question, so with some reservations, I confessed, "I might not be good at it."

It was a recurring fear of mine. I wanted a family of my own, many kids, but I was afraid that I would ruin them, much like my mother had ruined me.

"At what?"

"Being a mother, I didn't have the best role model."

What an understatement that was! The fact that I didn't end up in the loony bin was a miracle. At least it would make a good story for the grandkids, so I've got that going for me.

"Think of it this way—you know exactly what not to do."

Poof—just like that, the fear vanished

"True." I gave him a weak smile.

"Soooo," he dragged. "Kids?"

"A bunch," I blurted.

I want a loud home, filled with laughter and chaos. I want to give all the love I have to a little human who looks like you. I want us to grow old together.

There was so much I wanted to say, but before I could think of where to start, Mateo's gentle voice cut through. "Don't you want us to share the last name?"

"I guess it would make most sense," I muttered, bobbing my head. "Sabrina Hart," I chirped, taking it out for a spin. "Has a nice ring to it."

I repeated it over and over in my head, the words coming together like a lovely song.

"Sure does." He smiled back at me with that sexy, stupid grin of his that I loved to hate so much.

"Better than what I had in mind," I teased.

"Which is?"

"Sabrina Vamp," I deadpanned, making him chuckle. Then he kissed me with the same fire as always, one I hoped would never extinguish.

Sabrina Hart.

It had a nice ring to it; however, something didn't feel right.

Chapter 50

Mateo

Standing in the middle of the John Adams Courthouse, I stared at the beauty that was now Sabrina Hart. Yup, she took my name, but not before she'd asked for approval from the rest of the family, even if I'd told her it was unnecessary.

Her finger grazed over her new name, and her posture stiffened.

Fuck! Is she regretting it already?

"I don't like it." She scrunched up her nose. The badass Vamp was wearing tight black jeans and one of my t-shirts, which she'd tied up to fit her better. I thought she'd be happy about this, especially since she'd pulled some strings to get everything done in record time.

"What?" It came out more like a squeak.

"My name. Like this."

"Like what?" I was beyond muddled, with a mixture of panic.

She turned the paper to me, pressing her finger under the part where Ms. was written.

"Like this. I don't like this title." She kept tapping her finger on the same spot.

You know, I could try to come up with an excuse as to

why I was the dumbest man alive, but it would be pointless. I was plain out oblivious!

"I don't get it." I really, really didn't...

"This right here—" she underlined the part again "—says I am a woman of an unknown marital status. I want to change that." It sounded like she was encouraging. Who or what, I wasn't sure.

"I don't think it works like that."

She smacked me over the head—hard.

"I. Want. To. Change. It!" She raged, staring at me like I was this dunce fool who couldn't figure out what 2+2 was...

"I know you just rattled the whole justice system, but you can't change *this* law with a snap of your fingers," I pointed out.

Another smack across the head—this time harder, with a nice echo to it. The woman behind the counter snickered.

"She's asking you to marry her, sweetie," the woman said in that 'duh' voice.

The fuck?

"Wait, what?"

"Ding! Ding! Ding!" Sabrina sang.

Am I dreaming? Is this really happening?

I pinched myself. It hurt.

This is real.

"But you said—" Her finger on my lips interrupted my thoughts.

"Babe, take the win here!"

Another thing, I was a walking, talking blob.

She grabbed my hand and pulled me to the counter, where the eye-opening woman was working.

"We want to get married. What do we need?"

The woman explained everything, and Sabrina went into action, entirely in operation mode. She obtained the necessary papers, moving from counter to counter, filling out paperwork, all that with a phone between her ear and shoulder, while I sat there, like the moron I was.

In the background, I heard her shout "expedite it" and "rush." Also, there was some name-dropping involved, but all in all, Sabrina had worked her magic in getting it all done.

"Here." She handed me a blank piece of paper and a pen.

"What's this?" I asked, still shocked by the turn of events.

"Write your vows! You have fifteen minutes," she ordered, no explanation whatsoever.

What the hell is happening right now?

"Blackbird?" I said through a breath. I had so many questions.

Don't you want our family here? Don't you want more? A big, extravagant wedding?

I didn't want her to do this for me, didn't want her to miss out on anything. I didn't want her to settle.

"I already called everyone. They'll be here in twenty with something nice for both of us to wear… so chop-chop!" She followed the command by clapping her hands. When I didn't move, she turned to face me. "All I want is you and our family. It's all I ever wanted. Now go, you have fourteen minutes, and you better make me leak, or I will not be a Mrs!"

The threat worked, and I jumped to my feet.

Less than an hour later, we were standing across from each other in courtroom 4. She was wearing a simple white sundress, and I was in the same pants and shirt I had worn the night I saw her at the Greek restaurant.

I took out the paper, clearing my throat to read the words that poured out.

"It's obvious I fell hard and fast, but it was impossible not to. You've made it impossible. With that big heart of yours, the adventurous spark, and not to mention all the evasiveness, keeping up with the mystery. Growing up, I had a knack for figuring stuff out. I spent way too many hours opening up appliances in our house to see what made them tick." I glanced at my Mama, remembering all the times she'd yelled at me when she'd found me on the floor with another electronic device reassembled. Her hand covered her chest, and I smiled at her before I turned to the vision in white.

"So when you waltzed in, this beautiful enigma, waking up the explorer in me, what was I to do? I had to fall; I mean, look at you."

She blushed, and I took it as a good sign to continue, "Then you opened your mouth and made me fall even harder. The more pieces you revealed, the harder I fell, kept on going, never hitting the bottom. As it turns out, I wasn't falling at all; I was flying, and I've been doing it ever since. So, trust that I have everything I need here with you, that I am all yours, and even though it took you a while to admit it, I am the luckiest bastard and so fucking happy that you love me back." My voice cracked at the end.

"Language," Mama yelled, and we all chuckled through our tears. Everyone closest to us was here—my family, Aria, Nala, and Simon holding his partner's hand, all full-on sobbing.

"My dress has pockets... woohoo!" Sabrina squealed,

taking a piece of paper from her pocket, locking her earthy greens back on mine, not able to control the tears.

"At the beginning of our story, I didn't realize what I had, didn't quite know the worth. Still, your stubborn ass kept on pushing, and I am so grateful you never stopped. I thought that you were just a pit stop on the way, but now I know... You were the destination."

We both swallowed, eyes firmly locked in place.

"Growing up, I had this big fortune, everything money could buy, and not a single care in the world. The moment you opened your heart to me was the moment I figured out the value of it all. All the fortune, all the money, the security meant nothing... But you... You mean everything... You *are* everything. You jump-started my heart and gave it a home. I love you so freaking much. You are my most prized possession."

"I kind of feel objectified now!" I tittered, and she pushed me, hard enough for me to lose some balance. When I found my ground, she looked at me, a full smile on her face, and chortled, "Shut up and marry me already!"

We entered the small hall reserved for parties at the Apollo. Balloons were blown up, a DJ was set up in the corner, and there were candles lit all around the room. How

Aria and Nala managed to pull this off was beyond me, but it was much appreciated. Twelve white chairs surrounded a long table with a floral centerpiece. We didn't get the chance to sit before we were called for our first dance.

With Sabrina's hand in mine, I guided her to the improvised dance floor. Honestly, if we had more time to plan it, I couldn't see it turning out any better, because this, her... it was all just—perfect. And now, as I was swaying with my wife in my arms to the sound of Zara Larsson singing our tune, it was impossible to imagine it any other way.

"So, I was thinking about our honeymoon." She played with her lashes, fluttering them seductively.

I cocked a brow in amusement.

"What can I say? It started with me picturing you naked," she practically moaned. A slight touch of her lips sent impulses to my southern area.

"Of course it did." I shook my head. "So, what did you have in mind?"

"You, me, our bike, the entire coastline. Fucking under the stars..." she trailed off, allowing my imagination to do the rest.

"Mmm, I like the way you think." I raked my lower lip, marveling at the way her eyes traced the movement.

"Have you ever read the Addicted series?" she asked, continuing to torture me by biting on her lower lip. I have, but I'd undergo a quick reread after she'd told me who her favorite book boyfriend was. However, I knew my wife; I knew where her mind took her. I couldn't remember which book it was exactly, but there was a scene where the couple had sex on a motorcycle. I would be lying if I said I'd never thought about reenacting it.

"Baby, you should know by now..." I bit her earlobe, making her shiver. "Whatever perverted thing you want to play out, I am here to make all your fucking wildest dreams come true." The *fucking* part was for emphasis, since it was her ex-book-boyfriend's favorite word. A loud moan escaped her, and I pressed closer to her, letting her know what her voice did to me.

"You know something?" she quipped, lifting her eyes to meet mine.

"Hmm?" I hummed.

"Our initials are S and M," she pointed out, and we both chuckled, while I shook my head.

For a minute or two, we contemplated running to the bathroom, but figured we had a lifetime of those, so we just kept on dancing.

Soon, food arrived, and we enjoyed the time with our family and friends. Conversation flowed, smiles were spread, and love filled the air. When we couldn't take any more food, we decided to take the party to The Brick, with Nala securing us a VIP lounge area.

Luka drove his pickup, with Mama up front between him and Tristan, and my wife and me in the back. When we stopped at a red light, Sabrina took a selfie of us. "Look at us, husband. A real power couple." She showed me the photo and gave me a small peck on the lips.

Her eyes had that twinkle reserved solely for me.

"You know there's no backsies now? I can annoy the hell out of you, and you can't go anywhere." She pulled on my tie, leaving no space between us.

"Wasn't planning on it," I whispered, grazing her nose with mine, making her face wrinkle.

"I will annoy you!"

Oh, I knew she would, just like I knew I would be loving every minute of it.

"Bring it on," I taunted, meaning every word.

"I'll ruin you!"

You already have!

"Please do!"

She turned to the front, tapping on Mama's shoulder. "Hey, what did we win?"

"Sorry?" Mama turned around, eyes narrowed.

"The bet? We beat Luka to the punch. So what did we win?"

Luka growled while Tristan and I chuckled.

"Fifty bucks," Tristan answered, and Sabrina frowned.

"Oh, well, you can keep it." She slumped back into the seat, sporting the cutest little pout I've ever seen.

I took her hand, my thumb grazing over the ring that covered the barrier I had broken down, and she smiled.

"Hey Eva, can you please turn on the radio?" my wife croaked.

"Of course, honey."

With one click, we were both in a heavy lip lock, the sound of Ed Sheeran's 'Small Bump' firing up our hearts.

The End

Chapter 1

Aria

Fuck—my—life!

And add three exclamation points for emphasis!!!

"Oh, don't be so dramatic, Aria." John wiggled in his almighty leather chair across from me.

"You think that *this* is me being dramatic?" I took a step back to restrain myself from punching him in the face, no matter how much I loved the man.

John, also known as Mr. Wright, was my father's business partner and a long-time family friend, essentially my second dad. He had my utmost respect right up until about a minute ago, when he and my beloved ex-father laid out their plan.

My father and John were the CEOs of the W&B Corporation. They owned the majority of the mines around Boston and had businesses in almost everything. The company was listed on the Fortune 500; a plaque stating this was displayed on the wall behind me.

Yours truly was an only child in line to inherit half of the fortune, including my father's seat at the table. I was in my last year at Northeastern University's D'Amore-McKim School of Business, where I was learning everything there was to know about running one, even though my father had been preparing me for the role my entire life.

On the other hand, John had three children: two sons and a daughter, to be more precise. Mario was the oldest and set to inherit his father's seat, but one drunken mistake put that all in jeopardy, making the youngest child, Cillian, next in line. Their sister Helen had no interest in that world, which was a moot point since she was blissfully married with a third child on the way.

We've all grown up together, like a big, happy family, only to grow apart over the years. We spent every major holiday together, but other than that, we didn't see much of each other.

The dumb and dumber sitting across from me just informed me that they'd managed to "misplace" a large sum of money and were afraid of the board finding out. And that was not even the best part. The best part was their plan for a get-out-of-jail-free card in the form of a marriage contract. More specifically, an arranged marriage between Cillian and me would incline them to the other half of our trust. When we were kids, our family lawyer had drawn up the agreement, which was divided into two parts: one we inherited when we started college, and the other we would receive on the day we got married. Although it was never explicitly stated that we had to marry each other, the scenario was intended solely to double the money.

"You can't be serious?" Cillian finally yelled after being late to this spectacular charade of a meeting, but it was only 25 minutes, so no big deal—his words, not mine.

We exchanged disapproving looks as his frustration met

mine. He'd rushed in late per usual—a fascinating fact considering he was a freaking soldier. The bastard defied nature, smelling awesome while also glistening with sweat. And I hated myself for even noticing it. He'd barged in, wearing a yellow t-shirt and navy shorts, with a golden eagle logo plastered on both.

"Oh, Hades, and to think you ran away from practice for this. Does the coach know?" I teased as if my life depended on it.

"Brooks, always a pleasure," he gibed, barely acknowledging my presence; no, make that my existence.

"Oh, come on now, say it like you mean it," I hissed, and his head flew to the ceiling with a frustrated growl.

Yes!

My life's mission was to make him as miserable as possible.

"Why would I, uh, m—" he waved his finger between us "—*we* ever go through with it?"

Cillian glanced at me, then back at our parents. "This was your mistake, deal with it like the adults you're supposed to be!"

I hated his voice, but agreed with his words.

Cillian was my age, but he acted way older, always serious… as opposed to me, who pretty much acted like a child, but in a good way. He was a marine, some big shot lieutenant on top of the world till about a year ago, when he'd risked his life to save his friend, injuring his back in the process. He was still in the Navy but not on active duty.

"Look, kids, we screwed up, we know, and we are asking for your help. This is our last resort. It is just for a year." My father stood up, setting his hand on his desk as Mr. Wright finished. "You've known each other your whole lives; you can make it one year faking a marriage."

They were oblivious to how much Cillian and I hated each other. The saddest part is that we used to be best friends. Now his ego sucked all the air out of the room, making it hard to breathe.

With that, my eyes betrayed me when they glanced at all of his muscles put on display. *Hey, I'm only human, and I do have eyes*, so naturally, they got drowned in the unmistakable eye candy. And despite Cillian's personality, his body was impossible to ignore, no matter how much my brain protested it.

Clearing my throat, I pointed a serious look at the two men sweating their asses off. "If, and I mean *if*, we decide to do this, walk me—us—through everything."

Cillian choked on my request but listened to their plan without making a single move.

They took turns laying out the groundwork; it was a matter of two signatures, and just like that, we would be inclined to $2 billion—each. There was some talk about a big, fancy wedding to show how strong the families are, but I tuned out a bit at that point. It was relatively simple, not that hard to do. I mean, I could smile for the camera and pretend I didn't want to kill the groom. The problem with it all was the year we had to pretend to actually like each other, love each other, in order not to raise any suspicions. The pretending part would also entail living together for a whole year, and that was something I couldn't be persuaded into, no matter how much I loved my dad or John. The mere thought of being under the same roof as him disgusted me to my very core.

"How did you 'lose' the money?" I air-quoted the word lose.

"That is not important," John said, enraging my already boiling blood.

"This is unacceptable," Cillian said before storming out.

"Wow, his future wife is one lucky hell of a gal. Oh, wait!"

Sarcasm was me, me was Sarcasm. I lived by it, to it, and for it. Without it, I don't think I could cope with a mere act of blinking, as it was the only thing that saved people from me killing them. Cillian being on top of my kill list.

"Look, Peanut, I don't think you understand how much trouble we could potentially be in. We could lose the company altogether or face prison. It's just a piece of paper, and it's only a year. Please think about it." My father stooped so low that he resorted to the puppy-dog-eyes trick on me. And it almost worked. Almost.

It wasn't lost on me that my father's nickname for me was the one thing that had the power to kill me in an instant, even with his endearing tone.

"Aria, don't you dare eat that, it has nuts," my dad shouted, Mario's hand mid-air with a cracker ready. Cillian jerked it out of my hand, making it fall to the ground, and I burst into tears. My dad ran to me so quickly that the first tear didn't even get the chance to touch my lips. "Come here, Peanut, don't cry," he gasped, dropping his pipe on the grass. "Cillian, why would you do that?" my dad yelled at my best friend, then focused back on me. "You have to be careful, you can't go around taking food without knowing its contents." He

*grazed my hair and held me tight, the mix of mint and tobacco
filling up my nostrils.*

I snapped out the memory that should've been my first
indication of Cillian's true nature.

"I'll think about it, but I can't make any promises," I said,
losing my energy.

"That is all we ask. Thank you." John pulled me into a
hug, and I took a whiff of his scent, letting the nostalgia hit.

Chapter 1

Ty

"Come on, dude, you've got 2 minutes to shower, and we need to sprint out!" Ben yells as he breezes by me to get the first empty cubicle.

"Where's the fire? The class is not for another..." I look at my watch: 35 minutes.

"Yeah, but theirs is still going on, so we have to hurry!" he shouts back. The room is filled with the whole team, each under a showerhead, scrubbing at full speed.

"Whose?" I remove my shirt and toss it on the bench by the wall.

"The girls, dumb-ass," someone screams from the showers.

Now it all makes sense.

"You guys are crazy." I shake my head, turning on the water, setting it to just the right of lukewarm.

"Trust me, Ty, you *want* to be there," Cole says, his brows dancing up and down.

"I am nothing if not a team player." I give in and join their fast pace.

"That's the spirit," Parker yells from across the room.

"I thought you were gay?" I quickly work, scrubbing my hair, loving the sensation on my scalp.

"True, but I am nothing if not a team player!"

"Touche!" I holler back.

All at once, as if an alarm has gone off, we turn the taps and start getting dressed. The next thing I know, we're power walking to the performing arts hall.

"Thank God it's still not over," Ben sighs with relief the second we get in the hall overlooking the large mirrored studio, filled with girls in the middle of a dance. The entire Basketball team is glued to the glass, focusing on said girls. Amused, I join them, allowing my eyes to be blessed by the view. Girls in short shorts, tights, tops, tight shirts… Girls with different body types, hair colors, all hot in their own ways… following Ms. Lynch at the front.

The team is well acquainted with Ms. Lynch, the woman assigned to carry out our punishment for the fight we caused during the first game of the season. The only thing the coach could think of to punish us was to embarrass us; his words were around *'If you can't act like men, then maybe I should indulge you'* right before he laid out his master plan.

Subjected to two and a half months of dance lessons, all so that we can perform a formation-type choreography in front of our friends and family at the Christmas benefit. For the last month, we've been practicing the cha-cha twice a week, and today is the day we're supposed to have our first practice with our forced-on dance partners.

Right now, I am looking at all the potentials focused on

their reflections.

Well, all except one.

Love at first sight. I've heard of it, read about it, seen it on multiple screens, and witnessed it happen to my brother. On the other hand, I haven't had the pleasure of experiencing it. That is, until I laid my eyes on a blonde wonder.

Right there, overlooking a crowded room with bright lights and loud music, I get struck.

Experienced symptoms: all-around butterflies, shortness of breath, stopping of the heart, stiffness of the muscles, chest pains, temporary focused blindness (as in - not able to see anyone or anything else other than her), tightening of the throat, arousal, and spiking high temperature. To sum it all up - the whole nine yards.

A special kind of lighting strikes me, and my body goes into shock. It's that kind of thing that no doctor can fix, no remedy for the illness, no cure, no way of ever going back. In all honesty, I'm not planning on going back. I like the feeling, the moment it has its hand in consuming me, I am done for. The problem is that I want, need, and am determined to get more.

The entire room blurs out, making her the sole focus of my view. She is the only one not showing off her body, wearing a loose t-shirt with her sleeves pulled up over her shoulders and basketball shorts. Her blonde hair is tied in a ponytail, swinging from side to side. Her mouth opens to the lyrics, and she moves in sync with each beat. It's as if she's feeling the music, immersed in it with closed eyes, all the while nailing every step. I forget how to breathe, looking at her, transfixed, and I swear, time stands still for a moment. A bit of frustration comes over me due to her closed eyes, making me desperate to see them - the color, the shape, her soul.

Noticing the direction of my stare, Ben snaps me out of the trance. "Don't even think about it, man."

"What's the story there?"

Ben takes a deep breath, the warning kind, before he says, "That's Maddie, the volleyball captain, and you don't stand a chance. No offense."

"Some taken, but tell me more," I demand, intrigued.

"Look, Johnny, trust me when I tell you, don't go there."

I chuckle at the name drop from before either of us was born and fight the urge to sing out the timeless tune.

"Points for the reference, but if you don't mind, indulge me." I am practically begging, ready to go down on my knees even.

"Fine, your funeral," he gasps, then gives me what I need, placing his arm around my shoulder. "She's the all-around player of the year, number one in the state, and doesn't do basketball players. Trust me, we all tried and failed miserably."

Of course, she isn't going to make it easy, and we haven't even met.

"Minor setback," I deflect. "Keep going."

"You have a death wish, I see," Ben sighs, shaking his head. "She got here on a basketball scholarship."

"But I thought you said she plays volleyball?"

"Patience, brother, patience, I was about to get there." He rolls his eyes for emphasis.

"Did you ever read about a big-shot high school player

that all the majors wanted to draft, and she turned them *all* down?"

"Yeah, from Chicago, Stevens something."

I stare at the beauty, her eyes still closed, entranced in her world. She looks breathtaking, and the info dump I was just overstimulated with makes her unreal. But there she is, flesh and bone, intimidating and inviting all at once.

Ben squeezes my shoulder and points at the person I'm developing an obsession with. "Meet Maddison Stevens."

"Damn," I mutter.

"Yeah, bro," Ben agrees, praising how she quit basketball and turned to volleyball to keep her scholarship. He didn't say anything about the reason she quit basketball, only how she spent the summer training for a whole new sport before trying out for the volleyball team and making the second string. By the following season, she was crowned captain.

Impressive is too small a word to describe her.

The music stops, and all the girls scatter to the corners, grabbing their towels and bottles. I check the time; it's probably just a break, since there are fifteen more minutes till our torture starts. Unable to look away, I soak her in, and the switch. Taking a place in the right corner, she grabs a blue bottle and chugs it right before she spits some of it out, bursting into laughter over something a tall redhead says. Her smile is even more captivating than I imagined.

The clapping of Ms. Lynch's hands gets all the girls to momentarily stiffen before they go back to their former places. The redhead and Maddie do a cute handshake with wiggling fingers and their tongues sticking out right before they take their positions. Her eyes close the moment the music starts, and her fingers start drumming to the beat, tapping the side of her thigh, and when she begins her steps, I can't look away. Diverging from the dance before the break, she moves more sensually, swaying her hips, deep diving into the salsa rhythm, and it is the worst - slash - best thing any man could witness.

"Does she have a boyfriend?" I turn the question to Cole.

"Are you deaf or just need an ear cleanse?" It's Ben who drawls, "It doesn't matter; she does not do basketball players."

"Not what I asked, Ben."

"As far as I know, she's a free woman."

That she sure is!

Also by Lena Knight

Brick-ed series
Averted
(Sabrina & Mateo)
Anticipated
(Aria & Cillian)

Fostered H(e)arts series
Nothing's fair in Love & Basketball
(Ty & MJ)
Nothing's fair in Love & Marriage
(Luka & Norah)

Acknowledgements

First, I would like to thank my sole support system: my husband. Without you, I never would've taken this step. Thank you for believing in me and being my rock.

To my kids who made my dreams of becoming a mother come true… Mommy loves you the mostes.

I want to thank each person who took the time to read my words.

To Sunny, the first person who read my stories and gave me the push I needed to continue my journey.

To my beta readers and editors for helping me make the story better

And last but not least, I want to thank the Holy Trinity of BookTok for getting me back into reading, which eventually turned into me writing…

Lena

ABOUT THE AUTHOR

Lena is a wife and a mother of two, and somewhere along the way, she lost herself in her roles. She has a master's degree in Physical Education, but after her son was diagnosed with autism, she proudly pulled on her stay-at-home-mom shoes. She rediscovered herself through books and the new worlds they opened up. Reading turned into writing, and a new passion was born. Lena grew up never believing in herself, but thankfully, there are people in her life who gave her the push she needed to try... so this is her... trying.

You can find her on:
Tik Tok - authorlenaknight
Instagram - authorlenak